Pavlos Matesis is a prize-winning Greek playwright, novelist and translator, who has been described by *Corriere della Sera* as 'the most talented Greek writer today' and by novelist Alan Sillitoe as 'a master of the art'. His fiction includes *The Ancient of the Days*, *Always Well* and *Sylvan Substances*. His novel *The Daughter*, an international bestseller in nine languages, has sold over 150,000 copies in Greece alone.

His plays include *The Ceremony* (winner of the National Theatre Award) and *Nurseryman* (City of Athens – Karolos Koun Award for Best Play of the Year), *Guardian Angel for Rent*, *Roar* and *Towards Eleusis* (the latter four plays published under the title *Contemporary Greek Theatre Volume 2*, edited by Theatre Lab Company and published by Arcadia in 2002).

Pavlos Matesis is also a noted translator into modern Greek. Classical authors he has translated number Aristophanes (commissioned by the Epidaurus and Athens theatre festivals), Ibsen, Ben Jonson, Molière, Shakespeare and Stendhal. A listing of contemporary writers he has translated includes Peter Ackroyd, Antonin Artaud, Bertolt Brecht, William Faulkner, Jean Genet, Eugène Ionesco, Frederico García Lorca, David Mamet, Arthur Miller, Joe Orton, Harold Pinter, Sam Shepard and Tennessee Williams.

Pavlos Matesis lives in Athens.

About the translator: **Fred A. Reed** is Canada's foremost authority on Islamic Iran. His books include *Persian Postcards: Iran after Khomeini*, *Salonica Terminus*, *Anatolia Junction* and, with Massoumeh Ebtekar, *Takeover in Tehran*, the first eye-witness account of the takeover of the US embassy by Iranian student militants in 1979. He has reported extensively on Iranian, Balkan and Middle Eastern affairs for *La Presse*, Canada's largest French-speaking newspaper.

Fred A. Reed ranks high among Canada's literary translators. In 1991, his translation of Thierry Hentsch's *L'Orient Imaginaire* won the Governor General's Awards. Writers he has translated from the Greek include Giorgos Ioannou, Nikos Kazantzakis, Pavlos Matesis and Kostas Mourselas.

Also by Pavlos Matesis

Fiction

Aphrodite
The Ancient of Days
Sylvan Substance
Always Well

Theatre

Biochemistry
The Ceremony
Deposition
The Ghost of Mr Ramon Navaro
Her Highness' Football Evening
Lower Civil Law
Wolf, Wolf
Exile
Nurseryman
Towards Eleusis
Roar
Guardian Angel to Rent
The Hum
Contemporary Greek Theatre Volume 2 (Arcadia Books)

The Daughter
a novel

Pavlos Matesis
translated from the Greek by Fred A. Reed

ARCADIA BOOKS

Arcadia Books Ltd.
15–16 Nassau Street
London W1W 7AB

www.arcadiabooks.co.uk

First published in the United Kingdom 2002
Originally published by Kastaniotis Editions, Athens 1990
This B format edition published 2010
Copyright © Pavlos Matesis 1990

This English translation from the Greek, *I Mitera Tou Skilou*
Copyright © Fred A. Reed 2002

A catalogue record for this book is available from the British Library

ISBN 978-1-906413-58-3

Typeset in Ehrhardt by Northern Phototypesetting Co. Ltd, Bolton
Printed in the United Kingdom by Bell & Bain Ltd, Glasgow

Arcadia Books Ltd acknowledges the financial support of the Arts Council of England and of London Arts. This book is supported by the Hellenic Foundation for Culture, Athens, and the Hellenic Foundation, London.

Arcadia Books distributors are as follows:

in the UK and elsewhere in Europe:
Turnaround Publisher Services
Unit 3, Olympia Trading Estate
Coburg Road
London N22 6TZ

in the US and Canada:
Independent Publishers Group
814 N. Franklin Street
Chicago, IL 60610

in Australia:
The Scribo Group Pty Ltd
18 Rodborough Road
Frenchs Forest 2086
Australia

in South Africa:
Jacana Media (Pty) Ltd
PO Box 291784,
Melville 2109
Johannesburg

Dedicated to Martis

CALL ME RARAOU if you don't mind.

Roubini's my Christian name, of course, but when I made my theatrical debut they baptized me Raraou and now that I've arrived – look, I've even got it jotted down right here on my identity card: 'Mademoiselle Raraou. Thespian', so they'll carve it on my gravestone, too. Quite honestly, I don't care if I never see Roubini again. Don't want to know about her. Same goes for my last name, Meskaris. Crossed it out long ago.

I was born in Rampartville, the capital city, even if it's only a provincial capital. Guess I was around fifteen when we left the place. Me and my ma and half a loaf of dry bread between us, a couple of months after they made a public spectacle of her it was, they were still celebrating that so-called Liberation of theirs. Not even wild horses could ever drag me back there. Ma neither. Buried her right here, I did, in Athens, the only luxury she ever asked for, her last will and testament. 'My child, I'm dying, but grant me a last wish, bury me here. I never want to go back there'. (She may have been born in the place but she never said the word 'Rampartville'.) 'I don't care how you do it, just get me a lifetime grave. I never made you do anything else. Don't you ever let them take me back, not even my bones.'

So I bought the plot, nothing special really. And visit her now and then, maybe take her a flower, or a chocolate, or sprinkle her with a few drops of cologne – that I do on purpose because as long as she lived she never let me, not once: that kind of thing was for sinful women she said. Once in her life she wore cologne I think. At her wedding. Well, now I sprinkle on all the cologne I want and, if she doesn't like it, just let her try and stop me. The chocolates are because she was always telling me how she used to dream of chocolate during the four years of the Occupation: just one piece of chocolate of her own to eat, that's all she wanted. But afterwards the bitterness came over her, real bitterness; she wouldn't even glance at chocolate.

So I've got my own little apartment, two rooms plus hallway, and my government pension as daughter of a fallen hero of the Albanian campaign. My actor's pension should be coming through any day now too, just as soon as all the forms get approved, and generally speaking I'm fortunate and happy. Got no one to worry about, no one to love, no one to mourn. I do have a stereo and records, left-wing songs mostly. I'm a royalist myself, but those left-wing songs just turn me to jelly. Fortunately I'm so fortunate.

My father, he was a tripe washer by trade, but we never told anybody. He used to buy the tripes and the guts from the slaughterhouse, rinse them out and turn them inside out one at a time for making spiced liver sausages to roast over the coals. I remember him as a young man, he would have been what? around twenty-four at the time? What I mean is. I remember his 1932 wedding picture; if you really want to know, I don't remember what he looked like. When they called him up in 1940 me and my two brothers were already born: one of them is older than me. He's still alive somewhere. I think.

My only memory of my father is from the call-up when Mother and I saw him off at the railway station. He was so afraid he'd miss the train he went rushing on ahead with Mother hurrying after him, dragging me along behind her: the tears were pouring down her face but she didn't care what people would say. I remember seeing my father standing there in the railway carriage going off to war, and us, all we had to our name was that one twenty drachma piece. Mother tried to hand it to him but he wouldn't touch it. Then she threw it through the train window; at first he was crying, then he starts cursing and throws it right back at her, and Mother picks it up off the ground and heaves it into the carriage with all her might. All the other recruits are laughing, but the coin drops inside. She yanks me by the arm and we leave on the run. Now, did he ever pick it up, or did someone else grab it? We never knew. That was the last time I can remember seeing my father as a young man, from the front. Mostly I remember his back as he sat hunched over, rinsing out the guts. So I keep in touch with his face in that old wedding photo. I forget dead people, people who disappear from my life, people like that: what I mean to say is, I forget what they look like. All I know is, they're gone. Even Ma. She was over seventy-five when she died, but when you come down to it I never really had a good close look at her, so I keep in touch with her in the wedding photo where she's a girl of twenty-three, that's a good forty years younger than me. So I'm not bashful about taking her chocolates, now she's like my daughter. Age-wise, I mean.

Thank God, for the war in Albania I always say. At least I got a pension out of it. Frankly I couldn't care less if our nation was defeated. Anyway, you think maybe it's the first time? Me, I'm as nationalist and as royalist as they come, but a pension's a pension. Who's going to look after a poor orphan girl like me?

So when Father went off to the war with the twenty drachmas, we went home, tidied up the place, bought some bread on credit and Mother took on a job as housekeeper in a good family and did sewing at night on that little mini sewing-machine of hers, the manual one. She wasn't a real dress-maker, mind you: did things like blouses, underwear, kids' clothing, helped out at funerals too – she made winding sheets for corpses. Every now and again we'd get a postcard from the front saying I am well best wishes. I would write the answer: I was just finishing my elementary school at the time. Mother never went to school. 'Dear Diomedes, the children are well I am working hard please do not worry take care of your health I kiss you by the hand of our daughter Roubini your wife Meskaris Asimina.'

I could never get it out of my mind that those cards of my father's smelled of guts. That's how I never could eat tripe, it

3

always reminds me of how human bodies smell. Couldn't eat Easter soup either, even if I am a God-fearing person. Why just last year this impresario was making fun of me and saying How am I going to fit you into our new review Raraou? Nowadays people like to hear dirty talk but you, you're such a little goody two-shoes.

Well maybe I am but the men always lusted after me. Still do, in fact.

This was the same impresario who used to stick a piece of styrofoam into his underpants to make a more manly bulge. Even on tour when we wanted go for a swim he used to stick a hunk of it in his swimsuit. All us girls in the troupe knew it so some of us would go feel him up, pretend sexy, but actually knock it out of place. But any girl who made that mistake would never work for his troupe again. I lost my job because when he started cursing me, Why you little slut and your bitch of a mother, for two cents I'd ... I tell him. What with, smart ass? Styrofoam? So twice he kicks me in the behind. Big deal. Go on, kick away I say, you, you're stuck with those two inches of yours till you croak and ain't no plastic surgery can change it.

Well, maybe my father was skinny and hairy but he was all man. Our place only had one room with no partitions and an outdoor toilet. One time I saw him naked changing his underpants and let me tell you I really felt proud even though I didn't understand why back then. My older brother, he couldn't get along with my father. He was just a kid but he was always talking back: one day my father told him something when he came back from work, which he didn't do much; usually he just went out into the back yard and rinsed out some tripe; brought the work home, you see. So my brother, he goes and throws some dirt into the big tub with the clean tripe and just like that he pipes up, 'You ain't a man.' Remember, this is a thirteen-year-old kid talking. Anyway, that's when my father speaks up. You're no son of mine he says. Well, you ain't no father of mine you gut sucker, says my brother Sotiris. So go find yourself another father says my father and he goes into the house. Sotiris follows him inside, throws open the window and starts yelling Father! father! at every Tom, Dick and Harry passing by. And crying. Just imagine somebody going by in the street and hearing that. Then Mother gets up, closes the window, goes into the yard and rinses off the tripe. All set, she says: and he throws the tripe over his shoulder and leaves to deliver it to The Crystal Fountain, that was the name of the restaurant. Ma wipes her hands, covers the sewing-machine with a pillow-case and leaves; she had a neighbour woman's body to wrap for burial. Mind they don't go killing each other when your father gets back, you hear, she tells me. So when my father comes back he sits down on his bench in the yard pretending to smoke but I tell him, Come inside Pa, Sotiris has gone. And Father comes in and when Mother gets back from work she's got sweet rolls for us. They're in mourning, can't eat sweets, she says. So we eat the rolls and Mother leaves again, We're going to sit night vigil over her she tells my father, I'll make the coffee, you go to sleep.

My brother Sotiris spent his evenings hanging around outside a house of ill-repute, Mandelas' brothel it was called. Rampartville had three whorehouses all together but this was the place with the high-class patrons. I already knew what a whorehouse was and what they did inside. I actually set foot in one, during the Occupation. Must have been around thirteen I suppose: some Italian sent me on an errand. But I didn't see anything reprehensible; they even treated me.

One other time I went calling on the whores, a couple of months later. Our parish priest, name of Father Dinos, sent me, from Saint Kyriaki's church. Our house was right behind the sanctuary, you see, and every morning on the dot of half past six Father Dinos appeared. He was our alarm clock. And on the dot of half past six, he'd go round to the back wall of the sanctuary

5

for a piss before mass. Time to get up for school, Ma would call out. 'Father Dinos just pissed.' On account of we didn't have a clock at our place so that was the only way we could be on time for school; if we were late the teacher would whack us with a ruler, five times on each hand. So one day during the Occupation, back when we were just about to break our record, twenty-six days without bread – boiled weeds was all we had to eat – and we were really curious to see how long we could last … like I was saying, on the twenty-sixth day, Father Dinos calls me over, 'You're a good girl', he says. 'I want you to run an errand for me, but you mustn't tell anybody.' He takes me into the church, and then into the sanctuary, I knew women weren't allowed in there. Don't be afraid, come on in, Father Dinos says. You're still without sin. So he plunks this chunk of holy bread wrapped in an embroidered cloth napkin into my hands. I try to refuse, I'll sell myself before I'll feed you on charity was what Ma used to say. But the priest wouldn't take no for an answer. You know The Crystal Fountain restaurant? he asks. Of course I did: the Germans were using the place as a canteen. Go and ask for Madame Rita and give her this. Tell her it's from Father Dinos, she'll understand.' And I stand there gaping at him. 'She's a poor woman without any means of support and it's our Christian duty to assist her. Off you go now, and be careful nobody steals it from you, and don't forget to bring back the napkin; it belongs to my wife.'

I knew who Madame Rita was, all right; she was the number one whore in Rampartville, and she worked in the highest-class whorehouse, plus she did Germans on the side. She was rich, and she was tall. Walking along all I could think of was how scared I'd be because I'd never seen a German so close up; I was so scared I forgot to smell the crusty white holy bread. All of us were terrified of the Germans because they never spoke. The Italians we got to like because they laughed, teased the women in the street and sometimes threw bread to the kids. Little

6

loaves of army bread they called *paniota*. So when I got to The Crystal Fountain my legs were like rubber imagining how scared I'd be. From hunger too, maybe. Ma wouldn't let us walk unless we had a very good reason, every step is a wasted calorie (that was a new word she'd learned) and every step was one step closer to the Grim Reaper.

So anyway I walk into The Crystal Fountain. The place is full of Germans eating, fortunately, they didn't even turn around to look at me: the waiter comes over, a Greek he was. What do you want, little girl? he asks (For reasons of hunger I was kind of underdeveloped for my age, didn't start my month-lies until I was seventeen, if you can imagine.) I ask for Madame Rita. The waiter gives a kind of vulgar laugh. Hey Rita, another surprise from the reverend! he calls out. And Madame Rita gets up from another table. She's all woman, but nice, really nice. What do you want sweetheart? she asks me. I give her the message and the holy bread. Ah, from the good father, she says. Here, sweetie, Mmnnh. And she gives me a kiss. What a nice lady, she looked like she was so happy. Pretty old too, I think to myself. Old to me the thirteen-year-old is what I mean to say. She couldn't have been more than twenty-six at the time. Anyway, it was a big thing for me to meet her, like being socially accepted in a way. Why, I was so excited I even told Mother, even though I swore to the priest I wouldn't tell a soul. During the Occupation my mother stayed at home. There was no work, only two or three homes in Rampartville were hiring cleaning ladies, besides, who needed a seamstress for things like breeches and kids' clothing? They didn't even sew up the dead in winding sheets any more. People were buried wearing whatever they had on when they died. Mother still did the night vigils out of respect for the departed but she could only come back at dawn. The curfew was in force back then, from seven o'clock at night.

I hardly get Madame Rita's name out before Mother slaps me. You should have brought it here, she said. That was the first time she ever ordered me to disobey, a priest too. I cried, because it was cold as well. Mother was working at the sewing-machine and to comfort me she let me give her a hand. She was unstitching our flag, the one we hung up beside the front door the day my father left, and one other time, too, when our army took some city or other somewhere in Albania. Korce I think it was. Now was the Occupation and the flag was worse than use-less, it was downright dangerous especially if they ever searched our house. They searched all the houses, a Greek interpreter and two Germans. At first they sent Italians, but the Italians always got involved in small talk with the Greeks, so the Ger-mans relieved them of that job. But they never got around to searching our place, which I took as some kind of social humil-iation. Anyhow, on the subject of flags, I never kept one around the house again. I may be a nationalist but I never could figure out what good they're for, except maybe in a patriotic number or two in some musical review or other.

So there we were, my mother and me, unstitching the flag. Lucky for us it was a big one; I can still remember how my father got it, years before. This butcher he worked for went bankrupt, owed Father for three days' worth of washed guts and tripe. So Father requisitioned the flag and a scale, the kind where you hang the meat from a big hook to weigh it. He was too late for anything else, everybody else had got there first: the only thing left in the shop was the flag and the scale. When we unfurled it on October 28th, the day my father went off to war, it just about covered the whole front of the house. Reminded me of one of those patriotic songs we used to sing in school, the one about Mother Greece with her blue eyes tucking in her children for the night. Fortunately for us, Ma remembered we had the flag. At first we used it for a bed sheet. Now, after we unstitched it Mother cut it into four shifts and two pairs of drawers each. In fact, I remember mine were cut from the middle of the flag, the part with the cross: we couldn't unstitch that part, so I ended up with drawers in our national colours with the cross right in the crotch. Anyway, we wore those undies all winter long. And there was no danger of them finding a flag in our house – if you had one, you were resisting – if ever they searched us. Still, I'd given up hope of that. But when Father Dinos spots our underwear hanging out to dry on the line behind the church one day, he figures everything out. How could you, woman? he asks our Ma. And Ma snaps back Alexander the Great would do the same thing if his kids didn't have any clothes to wear. The priest never breathed a word about our underwear again.

Truth to tell, the Authorities did come calling – once. Before the Occupation it was, during the Albanian war. Five months after my father left, he stopped writing. Mother sent me over to some neighbours who had a radio on the chance I'd catch his name in the dead and wounded bulletins. Maybe altogether ten houses in Rampartville had radios back then, all good families. The neighbours were theatre people which we called the Tiritomba family because they played in our town in a musical called *Tiritomba*, you remember that song before the war that went 'tiritomba tiritomba'. They were really from Rampartville all along, but it was pure happenstance that they happened to be passing through town on tour when the war broke out. So they had to stay put. Good people, especially Mlle Salome, the impresario's sister-in-law. They had a place of their own in Rampartville, an inheritance. Nice folks, I'll tell you all about 'em later. The house is still standing today, not a brick touched. Seems they forgot to sell it.

Mlle Salome we asked to listen for the casualty reports so I wouldn't go wasting my time for nothing. Went to police head-quarters and to the prefecture too, looking for information. Were we supposed to put on mourning and hang the black crepe over the front door or weren't we? But nobody heard my father's name. Don't worry, said Mlle Salome. If the unthinkable's happened, the Authorities will inform you for sure, and you can pick up the medal.

That's why we didn't put in any black curtain cords either.

So, one day a gendarme and a guy in civilian clothes come knocking, asking Mother if she heard any news, or if she knew anything about Father's politics. We showed them the postcards from the front, such as they were; what else were we supposed to show? He'd been absent without leave from his regiment for more than a month, they said.

As soon as Granny found out she rushed right over: just about tore my mother's eyes out, in fact, on account of we had-n't put up the black crepe. Granny wore black the whole Occupation: one day she managed to lay hands on some wheat, so she boiled it up as an offering for the deceased, sent us over a plate and for two days we had food to eat.

But we never hung up the crepe or wore mourning.

You won't catch me mourning him unless I get orders straight from the government, besides, it's bad luck Mother said. Later, a lot later, after Liberation, we finally got a letter from the government saying that my father Meskaris Diomedes had been declared missing on the field of honour and that his family was entitled to a pension. Well, it just wouldn't have looked right to go into mourning then. Besides, the religious waiting period was long over. That's the pension I still get to this day, but we only started collecting it much later, of course, after we left Rampartville for good.

Those two were the first officials ever to set foot in our house. Later, around the end of the first year of the Occupation they finally came looking for weapons. Italians, this time. They rum-maged through the chest-of-drawers and then checked out the floor, some floor, nothing but hard-packed earth, wall to wall. One of the Italians took a long look at Mother. My name's Alfio, he said, you can find me at the Carabineria. Looked like a nice man, the homely type; shy too. He spoke a few words of broken

Greek. After they left, my brother Sotiris called her a slut and I smacked him one.

That earth floor of ours was nothing but trouble. Ma was a real housekeeper; like mother like daughter, I always say. We had to keep the floor damp all the time. If we used too much water it would turn to mud. So we all took a mouthful of water and sprayed it over the floor to keep down the dust and make it hard like cement. Sprayed it during the winter time, too, all of us together. And after the spraying came the tamping. We'd lay down a board and all of us walked up and down on it, then we'd move the board to another spot and start all over again. Because if we didn't look after the floor it would turn back into dirt, and weeds would start to grow, mallow mostly, but once a poppy sprouted right next to the sink.

I know, I know it's sinful to say, but I always loved that earth floor of ours. Maybe because I always had a love for earth, ever since I was a kid; figure it out if you can. I was always dreaming I had a little piece of earth all my own. Always carried this lump of earth around with me in my school bag. And I had this little corner in our backyard all to myself, called it my 'garden', built a little fence with sticks and planted green beans, but they never grew, planted them at the wrong time of year it seems. After that, I set up a little garden, right under my bed.

In winter we kept the floor covered with rag rugs and dusters but it was no use, the weeds kept popping up. One day, early in the morning it was, I look over and I see the rug moving, rising up: it's a snake, I say to myself. I lift up a corner of the rug and look: it was a mushroom! Like the sun rising right out of the floor.

We did our best, whitewashed every Saturday and dusted every day, but there were always fresh cobwebs in the corners. But the spiders always popped right out and wove their webs all over again. Leave them, Mother told me one day, they don't hurt nobody and they eat the flies besides. What's more they keep us company.

Must be from back then that I get these dreams of mine about snow falling in the house. Here I sit in my apartment in Athens, and there's snow right in the house. Snow in the corners, snow at the feet of the console, snow on top of the chest-of-drawers and all over the washbasin. How can that be? I say to myself: doesn't the place have a roof? Then I wake up. Sometimes I dream there's snow in Mum's grave. It's nothing but a little hole in the ground: can't imagine how I'll ever fit in when the time comes. There are snowflakes in the corners. Nothing else. Not even debris from the casket; nothing. Nothing's left of Mum but snow.

So, we're in the second year of the Occupation, and one day I burst out laughing. Let's make a bet how many days we can last, I tell my brothers. Twenty-six days without bread, weeds and raw coffee, coarse-ground coffee was all we had to eat. A couple of days before there was a grocer's break-in, but all I could grab was some coffee. We had a handful each to eat every afternoon, then go outside to play. Ma didn't like us playing because we fainted a lot: we weren't hungry any more, but we walked really slowly. The shop break-in was the first; up until then, self-respect was all that held us back, the whole population. But that day the Red Cross was supposed to distribute free food. The three of us queued up from eight that morning; I didn't go to school that day, in fact we didn't go to school much any more. Mother never went to a food handout, I don't know why, maybe she was embarrassed. But she gave us permission, as long as we were clean.

There we were, queuing. Around half past three they announced there wouldn't be any food distribution. Then all of us, must have been close to 300, kind of shuddered at the same time. Silence. Then we all turned back and broke down the doors to three shops, pushing with our backs. One was a ladies' drapery that had been closed for a long time. We snatched whatever we could lay our hands on. There were civil servants' wives, and even Mlle Salome, strutting around dressed to the nines. People were trampling over someone lying on the ground. It was my brother Sotiris; but he wasn't hurt, he was just lying there letting the people walk all over him while he stuffed something into his mouth. I managed to snatch a can, turns out it was full of that coarse-ground foreign-tasting coffee; the only kind of coffee we ever had at our house, before the war that is, was the Turkish variety. Like an apparition I see Mlle Salome come sashaying out of the ruined shop just as pleased as punch even though they'd ripped the fur collar off her coat. Always the charmer, she was. She'd looted some cosmetics, some rouge, a box of Tokalon powder and a lipstick, she showed it all to us afterwards. Found out later she was in the Resistance, even if she was from a good family. But what do you expect from an impresario's sister-in-law after all.

It was our twenty-seventh day without bread. The coffee was gone too. Mother had been gone all morning and the three of us were huddled in bed together, trying to keep warm, if only we had the pullet to sit on our feet and keep us warm. Poultry give off more heat than people, you know.

The pullet was a present from Mlle Salome, bless her heart, wherever she might be, even though she never made it to Athens. Broke into somebody's chicken coop, stole the bird and passed it on to Mother. Boil it and feed your kids the broth, she said, their glands are starting to swell.

The pullet had bright-coloured feathers and a long neck; a lively bird she was, too. Didn't have any idea we were in the middle of an Occupation. Ma please let's not kill her, we begged. All right, we'll let her grow a little, maybe we'll get an extra portion. Maybe she'll even lay an egg or two. But the first eggs we had to eat were when the English marched in to liberate us. So we kept the pullet about six months, tried to feed her, and I even dug up the odd worm: put her out to peck around for weeds and bugs in a vacant lot up the hill. We had to make sure

13

nobody would steal her so the three of us carried her hidden under Sotiris' overcoat. We had to carry her, it was all she could do to stand up she was so exhausted.

That day when we get to the vacant lot I put her down to scratch for worms but she flops over on her side and looks up at me, too weak to scratch. I give her water but she can barely drink. Kids, I say, she's not long for this world, let's get back home so we can cut her throat before she croaks. But Ma says, No I won't do it, and later that afternoon the chicken looks me in the eye one last time and drops dead. From hunger. I picked her up; she was heavier dead. You're not going to bury her? You're crazy, you think you're rich or something? Mlle Salome shouts from her balcony when she spies me digging a hole in the yard. She's still warm, come on, pluck her and boil her! A whole chicken going to waste!

I go back inside. Saying, Ma, where's the trowel? My brothers pull back the bed and I dig a hole right in the corner I was saving for my little garden and buried her nice and pretty then we put the bed back, just so. Every morning after that I moved the bed so I could have a look. One morning I found a snail right there on top of my pullet's grave. Now you decide to show up, says Ma. Where were you when the chicken could have used you for food? And she picks it up in the palm of her hand and puts it outside in the grass. O she talked lots about the chicken, we even had a name for her, but I can't for the life of me remember what it was, now, decades later.

So there we were the three of us, huddled in bed trying to stay warm. In the afternoon Mother came back from the nearby villages where she'd been making the rounds and she had some fresh broad beans and a pocketful of wheat which she boiled up for us to eat. There's no olive oil? asks Fanis, the youngest of the lot. Of course he knew there wasn't any. No, says Mother. But if we had any you'd give it to us, isn't that so Ma? asks Fanis, looking for reassurance. But Sotiris gets to his feet. Ma, I'm

14

going to puke, he says. And Mother pops him one. It's a sin to throw up good food, she says. You'll go straight to hell. You don't respect me, isn't that so? Try to pick a few beans for you and get shot for my trouble. It was true: her head was spattered with blood, there, around her bun. Sotiris blushes, then pukes anyway. Ma slaps him without so much as a word, marches him over to the sink and washes out his mouth, and sits down on the window-sill. When night comes she gets to her feet, opens her little chest and pulls out her face powder – it was her wedding present – and powders her face. Then she takes her big sewing scissors and lets her hair down. She always kept her hair in a bun. That hairdo makes you look older Asimina, Mlle Salome would tell her. You look like a little old lady.

When Ma let down her hair it fell almost to her waist; me, I get my lovely hair from my mother, that's for sure. So, as I was saying, she goes over to the sink and starts to cut off her hair with those sewing scissors of hers while we look on wide-eyed. As soon as she finishes she cleans up the sink, twists the cut hair into a braid and throws it into the garbage can and tells me, Go ask Mlle Salome if she'll lend me her lipstick.

Mother never ever used make-up. Before that afternoon not once. And never since. Only one other time they smeared lamp-black all over her face when they publicly humiliated her right after Liberation it was. Last year at the funeral, as they were lowering her into the ground. I dropped my lipstick into her casket beside her. Just to do it my way, for once.

Mlle Salome was the impresario's sister-in-law, I think I mentioned. 'Artistes' we called them, but they were fine people all the same. We are the Tiritomba family, Mlle Salome liked to declare with a simper. She had a sister, Adrianna, widow of a certain Karakapitsalas. An actor, he was, her late husband, and together the two of them toured the provinces with their troupe. What a life! He was the one who discovered my, shall we say, theatrical talents. Come October 28th, the day the war started, they just happened to be performing in Rampartville. The impresario enlisted then and there. But no sooner did he get to the front than he bit the dust: stray bullet. That's what they told Adrianna to console her. But the truth is a mule kicked him in the head and he died on the spot. The troupe broke up. Some troupe! I mean, they were mostly relatives. Whenever one of their leading ladies would dump them in the middle of the tour to marry some guy in some small town or to work in some whorehouse along the way, which was pretty often, they had to fill in the role themselves: mostly it was Mlle Salome who took over the role, besides, she could play the mandolin. One time, in Arta I think it was, and Adrianna was still weak from childbirth. Anyway, there she was, playing the role of Tosca. But she was still nursing the kid so they had to change the title to *Tosca, indomitable mother*.

So I nip over to Miss Salome's place and she's delighted to lend me the lipstick. Fortunately it was wintertime and she had it in the house. In summertime she kept it in the ice box at the coffee house down the street to keep it from melting. Mlle Salome taught me the trick, bless her heart. When I became an actress in a road company I'd butter up the coffee-house owner in this village or that so he'd look after my cosmetics: by then they had fridges, not ice boxes. Even today I always keep my lipstick in the fridge.

Anyway, I get the lipstick from Mlle Salome and take it to Mother. By now I'm really curious. She puts on some lipstick, the short hair really did wonders for her but she didn't realize it. Then she puts on her coat. Back soon, she says, be patient. And sure enough, she came right back with a determined look in her eye. Listen to me, she says, there'll be a gentleman coming any minute now. You go out and play in the yard, and in about a half hour I'll call you. If it rains wait in the outhouse or the church. And she filled the washbasin with water and got out a clean towel.

We went outside and picked some buds from Mrs Kanello's rose bushes, peeled off the outer leaves and ate them thinking how it wouldn't be long before summertime and we could eat the buds from the grapevine, they're really delicious: rosebuds are too sweet. And we hid behind the garden wall, because the man we saw going into our house was not some Greek gentleman it was Alfio the Italian from the Carabineria. Mlle Salome was hanging out laundry on her balcony. God help us, she says. Look at this Adrianna, come quick! Adrianna appears and Mlle Salome shouts at us, Hey kids, they're searching your house, but her sister says, Shut up Salome, don't go judging people, and shoves her back into the house.

We were getting impatient and so hungry even the rosebuds didn't help, so we went into the church. Not long after that we saw Alfio go by, then Mother called us Come on in kids, and we went back to the house.

Mother slides the washbasin full of rinsing water under her bed and tells me to set the table. And she puts out bread – *paniota* it was – and margarine and a big can of squid. We said grace and ate so much there were still crumbs left over. Then Sotiris gets up from the table, throws down his napkin and says to Ma, You're a whore. Ma didn't say a word but I stood up, I was ready to scratch his eyes out. I smacked him, then he opened the door and walked out. Twenty-eight years later I ran in to him in Piraeus. He didn't say a word. Never saw him since. Mother never saw him again; never even tried.

Anyway, I cleaned off the table that night and we slept as sweet as can be, with full stomachs, and you know something? From then on Fanis and I slept better, just the two of us, instead of three in the same bed. Before we went to sleep I say, Ma you want me to empty the water? No, she says, I'll look after it. And she thanked me. From that evening on I always spoke to her in the polite form, until the day she died. And today, when I visit her on All Souls' Day, I speak to her in the polite form.

17

Before bedtime I returned the lipstick to Mlle Salome, washed the dishes and shook out the tablecloth. But the crumbs I kept, and scattered them underneath the bed where my pullet was buried. That night I got up on the sly and helped myself to more bread and margarine.

From that day on we were never hungry again. Signor Alfio started feeling more at home, and Ma didn't have to put us out before he came any more. When he came visiting right after sundown twice a week he brought us a little of everything: olive oil – not much, mind you – and sugar included: he liked a cup of coffee afterwards. He would come in and wish us all a good evening and we would greet him politely, then I'd say to Fanis, Let's go outside and play and out we went. One day we had to play in the rain because the church was locked up tight. Mrs Kanello was just coming home – she had an umbrella – and she says to us, What are you poor kiddies doing outside in the rain? you'll catch your death. Shame, you bring shame on our neighbourhood, shouts Aphrodite's mother from across the street. What did she ever do anyway besides crocheting lace for her precious Aphrodite's dowry? Before the war all she ever did was sit there on the stoop and crochet by the light of the street lamp just to save on electricity. Now was the Occupation and the blackout and she's still at it: you can't teach an old dog new tricks I say. Where was I? So Mrs Kanello goes up to our front door and calls out, Asimina, your kids are safe at my place. Then she turns to us and says, Come on my little lambs, and we huddle under the umbrella and she takes us to her place, a two-storey house it was. She gives us sage tea to drink, with dried figs for sweetening. We drink the tea then we eat the figs. All the while Mrs Kanello is looking out the window: finally she says. You can go home now, off you go.

One day Mrs Kanello comes up to me in the street and says Child, from now on you show your Ma more respect; take no notice of the neighbours.

Mrs Kanello was in the Resistance and everybody knew it. But even if she was, she still got on just fine with our family, always had a cheery good morning for us kids. She was a gorgeous woman with curly hair like the goddesses from the museum at Olympia where they took us on a school trip before the war. Only she wore pins in her hair, big thick hairpins made of bone, and I don't remember seeing any goddesses with hairpins, I noticed them because my mother's were made of metal, more like wire.

Mrs Kanello was tall and built like a man, and when she went by you could feel the earth shake. She worked as a telephone operator at the Three Ts, which is what we called the phone company back then. And today, even though she's over seventy, she walks like an amazon, now there was a woman for you, even though she doesn't have any of my, shall we say, femininity. Before the war, in the evenings, she and her sister used to sit on the front stop and croon 'Those eyes of yours', or maybe 'Don't shed your tears, it was just a wild fling ...' Every evening they'd sing but they never seemed to get any better: still, they were honest girls, even if they couldn't carry a tune in a bucket. But when the Occupation started, the singing stopped. Her sister disappeared. Went off to the mountains to be with her fiancé people said.

Nowadays Mrs Kanello can sing to her heart's content. Mind you, I don't approve of her songs politics-wise, I mean to say. She's still living there in Rampartville, but her children are in Athens. So when she comes to pay them a visit, she drops by to see me too. There I'll be, in the kitchen brewing coffee and I overhear her singing to herself, just as off-key as ever, but I don't mention it because she's kind of sensitive, always thought she was some big deal as a singer. Her kids grew up just fine though; why she's even got a married daughter living in Europe, but she never took on airs, socially speaking. A good-looking woman, widowed, with a pension, which she got strictly on her own; one look at her from behind and you'd swear she was my age, that's what I say to make her feel good. Got the idea from this psychiatrist after the time I had a fit on stage; since then it's tough to find work with a reputable company. Anyway, my director takes me to this psychiatrist, you can bet your life it's on my health insurance card. Don't you worry, dear, the doctor says, go on a pension and take a long rest. And say nice things about people. Saying nice things about people is the best medicine. You artists are always saying nasty things about people, especially you actors, that's why you're all so unhappy.

After that it takes more than a little fit or two to faze me. I don't even stick my head out the window any more, just close it and wait, what's there to worry about? It's just a fit, it'll soon be over and done with; five or six hours and it'll be finished. Why, I even bite into a hand towel so nobody can hear me, learned that trick at the movies. That's why I say nice things about Mrs Kanello's waistline and her appearance too, and besides she's a fine lady, with a fine pension.

She married before the war, fine looking man, and a hard worker too. They had four children, one after the other, but come the Occupation there she was, stuck with the little tykes and a husband who couldn't work any more. The way I hear it, he opened the window one night around midnight and, all of a sudden, he was bewitched, wham, right in the eyes, may even have been the evil eye; people are always jealous of good looks and happiness. Anyway, from then on the poor man suffered some kind of phobia, never left the house again; imagine, barely thirty years old. A fine, handsome man, for sure. He helped out with the housework, looked after the kids while his wife was working at the TTT, even learned how to repair shoes; he fixed ours for free! Only you didn't dare ask him to stick his nose outside. He got as far as the balcony maybe twice, after Liberation. Finally, thirty-four years later he left the house with honour and dignity, his own kids carrying him in an open casket. They held the funeral at the town cathedral – Mrs Kanello spared no expense. She used to work double shifts at the TTT, then line up for the public soup kitchen, bring home the boiled wheat in her lunch bucket, feed the kids, do the laundry and next morning off she'd go to work at seven o'clock sharp.

On Sundays, she and Mlle Salome used to scour the countryside for food to steal. Aphrodite tagged along too, coughing: that was while she could still get around. Pieces of fruit from garden fences, or vegetables from garden plots, you name it, they grabbed whatever they could lay their hands on. It was a scary business. Let me tell you; the peasants had illegal guns and they'd start shooting at the drop of a hat, before you even set foot on their land. Anyway, one time they came across a grazing cow. Hey, there's one they missed, says Mrs Kanello and she lies down right smack under the cow's udder and milks it into her mouth, then she gets up and holds the cow while Mlle Salome and Aphrodite take their turn at the tit. After that incident she always carried this little bottle around with her, but she never ran into a stray cow again.

One thing we never could figure out was how come they were always toting bags or baskets full of vegetables on those country outings of theirs. Later we found out the baskets were filled with hand grenades. They were really secret messengers all along – Mrs Kanello was the leader – and the grenades were for the partisans. Who would ever suspect a couple of half-starved women? And Aphrodite was only seventeen at the time. Mlle Salome even brought along her mandolin, they made like they were going for an outing in the country, downright batty they looked. The grenades they handed over to Thanassis, a retarded kid about my age, the schoolmaster's son from a village name of Vounaxos.

Half the TTT was occupied by the Italians. In the meantime, Mrs Kanello managed to pick up a few words of Italian, learned it from a Teach Yourself book – what a gal! – the better to eavesdrop on the Occupying Powers. She wrote everything down on scraps of paper she dropped off at the public urinals. That was another scandal, a woman hanging around in the men's urinals, a lot of people were whispering about immoral behaviour. In fact one old fellow gets all confused one day and asks her, What are you doing here, you virago? But she fires right back at him, Come on, old man, button up, you ain't got much to show there.

All that I found out later; I heard they even gave her a medal, when the Republic came in. But still, people say that on account of her lousy Italian she passed on mistaken information and they blew up the wrong bridge, but they were probably saying that out of jealousy; people were jealous of her because she was a linguist. Anyway, back then, every so often some peasant or another would come by the TTT during work hours and drop off a basket of potatoes or mustard greens. From your Godmother he'd say. The rumour was that Mrs Kanello had a lover. Only my mother didn't believe it and took her side (Signor Alfio was visiting her regularly back then). Mrs Kanello a lover? Can't be: she's an honest woman. Finally Mrs Kanello finds out and says to Ma, Shut up Asimina and let 'em talk. I sure as hell don't want 'em thinking I'm doing anything else. Because she was one patriotic lady, let me tell you. The baskets were crammed full of grenades, bullets and all kinds of ammunition hiding there under the potatoes. And she'd go strutting by – can you imagine, she had to be crazy! – in front of the Carabineria just as proud as you please carrying those food baskets of hers; after all, it was right on the way to her house. Had to rest every so often, too; those baskets weighed a ton. The Italians at the Carabineria knew her; half of them worked with her at the TTT in fact. So one fine day, one of them comes up to her when she sets down the basket right next to the sentry post in order to catch her breath and the sentry says, Signora, let me give you a hand. She was pregnant again, by the way. That's very nice of you, she says, and together the two of them lug the basketful of

22

ammunition all the way to her door. Mangiare, eh? says the Italian (that's how they say 'eat'). What am I supposed to do with four and a half bambini to feed? she says. Talk about a dingbat!

When her belly starts to show Aphrodite's mother pipes up, Are you crazy? Getting yourself knocked up when everybody's going hungry and starving! How are you going to manage? I really wasn't all that wild about it, says Mrs Kanello. I'll have a tough time hauling the ammunition, but my husband's indoors all the time, he can't go to the movies, can't find his favourite sweets, what's he supposed to do for entertainment? Still, she wouldn't hear of getting rid of it, no matter what Plastourgos's wife said, even if she was a trained midwife and an honest woman besides. So Mrs Kanello went about her work with a bulging belly, not to mention those Sunday outings of hers with the hand grenades.

But one day they call her into the Carabineria for questioning. Seems someone squealed on her about the outings with the mandolin. What I really mean to say is. I know who – a woman it was – squealed on her. She's married to a member of parliament now, so I don't want to get involved and maybe get my pension cut off.

We knew all about the Resistance; but even if they slit the throats of our dear ones we would never breathe a word, even if we were nationalists back then. Mother sent me to find Signor Alfio before it was too late, but I couldn't find him. So they held her, questioned her for five hours in the Carabineria, even beat her, and her seven months pregnant. Fortunately Signor Alfio finally appears, I know the signora from the TTT, he says, she's all right. And the whole time that dingbat Kanello is screaming at them, Let me out of here, it's my shift, I'll get fined! Finally they let her go. She lost one of her shoes in the beating – we all wore clogs with thick wood soles back then – and when they told her, Get going, off with you, she hustled down the stairs as fast as her legs would carry her.

23

When she reaches the street she realizes she only has one shoe. Corporal, give me back my shoe! she shouts. An upstairs window pops open and the clog comes flying out, hits her smack on the forehead, you wonder how it didn't knock the poor woman out – those women's clogs weighed a good five pounds each. Anyway, she slips on her shoe and stalks off swearing, with a goose-egg this big on her forehead, cursing Italy up and down like you can't imagine.

Like I say, all the women wore open-heeled wooden shoes back then: you tell me where were we supposed to find shoe leather – any kind of leather – for soles? When all their pre-war shoes wore out, the women changed over to clogs. Before, the only people who ever wore them were washerwomen, poor washerwomen at that, to keep from slipping on the soapsuds. But during the Occupation they were all the rage, even ladies from the best families just had to wear them. They made the soles from a solid piece of wood, with thick, high heels that looked something like upside-down castle turrets, and the uppers they wove into patterns taken from curtain material: then the women would take them to the shoemaker and he would tack them together, and hey presto, you'd have your year-round open-toe, open-heel model. In wintertime women wore them with long woollen stockings plus ankle socks against the cold: chilblains were the biggest problem. And when you'd get three women walking down the street together, the Italians would rush out on to the balcony of the Carabineria with their guns at the ready. The drumming of clogs on the pavement sounded like a machine-gun going off. Not to mention the howls of pain from inside the houses from sprains and twisted ankles and suchlike. What did they really want with those massive five-inch wood heels anyway? So you take the high heels and hunger, and people got so dizzy that the streets were full of women with dislocated joints, high society ladies too. Me, I wore clogs for the first time just before the so-called Liberation, when I began to be a little miss.

Six weeks after the beating Mrs Kanello gave birth. The pains came at night but it was curfew; what a dingbat, always doing things topsy-turvy, just how were they supposed to fetch her mother all the way from the other side of Rampartville? Sure, Plastourgos's wife volunteered. She was a trained midwife and as honest as they come. Lived close by too, but the women didn't trust her. She was too educated they said and, worse yet, she was too young: they wanted somebody with plenty of experience. Fortunately Signor Alfio was just leaving our place so he escorted me over to fetch her mother, who delivered her just fine. The old lady had me stay to boil water but when I opened the door to hand her the kettle she cursed me for bringing an Italian to her house. Now people will say I've taken an enemy of the Motherland for a lover, she said. Anyway, the baby came out just as fine as you could wish, a little boy. That's my last one, said Mrs Kanello. How was she supposed to know she'd have yet another one when the war was over, when Scobie was running the country.

Bright and early next morning Kanello is up and around, suckles her newborn, swaddles it and then herself; around ten she picks up her lunch bucket and an extra cooking pot and is just about to go out the door. Her mother is furious: You heathen, you're not going out? You still got thirty-nine days to go, you're unclean! But just try and hold her back, unclean or not: she wasn't about to miss the Red Cross soup kitchen.

The lady neighbours – Aphrodite's mother and the Tiritombas, you know, the impresario's family – spot her queuing for her portion of porridge, looking pale as a sheet and thin as a rail. Padded belly or no padded belly, it was no use: she was ashwhite from loss of blood and her eyes were glazed over. She did her best to walk like Scipius Africanus but she couldn't stand up straight. What's the matter? the impresario's wife asks her. What happened to your belly? They prod her and poke her just to make sure, then carry her back home, and she's braying the

25

whole way back about losing her ration. Just then Mother comes out on to the street. What with Signor Alfio she didn't have to queue at the soup kitchen. I'd go instead, with ration coupons; Sotiris was gone but we used his coupon anyway. So what, if it was illegal? The Red Cross ladies gave me his portion. They couldn't imagine how a cute little girl like me could be cheating them.

While Mrs Kanello was recovering my mother put in her first appearance at the food line, to pick up her rations for her. At first the Red Cross ladies drove her away, but Signor Alfio went over and told them something in a low voice and they dished up the rations for Kanello's family without saying a word; in fact, they even threw in an extra spoonful. It went on that way for a whole week, which was how long Mrs Kanello was bedridden. The other women in the queue made nasty remarks about Mother, here comes the collaborator, they'd hiss. Well, maybe we were collaborators, but Aphrodite's mother and the Tirit-omba family took our side. Poor Aphrodite, she couldn't come to the food queue any more because she'd just come down with consumption.

Just as soon the new mother could get around, Ma stopped going to the soup line. But Mrs Kanello, she talked to us, treated us like human beings, even when they humiliated Mother in public right after the so-called Liberation. Anyway, before we knew it, she was back on her feet, caring for Aphrodite too. The girl's consumption was getting worse by the day, but she kept on crocheting her doilies. One day Kanello tried to convince some village yokels to sell her a little olive oil. He kicked her out. Believe you me, was she fuming! On the way back to give Aphrodite's Ma the bad news, she runs into the daughter of the local newsstand owner, Koupas was the guy's name. Koupas' brood mare, we called her; well-built and plump she was, and as far as we were concerned that made her just about the best-looking woman in town. Get a load of the fat oozing off her, the men would say, drooling. But she wouldn't so much as glance at a man because she was shacked up with an Italian officer. Anyway, Mrs Kanello spies her coming down the street, shaking and shimmying, and out of the blue she grabs her and starts pounding her for all she's worth. And the poor girl stands there whining, Why are you hitting me, Madam? Who are you? Have we been introduced? What did I ever do to you? Introduced or not, fires back Kanello. Take that, you fat cow!

That was the best she could do for Aphrodite. And meantime, the poor kid was getting weaker and weaker.

Aphrodite, now there was a real beauty for you. With a real bust. She and her mother crocheted lace for other girls' dowries, but come the Occupation the customers dried up. I never had much of a bust myself, before or after the Liberation, and later when I was in the theatre, you know, my various lovers and admirers really let me hear about it, teeny tits they called me. Not only did Aphrodite have a bust, she had lovely skin, the colour of ripe grapes, and clear blue eyes, the only pair of blue eyes in the district, all the rest of us were darkies. Me, I only turned blonde since the Dictatorship. She had this warm laugh and hair that seemed to curl in the wind. A gorgeous girl. But six months after she got consumption all that was left of her was a shrivelled up sack of skin, like some saintly relic. Even her eyes went pale. Ma would take her margarine whenever Signor Alfio brought us some, but the girl kept getting thinner and thinner. Her knees where thicker than her thighs. Be brave my little one, her ma would tell her as they crocheted away, We're almost there, Mr Churchill says so. That was because we heard over the underground radio that Churchill was winning and Hitler was losing. Mrs Kanello told us the same thing when she'd come back from her ammunition delivery outings with a basketful of wild artichokes. She had bats in her belfry, that woman. One day, so she said, as she's slogging along bent double under the load, she reaches the top of a little hill. All around her, nature

27

(what does nature care about people's troubles, anyway?) is dolled up in its Sunday best; she turns to Salome and says, I'm going to celebrate, and blow off a hand-grenade. Been carrying them all this time, never once heard one of them go off. So she climbs up the hill, pulls the pin – that's what she called it – and heaves the grenade down the hill. All springtime echoes with the explosion. In fact, one of the strings on Salome's mandolin pops. Then two German soldiers come dashing out of the swamp at the bottom of the hill, underpants down to their boot tops; they must've been performing some unnatural act or other when the grenade went off. The Germans officers wouldn't let the soldiers go with local women, that's why they had to satisfy each other, so people said.

Mrs Kanello's front window was bright and sunny all day long. Later, when our Fanis came down with adenoids because he grew too fast and had to spend most of his time in bed, Mrs Kanello would invite him over and sit him down in the window, The sun's full of calories, nothing like it for what ails you, she said. We gave him a medicine called antipyrine, something like quinine powder but bright yellow and bitter. Our front window got no sunlight. We only had one floor and it was behind the church.

That's when Mrs Kanello got it into her head to bring Aphrodite over for some sunlight. But Aphrodite didn't care about anything any more, all she did was smile that faint smile of hers. She didn't even care that she wasn't getting any news from her father in the partisans. Plus in addition we had some unseasonal rain storms. Aphrodite would sit for hours on end at her window, with the curtains half-drawn, staring off into the distance, seeing nothing. As her condition got worse, her mother had to lift her up and carry her over to her chair. For hours on end she would draw invisible shapes on the window glass with her fingertip. I waved at her from the street as I went by, but I don't think she even saw me.

28

In the meantime the Tiritombas family left town, on tour, believe it or not. I'll get around to that in a minute, it's a whole story in itself. If you can imagine. A whole company going on the road on account of a goat!

We weren't hungry any more. Not that we were living like royalty, mind you, but with what little Signor Alfio brought us every week we managed to stay on our feet, and little Fanis got over his adenoids. Signor Alfio kept on seeing Mother: better for him than going to some streetwalker not to mention no worry about venereal diseases. Besides, he was married back home plus he was shy, he couldn't have made it with a whore, also he loved his wife, and praised her to the skies whenever he talked to us. So that's why he preferred to satisfy his sexual needs with a nice clean-living little housewife.

Leave the house? Mother wouldn't hear of it – except maybe the odd evening when Mrs Kanello invited her over for some chit-chat, or maybe to help hang out the washing. Meanwhile, the toughest regulations were lifted; the conquerors realized we were law-abiding subjects, the curfew didn't begin until midnight. The movies started up again: now it was all German operettas, of course, with Marika Rökk, and those Hungarian tear-jerkers with Pal Javor and Katalin Karady, plus the odd Italian item.

Fanis and me would go to the movies together. Signor Vittorio would get us in for free, he was from the Carabineria too – a replacement. Signor Alfio had gone back to his home country by then. It was cheap, general admission – only five million. Nothing, really, when you think that a box of matches went for three million, but where were we supposed to find the money? Anyway, I stuffed Fanis's pocket full of raisins and off we went to the five o'clock show. Before we went in we asked old Uncle Grigoris at the ticket window, Any food? And if he nodded yes, then we went in.

Because we only went to the movies that showed food.

29

Nobody ever ate a bite in the tear-jerkers. But in the operettas there were always banquet scenes, tables piled high with food, while the leads just talked, and no one ate, hardly touched a bite. It was so bad one day a man shouted out at Willy Frisch up on the screen, Eat something, for God's sake! People came to drool over the food scenes, and they burst out laughing. But this German soldier, he thought they were insulting the fatherland, so he ripped the man out of his seat and beat him.

We always got our fill with those movies, because there was a second food scene, where the star would take the female lead to a restaurant, or some swanky club to try and seduce her. At first all they would do was drink, and people would be getting impatient. But then would come the food. Mostly disgusting stuff like oysters and caviar – ever since then I can't even look at seafood. You think they ever ate things like bean soup or roasts or boiled pig's heads? In one film they did eat some eggs though. Most of the time when the food scenes were over, Fanis would tug me on the sleeve to go home because then came the love scenes and the mushy stuff. Since then, in fact generally speaking, I never cared much for love-making, it always seemed a bit like a kind of surgical operation there in bed, with the male of the species flopping around all over me, even nowadays, is what I mean to say.

Signor Vittorio, he wasn't as gallant as Signor Alfio. Even if he was an interpreter, too. Signor Alfio brought him by one evening saying he was going back home and he wanted to introduce his replacement to Mother. That evening he was so upset he forgot to bring us food. I'd say he was just about ready to cry when he kissed us, me and our Fanis. Anyway, he gave us some money, and we walked him to the corner so as to leave Mother alone with the new gentleman. Meantime, we could hardly wait for the introductions to end. Mrs Chrysafis, the lady with the narrow two-storey place just across the street, gave us a recipe book and in the evenings I would read recipes to Mrs Chrysafis and Kanello's kids. First would come the main course, then the desserts, all chock full of meringues and custards.

The money Signor Alfio gave us we clutched tight in our fists, and when Signor Vittorio left we hurried into the house. But Mother told me to get same paper, she wanted to write something. So I dug around until I found my school bag, pulled out my pen, my ink pot and tore a lined sheet of paper out of my exercise book, I hadn't opened the bag for three years. Roubini, she says, after your brother's asleep I need you. Fortunately our Fanis dropped right off and I wrote a letter to Signor Alfio just as my mother dictated it. Then I wrote it out again, clean, and the next morning Fanis delivered it to the Carabineria: fortunately Signor Alfio was still there, so he handed it right to him. The original I still have right here in my purse.

Respected signor Alfio,
I am the lady who you have been visiting for these last two years, just behind the church of Saint Kyriaki, Asimina by name, and I write you by the hand of my daughter Roubini being as how I am illiterate.
I thank you for such regular visits for two years now, for your kindness and for your food. Also I thank you for introducing me to your successor, as I am a homebody and I never could have found him all by myself.
Know that wherever you may be for the rest of your life I will always be thankful to you for rescuing my children from death by starvation, but also for giving me much satisfaction. I confess that as a man I esteemed you more than my spouse and primarily you made me a woman with the kindness which you showed me.
I am a married woman, maybe a widow even, but I had tender feelings for you which it never happened to me before in my life to desire a gentleman so much. I never revealed them but I am telling you now when you are not present and you will not come back again to my house. I do not condemn my maybe dear departed husband, but if we had peace I would

31

never take food from you. And the shirts and the underwear I washed for you I washed with pleasure, and I would happily wash them for you for my whole life. And as I was washing them in the soapsuds, I imagined you were my blessed husband, this you should know also.

I send you my blessings. You are the enemy of my nation but you have a little mother waiting for you I know that much. I do not know what nation means and I never saw what they call a nation.

I hope that you and your family will keep well, and that you have a safe return to your missus. She seemed so nice in the photograph you showed me. You were a real gentleman, and truly warm. That brought me comfort, especially in the wintertime, I felt so guilty with my children outside in the cold but fortunately you finished quick and neat. I want you to know that I only began this work with you, before I never did such a thing. And that with you I felt truly wonderful maybe it is not a patriotic thing to say it maybe it is a sin even, but I am not afraid for there is nothing above to punish me, for if there was, why did not it help me in my hour of need? Does the Above only exist to punish? Then it does not exist.

I hope that you are well pleased with our cooperation, you are a man of fine sentiments, I have heard that all the Italians are like that, by nature.

I wish you health and long life, and I wish for victory for your country and for mine also. And so you can understand how genuine are my emotions I end with two cheers Long live Greece, Long live Italy.

Your very respectfully yours,
Meskaris Asimina
(by the hand of her daughter)

I copied the letter out, then we broke down in tears and we didn't even know why, just sat there in each other's arms, crying hush hush, trying not to wake up my kid brother. I remembered the money from Signor Alfio, laid mine on the table and opened Fanis's fist in his sleep and took his. Then I gave it all to Mother and that night I slept in her bed for the first time, I didn't even ask her and she didn't ask me. She even let me empty the washbasin.

Back then we turned up money on the street too, small change, the odd 50,000 note. My teacher Mr Pavlopoulos – I wasn't at school any more – he lived right around the corner from the church but he still said hello and every 15th of the month he'd take me along when he went to pick up his pay. They paid him in bills, two gunny sacks half full, and we lugged them along, him carrying one, me the other. A bit on the short side he was, but a good looking man, my first love, I think, but at the time I didn't know it. Where could he be now? Always gave me a million drachma bill or two. The small stuff we found on the street, we saved it for the collection plate, Fanis and me, when we went to church on Sundays. Not that Father Dinos would scold us if we didn't give anything, that's for sure. Why we went to church every week was so we could take communion at the end which Father Dinos cut up into good-sized slices, plenty of people – and he knew it – the only reason they came at all was to get a bite of holy bread, he gave us two extra slices, For your parents, he said. But if the faithful didn't contribute he'd give them holy hell. So you can snatch the holy bread, but you can't quite reach the collection basket to help the church, eh! He knew what he was talking about all right; some of them were wives of black marketeers or peasants who bought houses in Rampartville with payment in kind, say, two cans of olive oil and two loads of wheat for a house with a courtyard, you know, the kind of people the partisans sent packing.

Sometimes we tried our luck at Saint Athanassios church, their parish priest was a saintly sort. He made us a sign to wait till after mass and then he slipped us a whole slice of holy bread. Still, we didn't make a habit of it, seeing as how every time his son Avakoum would go by swinging his censer all dressed up in his altar-boy get-up, he hissed in my ear how he wanted to talk dirty to me and me, I was supposed to sit there and like it. That's what all the men want from me anyway, generally speaking, but back then I just wasn't in the mood. That's all they ever want, you bet your life, maybe I do egg them on a bit, I admit maybe I am a bit of a tease, what am I supposed to do? Not come across?

After Alfio henceforth Mother never went to mass as she knew it would scandalize the faithful. Only one time she went for evening prayers and some woman hissed, Collaborators get out of church, Father Dinos cuts the woman off cold: breaks off the prayer and says, Now listen to me, do not judge your fellow man, the Church is big enough for everyone. But Mother, she never went again. Here in Athens even, the only church she ever set foot in was the chapel at the cemetery, in her coffin I mean. Generally speaking, I inherited my self-respect from her. Once on tour, up in north Thessaly I think it was, some smart-ass starts making remarks right in the middle of the performance, How much a one-night stand? he yells. Once he says it, twice, so I stop the show, step up front stage and say, Listen here mister, just who do you think you're insulting like that? I paid my money didn't I, miss? he shoots back, You're an actress, right? So you're a whore. Listen here, mister, I say. So maybe we're whores, but buggered out we ain't. We got our work to do, so sit down and shut up. That got a laugh, but afterwards the director comes up to me and says, Raraou you got a hole where your brain ought to be.

Not long after Signor Vittorio took Signor Alfio's place Aphrodite died, poor thing. Fought death to the last, she did. Hour after hour we waited, every night for two whole months, first my mother then Mrs Kanello spent the night at their place, so her mother wouldn't have to meet death alone; it was their first death. Her mother couldn't sleep, all night long she crocheted away on Aphrodite's dowry (after the Occupation she went and sold it all) and every so often she'd take off her glasses and check to see if her sleeping daughter was still breathing. Then back to her crocheting. Next to her my mother was nodding sleepily, and I was cat-napping with my feet all warm and cozy under Aphrodite's covers. Good girl, keeping her feet warm, Ma said, but Aphrodite couldn't feel the warmth. Couldn't feel the cold neither. I say to Ma, Ma wake me up if she dies when I'm asleep. I don't want to catch it. I thought you could catch death.

One time our little Fanis goes to their place on an errand and Aphrodite sends him away. Don't come in here, I've got the sickness, she said. The sickness, back then that was what they called consumption, it was kind of a fashionable sickness you read about in novels where the hero abandons the heroine and she gets consumption every time.

Not that I never saw a corpse before, mind you; far from it. Before the war it was an everyday sight. Back then in Rampartville if you went to take your appendix out, most likely they'd cart you out of hospital dead, from wealthy families too, this banker's son died in an operation and he was only seventeen.

I was just a little girl, maybe seven years old, when I saw my first corpse and believe you me I wasn't impressed. Looked just like everybody else, far as I could see. Lying there in the casket with the bearer walking alongside holding the cover and the priest following along behind, chanting and greeting people he knew on the street. Further back came the mourning family, and then altar boys carrying the church banners on the ends of long poles (sometimes they'd even start fencing with phem), and behind them came the mourners and the curious. They planned the funeral march so it would pass through all the main streets of Rampartville, that's what almost all the relatives of the dear departed insisted on, plus it was kind of a social recognition, a way for the dead man to bid farewell to the street where he used to take his Sunday stroll. Wherever the procession passed, the shopkeepers would close their doors for a moment

35

out of respect, make the sign of the cross, then it was back to business. People on the pavement would doff their hats and wait with bowed heads for the remains and the priest in his full church get-up to pass by.

So when Aphrodite died it was nothing special, just so I didn't go catching death from her. Ever since I was three I heard plenty of stories about dead people, how they climb up out of their graves at night and make the living do their bidding. Fairy tales, that's all it is, my godmother told me once. Don't you believe a word of it child, dead people are good people.

Later, what with the Occupation and the partisans, I saw plenty of dead people, forget the coffins. Saw a two-week-dead corpse all puffed up, hanging from the bell tower, back when the partisans liberated us and before the English liberated us. And I saw Security Battalion Home Guards, Secbats we called them back then, trussed up against the wall with their bellies sliced open in an X all the way from the shoulder and their trousers pulled down to their knees. Now that I'm over sixty (even if I don't look a day over forty – there was this man pulled out a condom so I wouldn't get pregnant, can you believe it!) and I'm shocked at the sight of a dead body, as I should be if I may say so. Well, a small town girl is one thing and a lady from Athens is another you'll say, and an artiste to boot, but these eyes of mine have seen plenty, you can be sure about that!

I didn't see Aphrodite dead because on the afternoon she expired I was playing outdoors, Mrs Kanello spots me and sends me off to a farm close by to fetch milk for our little Fanis as he was a growing boy.

When I got back, Aphrodite had breathed her last breath. Her lamp ran out of oil, Ma said, go pay your last respects. Me, by the time I reached the top of the stairs the door was wide open like it was some kind of name-day party, in fact two Italians had wandered in thinking it was a house of ill-repute. I look into the girl's room, but all I see is her feet, and Mrs Kanello rubbing them, trying to keep them warm, and Aphrodite's mother is sitting there still crocheting her lace. But just then Fanis calls out from downstairs, Come quick, partisans, They caught some partisans, let's go and see! We head for the square; nothing. When they brought in dead partisans they usually dumped them in the square, as an example. But this time they captured live ones and they were holding them at the gaol house, which was really a rented house.

There were even some women partisans. Small people they were, nothing but skin and bones and dressed in rags, I never saw women wearing army tunics before, they looked like peasants. The Italians let us stare at the partisans but then a truckful of Germans came roaring up and they shooed us off, *Via, via*, they said. We left. So, that was my first look at real live partisans. They had them locked up in the kitchen, more than twenty of them, don't ask me how they crammed them all in there. Anyway, you wouldn't catch me in an army tunic even if I was freezing to death, even if not one but ten Motherlands said I had to, back then I was fashion conscious and I didn't know it, that's why the men just couldn't keep their hands off me. Some can't even today.

Anyway the partisans, they really disappointed me, as men. All us women used to whisper about them among ourselves. I imagined they were all like some kind of Captain Courageous in those penny novels Mlle Salome used to read us: real giants ten feet tall, well-fed with victory smiles just like the American actors in the movies after the war who went around liberating exotic countries. Mlle Salome worshipped the partisans, makes sense you'll say, after all, she was from a left-wing family. Well, we used to get together at the Tiritomba family's place before they went on the road, and trick our hunger with jokes. Aphrodite's mother would be there with her lace, my mother would bring her mending, and Mrs Kanello would bring along

37

fried chick-pea cakes for snacks. Everybody talked about what Mr Churchill said on the radio the night before. Mrs Adrianna Tiritomba was hard at work knitting a sweater from unravelled wool, the Partisan's Sweater they called it, it was Mrs Kanello's idea, just as they used to knit Soldier's Sweaters when we had the war in Albania.

Mlle Salome was knitting a pair of breeches. One day she opens them out to measure, we do a double take, the things were a good six feet long, with a pouch the size of a kid's head right between the legs. What in the world's got into you, you made them big enough for three men, says Mrs Kanello. You're only saying that because you're a royalist and you want to bring down the Movement, snaps Salome. The partisans are giants and here you are, trying to tell me they're midgets? Well, says Mrs Adrianna as she points to the pouch hanging there between the legs, If you're starving you dream about bread. That set off a ruckus. But from that day on I got it into my head that the partisans were taller than normal people; that's why I was so disappointed when I saw my first live specimens in the gaol-house kitchen that evening.

After we left the gaol house I felt sleepy and went right home to bed, so I missed it when Aphrodite expired. Signor Vittorio even came by but I told him Ma's out and he left. After, I washed the dishes and cleaned up the floor, some little shoots were poking up through the earth again. In fact, over in the pullet's corner the earth had started to sink, as though the pullet was sinking deeper and deeper into the ground.

I only made it to the funeral but I didn't stick around for long, there was a memorial service close by, so little Fanis and I snuck over to get some sweets.

But I did go along on Aphrodite's last outing, about a month before she died.

About a month before she died Aphrodite ups and says, Ma, take me for an outing, I want to go to the seaside.

There was a little port about eleven kilometres from Rampartville by train, for the provinces back then it was an enormous distance, nothing like getting around in Athens these days with the trolley-bus. Of course it wasn't the first time for me; before the war our school went on a trip there. But Aphrodite had never seen the water before, not once, she was always making plans to go, back before the war, but somehow things just never worked out. Come the Occupation there was no way you could go. The Germans had requisitioned the train and the only civilians who had permission to ride it were the black marketeers. So all poor Aphrodite could do was to stare at the sea from the top of a hill just up from the church, where we used to graze our dear departed pullet. Then all of a sudden, a month before she dies she comes out with, Ma, take me to the seaside.

Her mother Mrs Fanny had the windows closed and the shutters barred from a couple of days back. Keeping out the cold draughts, she said. But down deep she was getting the house ready for mourning. Got to let my husband know about the girl, I was supposed to tell Mrs Kanello for her. That's when I discovered Aphrodite's father was in the partisans but they kept it hush-hush and Mrs Kanello made me swear on the holy icons not to breathe a word to my ma, seeing as how because Signor Vittorio might catch on. Also she let drop that Mrs Fanny wasn't getting along with her husband; an unfortunate marriage it was. Anyway, she tells me to tell the sick girl's mother, God help him, Mrs Fanny if your husband hears about it and tries to come into town they'll grab him and make mincemeat out of him.

On the spot Mrs Kanello up and leaves kids and husband behind, takes off from work just as bold as brass and goes off to look after her mother. (Now there's an old strumpet if I ever saw one, ninety-six and still flirting with her grandchildren if you please, a temptress right up to the last, old lady Marika was, and a real doll. I've got to admit it, I confess, even though she chewed the hell out of me when I went to her place with Signor

Alfio. But now she's gone to a better world by far, God rest her soul.)

At which point Mrs Fanny bars the front door too. The hunger was really something, but she was of good family so she wouldn't dream of asking for food or fighting for a place in the queue at the soup kitchen. What was the use, anyway? The consumption inside her daughter kept getting bigger. Things went on that way for about a month, me, I'd forgotten they even existed, what with their house closed up tight and not a word. Only at night, sometimes, I heard a kind of howling sound, like a wolf. It was Mrs Fanny howling in her sleep, from hunger. Instead of dreaming dreams full of food to let off steam, all she did was howl, at least that's how Mrs Kanello explained it to me after the war. I could hear the howling, for sure. If you're not getting enough nourishment you don't get a good night's sleep, you see, and I asked Mother, what's that noise? Go to sleep, she would say, it's a jackal in town, or maybe the Germans are torturing someone at the Kommandantur. (She never had a bad word to say about the Italians.)

And one morning in April Mrs Fanny throws open all her doors and windows like she won the jack-pot. Neighbours, she calls out in a voice that sounded like she was laughing and at the same time tears were running down her cheeks, let's go for an outing to the seaside. Doors popped open on all the balconies, but Mrs Fanny called on our little one-storey place first, and believe you me it was a big honour for my poor mother. Asimina, Aphrodite's mother tells her, she's lost all her blood, no chance anyone will catch the sickness. And she wants to go to the seaside.

And we all came out of our houses. How many women are we? asks one. They counted me as one of the women. Eleven altogether. My brother Fanis tagged along too. What with the train requisitioned by the Germans, we set out on foot for the port to give Aphrodite her first look at the sea and then say goodbye, that was always her wish before the war.

40

And the front door swung open and four lady neighbours carried Aphrodite out perched in a chair, and we set out, leaving the door open so the house could breathe.

And not much remained of Aphrodite. Her breasts are gone, I said to myself. Her legs were shrunk: just like a little girl again she was, like an eleven-year-old boy with malaria. Just as if when she was starting to grow taller and get bigger, her body took fright and tried to shrink back into itself again.

And we carried her sitting in her chair, the eleven of us, all eleven kilometres to the port, trading off carrying the chair every 100 paces or so. Along the way the villagers threw stones at us so we wouldn't steal their green crab apples or the buds on the grapevines along the stone fences. But little Fanis managed to swipe a head of lettuce.

And even me. I took part in carrying the chair along with three other women a couple of times. When I think about it, it was that day, on that very excursion, was when I was given the honour of becoming a woman. The others were all older than me but not one of them called me the kid or the dim-wit, nobody was afraid I'd tire myself out, nobody did me any special favours, not one. So by the time we finally reached the seaside, I wasn't a kid any more. I was a grown-up and a woman.

And we spread out our blanket on the sand right by the water just as Aphrodite wished. And we set her down; the day was cool with a brisk breeze blowing in off the water and all of us had goose bumps. The salt spray spattered Aphrodite, but her skin didn't feel anything any more, not even goose bumps. And she was like a piece of unclaimed baggage, like a trunk the morning steamer had left behind. That's how come I knew Aphrodite was dying, she wasn't getting goose bumps. The drops of spray and the salty surf, one big waste of time they were, couldn't get a rise out of Aphrodite. All she could do was smile that washed-out smile of hers.

And we sat down for a meal of raisins and two quinces cooked in grape syrup. Aphrodite, wasn't a bit hungry, clutching two fistfuls of raisins. Hasn't eaten a thing for a month now, said her mother. That was the only good thing about always having the taste of blood in her mouth: she wasn't hungry any more. All the rest of us ate. And Aphrodite stared out at the sea and clutched the raisins in her hands and soaked up the sunlight with her legs wrapped in a blanket, like a little kid's legs they were, and late that afternoon she let out a single cry of Viva! Then she clammed up.

And on our way back to town we had to trade off chair-carrying chores more often. Nobody had any decent food to eat for months and it was as if our strength had got smaller. Not one of us sweated because not one of us had anything left to sweat.

And by the time we stopped halfway back to town to pick wild greens the weather had turned cloudy. The hills had gone reddish brown and now they were turning dark grey. Little Fanis sat down next to Aphrodite, he didn't know what to pick, what did you expect from a man? so he was having himself a good time; after all, we were on an outing and when you're on an outing you're supposed to have fun, aren't you? So down he sits next to Aphrodite and he asks Aphrodite, how come you caught the sickness, what's the sickness Aphrodite? Always was a bit simple minded. Seems that's when Aphrodite finally admitted to herself that she was going to die and she says, The sickness is a little girl without a home and she likes blood to drink and she's always cold. And whenever she sees a good person asleep without anybody to watch over him she cuddles up inside his chest to keep warm and sucks his blood and never comes out.

We got back home that evening. Seventeen days later Aphrodite was dead from the excess of tuberculosis. They stuck a little paper flag on top of her grave: it was a greeting from her father. Afterwards, when the partisans liberated Rampartville, he came back and put a real flag on her grave, a cloth one. One year later during the so-called December uprising in Athens it was, just before the Civil War, they captured him and slit his throat. But Mrs Fanny his wife is alive and well, right here in Athens what's more.

Strictly between us, all this heroic business never made any sense to me. I always say, What if we just let the Germans through our Nation, just let them go about their business and leave them alone? Wouldn't it have been better? Wouldn't we have spared ourselves the Occupation, the starvation? I mean, just what do we have to show for it, family-wise and nation-wise, all that rushing off to Albania to the front lines and all the knitting sweaters and for nothing, the whole lot of it? The other countries, the ones who didn't try to stand up to the Germans, were they so stupid? That craphead Churchill, a curse on his grave, how come we were the only ones he fooled? And further-more, I always say, Exactly what did we get out of the so-called Liberation? A face-full, that's what we got. We take the money from the Marshall plan and we rebuild Mandelas's brothel in Rampartville and a night-club in Athens, the Neptune Club I think it was, on Syngrou Boulevard. They say it was the first building in Greece to be built with American Marshall money, back when we had the Tsaldaris government if I'm not mis-taken.

That's what I told one impresario and he gives me the boot smack in the middle of a tour. Being a bit of a queer wasn't good enough for him, no, he had to be a patriot, and me. I'm not patriotic too maybe? You can bet if I was a boy no way would he dump me right in that dead-end dump but I gave him a piece of my mind, and how, and he just stood there gaping with little bubbles coming out the corners of his mouth.

Three days after Aphrodite's funeral who should appear but Mrs Kanello with a newborn baby in her arms. The whole neighbourhood is stunned. Father Dinos gives her a tongue-lashing. Don't you talk to me that way, she tells him. Aris is his name and that's what you're going to baptize him. I shall never bless the name of an idol-worshipper's god, he roared; still, he could take a hint. Aris just happened to be the top partisan big-shot back then, so after things had calmed down a bit, Aris is what he ended up baptizing the kid. We all thought she was off looking after her sick mother. Mother's just fine, so don't start getting ideas, she'll last until Liberation and then some, said Kanello. The kid's my sister's. (Her mother lasted until Liberation and the first beauty pageant and the Dictatorship: one tough old bird, believe you me.)

What happened was that her sister the partisan went and got herself knocked up and it was just about her time, that was the whole mystery. Her husband hid her in a sheepfold seeing as how she couldn't very well keep up with the band in the rough country and take part in attacks what with her belly up to her eyeballs, what's more she was useless as a fighter. Plus, Captain, someone in the band piped up, she makes an easy target.

So they sent out a call for Mrs Kanello. She pads herself, pre-tending to be pregnant, strolls right through the German lines and delivers her sister's baby, another dingbat, that sister of hers. Her husband left her a rifle and a few hand grenades, just in case. So Mrs Kanello cuts the cord, everything's just fine, and then she goes and lobs a grenade over the top of the hill for good luck, anyway, the kid came out male, scared the bejesus out of the sheep, it was all they could do to coax them back into the fold. Boy, did I ever get my fill of milk up there, just like a snake, Mrs Kanello told us as she suckled away. Come on, you little outlaw, suck, she'd say, and she'd unbutton her dress and push the kid's face up against her breast until he found the teat. Mrs Kanello's milk was always flowing, probably because of all the kids. Anyway, she nursed the little guy until Liberation, today he's about to retire, a merchant seaman he is and a fine-looking man. A lefty though. Too bad.

44

Back then, before the war, the women used to suckle their kids right on the front step with their breast showing, and there wasn't a husband who said a word, of course I'm talking about the lower classes of women. But they were proper ladies in every other respect and if a stranger so much as looked at his wife sideways the husband would beat her black and blue if he was a bit of a pipsqueak. But if he had some muscle and some guy dared to steal a glance at his wife he'd whip the piss out of the guy instead. Even during the Occupation men didn't give nursing mothers a second look, not the locals anyway. Me, maybe I was only thirteen years old, but they were always gobbling me up with their eyes. In fact, a couple of them even invited me to the dance academy. Don't you dare or I'll beat you within an inch of your life was Mrs Kanello's advice when I asked her (I never asked my mother about matters of morality, since she considered herself a collaborator and a compromised woman, on account of how Italians visited her).

The dance academy used to be a former lumber warehouse. For the town pharmacist, a certain Mr Patris who rented the top floor, it was an affront to his personal honour, he had this French wife, you see, and she didn't really have much time for Rampartville high society. The dance academy was for men, strictly. Society mothers sent their sons there for social polishing. Girls learned to dance from their mothers, or arranged for private lessons at home from the academy. The dance master Mr Manolitsis taught the tango, the fox trot and the waltz mostly, plus the rhumba and the hesitation waltz. Come Liberation, he started teaching swing. He was plumpish, short and light-footed and he wore high heels and he always danced the lady's role himself, and when he went by on his way to church he always greeted us politely. After ten lessons the most advanced pupils danced with each other and Mr Manolitsis took on the next group of beginners. But even when the lessons were over and the pupils graduated, they didn't leave. They spent their afternoons at the academy, it was like a kind of social club and everybody there dreamed of dancing with a real woman, not with some classmate or other.

Still, a few girls managed to sneak in. But if they did they could say goodbye to their good name, at least till they got married. That's how you never saw a woman go near the place. Later in the afternoon grown men would show up. They would dance with one another, men and boys, taking turns leading, so nobody's masculinity would suffer. They even say high school kids used to smoke cigarettes in there.

That was one of the things the grown-up women talked about at our get-togethers at Mrs Kanello's place. In wintertime we sat in a circle, you see, we were used to sitting in a circle around a charcoal brazier. So there we sat in a circle, with nothing in the middle, who could afford charcoal? Aphrodite's ma would drop by too, always brought her crocheting, she did, the same old lace for the dowries. Can you believe it? after Liberation she actually found some customers, everything she crocheted for her daughter during the Occupation she sold as a good price, why even a British officer bought some.

So we sat in a circle around the charcoal brazier that wasn't there, each of us with a blanket thrown over our laps to keep warm, and to hide our flab, cracked Mrs Kanello. But she avoided making remarks about flesh if my mother was around; Kanello was what you'd call a born self-taught gentlewoman. She'd steer the conversation around to social life in Rampartville, or politics. At least we're rid of those bastards the royals, she said. Just wait'n see what happens if the Brits try and stuff them down our throats after we win, it'll be the partisans all over again. Then my mother would open her mouth and disagree, You can't have Greece without a king, she said.

At Mum's forty-day memorial service I got it from Mrs Kanello how right after her first Italian, Signor Alfio, she ran to Father Dinos to confess her sins and – this is the priest telling

Kanello, mind you – what was really bothering her worst was the royal family. (Father Dinos was the biggest gossip in the neighbourhood; if you wanted everyone to know your deepest secret, just go and confess, so be it.) Mother was a royalist. She believed the Allies would win and bring back the Crown with full honours. The worst thing for Ma was sinning with the enemy, said the priest; how could a turncoat and an adulteress like her bear to live in the same country with the royal family, that was so honest, such a shining example? Don't worry your head, Asimina, the priest told her – what a nut he was! – how are you supposed to keep your kids alive? If I was in your place I'd be a whore too. Get a load of this, Rita's sweetheart the whore-priest calling her a 'whore'. That's when Mother really hit bottom, said Kanello. She always knew she was a turncoat, but a whore? Never even crossed her mind. So when the priest called her one there went her self-respect.

Well, naturally, back then I didn't know what they were talking about, sitting around the imaginary charcoal brazier; all I could think about was that before the war we used to put aluminium foil over the coals to keep them burning longer. Politically speaking, I didn't have a clue.

The better class of people in Rampartville, they didn't think too highly of the partisans. After the first year of the Occupation, almost all the more affluent homes in town began to invite the Italians in. Some even opened their doors to the Germans, they were bullheaded, the Germans I mean, wouldn't set foot in the house of a conquered people. But the Italians, talk about friendly. Why, open your door and they'd come strolling right in, with all the gratitude in the world. They weren't even too proud for our place, dirt floor and all. I know, I know, Signor Alfio and Signor Vittorio, they weren't exactly the cream of the crop you'll say.

Homes like that, they didn't respect the partisans at all, that much I picked up from Kanello, and later from Salome. Sometimes, for their evening parties they hired the Tiritomba clan to put on a sketch, and Italians would be there. They were always good for a laugh, the Italians I mean, even if they didn't understand a word, applause too; as obliging as can be. One time Mlle Salome took me along for a bit role. You don't have a speaking part, she went; just stand still and I shove you towards Adrianna, and she shoves you back at me, nothing to be scared of.

Scared? Me? I knew what Italians looked like already, didn't I? So I played in the sketch, and if I do say so myself, from that night on I knew I was destined for the stage. By the way, I almost forgot to mention that they had food like in the movies, too. The minute the hosts went downstairs to show their guests to the door the troupe made a rush for the half-finished dinner plates. Eat, eat, said Mrs Adrianna, but if you leave grease spots on my good dress I'll whip the stuffings out of you. She had me dressed up in medieval dress, a *Cavalleria Rusticana* kind of stage costume or maybe it was an opera castaway. Anyway, I tucked my shift into my drawers, tightened the drawstrings (we didn't have elastic back then), and stuffed my corset with whatever I could lay hands on. No one even noticed; I took it all home and the family ate its fill.

Those fine upstanding citizens, the ones who made the Italians at home, they hated the partisans. Just you wait, when the partisans march into town one of these days heads will roll, that's how Mrs Kanello put it. Over the clandestine radio we kept hearing about the royal family's health; they were safe, somewhere in Africa I think it was. Why doesn't some cannibal do the Christian thing and eat them, said Mrs Kanello, and we shivered. I've got a confession to make, deep down I'm a republican, but I never held with the idea of getting rid of the royals. It was awfully discourteous, doing a thing like that and expelling the royal family like they did, in the plebiscite. Since then, us having no royals makes me feel like I'm on stage without my drawers on. I want to vote for them every chance I get, every election, whether it's for parliament or for city council, I don't care: whoever's on the ballot, I cry a little bit and I write, 'I vote Royal. Raraou.' Our member of parliament has my voter's registration book; I gave it to him when he brought us to Athens, all expenses paid. Still has Ma's too; she may be dead, the poor dear, but she still keeps on voting.

That's that. Fine with me, I mean, go ahead, be patriotic, with all the left-wing stuff and the trade-union talk and all the marches; me, I'll demonstrate and I'll go on strike just as good as the next man but give me the royals any day. Ever since they kicked them out I never really enjoyed Easter, even though I get my Easter bonus. Before, before the republic came in I mean, I used to go to mass at the cathedral every Easter and when I lit my candle, I told myself, the King was lighting his from the same flame! And the Commander in chief of all the armies would be there too! and after mass was over I'd go back to my little apartment, light my own little candle and keep the flame alive until the next Easter, even though I'm not a religious person. Nowadays, that's it for the candles. We want people to treat us as Europeans and we don't even have a royal family? I don't get it.

Nowadays I stay away from Easter mass. Not that I'm the religious kind; no more than I have to be. I used to think Mother was religious because she never said a word about God and all the rest. But one afternoon when she sent us over to the church so we wouldn't get wet from the rain while Signor Alfio was visiting, I told her I was scared of the church, especially in the dark with the saints up there on the altar, all full of spite, they looked downright uncivilized, and Mother says, Don't be afraid Roubini. God doesn't exist. Take your little brother Fanis and stay put or else you'll catch your death. That's all church is good for. Plus the holy bread the priest gives you every Sunday. So, she says, take our little tyke and wait there till I'm finished,

49

don't be afraid of the church, there's nobody there. It's your own home you should be afraid of.

That was the only catechism I ever got from my mother.

When she was on her last legs here in Athens, when I knew that she was on her way out I thought maybe she wanted to take communion, but I had to bring it up in a roundabout way so as not to make her suspicious, so I said, Mum, how about I call a priest to say a couple of prayers, what do you think? And she rolls over and turns her back to me and stares at her little bottle of pills.

Only one time I heard her cry, Holy Mother of God! The day when the Germans crushed our little Fanis's hand. That was before we knew Signor Alfio. I can still see it all plain as day, the whole neighbourhood was crazy with hunger. And Aphrodite's ma Mrs Fanny passes the word that Liakopoulos's warehouse is full of potatoes. Word spread like wildfire through the neighbourhood and we all congregated in the little square in front of the store, just a bit down the street from the church. I figure there must have been a good fifty of us, women and children mostly. It was around noon on a Sunday; some of the people had it in mind to break the door down, they were carrying pick-axes. But the Germans got there first: it was Liakopoulos himself who called them to come and restore order, the mob was threatening his goods. Get back, shouted Kanello. She had an axe in her hands and was about to lunge when we heard the truck. Get back, it's Germans, get back! They won't stop, they'll make mincemeat out of us.

We flattened ourselves against the wall across the street, the army truck came to a halt in front of the store and Mr Liakopoulos was standing there in the window, wearing a hat and a tie, if you please, staring at us, the idiot, as if he still didn't know what was going on.

The Germans pointed their machine-gun right at us. We weren't afraid, why should we be? Every day they pointed machine-guns at us. Then two of them climbed down from the truck, ripped open the metal shutter and went into the store-room. Then Mr Liakopoulos understood; he'd just tied his own noose. So, they tear open the shutter and what do they see? Inside the storeroom are sacks of potatoes stacked all the way up to the ceiling. The Germans started loading them into their truck. When Mr Liakopoulos saw what was happening, some-thing came over him: his daughters carried him back into the house, one of them even splashed water over his face.

'Maybe we won't be eating your stinking potatoes, you son of a bitch,' shouted Kanello, 'but you won't be selling them on the black market either!'

'Watch how you're talking, lady,' one of Liakopoulos's daughters shouts back at her, 'or I'll turn you in to the Kom-mandantur.'

'Go ahead and try it you slut,' Kanello yells. 'The partisans aren't far away. I'll have them burn your house down and the lot of you along with it, I've got my ways!' (Sure enough, their house went up in flames when the partisans attacked the town; coincidence, most likely.)

So there were the Germans emptying the storeroom; it was a regular potato requisition. And there we stood, petrified and drooling. I hope they turn to rocks in your guts and plug up your ass-holes, shouted Mlle Salome, but in a low kind of voice, more like a mutter.

No one made a move. The truck was parked right in front of Liakopoulos's door. Across the street was us, crowded together, and between us, the little square, empty. We didn't want any-thing to do with the Germans. Just kill them. I try not to think about Germans because I only get upset and lose my sleep, even today.

Three potatoes popped out of one of the sacks as two Ger-mans were loading it into the truck. Huddled against the wall we let out a groan. Nobody move, said a man's voice. The Ger-

51

man with the machine-gun on the truck smiled at us and pointed to the spilled potatoes with the barrel of his gun. Don't let them fool you, don't move an inch, said the man. The other Germans stopped their loading, watching us, waiting to see what would happen. As for me, it was as though I could hear us breathing. They'll crush them when they back up, said Mrs Fanny. They'll crush them, the pigs.

The Germans stood there, smiling. And we stood there.

And then poor little Fanis comes running out of the crowd and makes for the middle of the square, ungainly as a plucked chicken. We stand there petrified. Little Fanis looks at Mother with a faint smile on his face and makes a bee-line for the potatoes and picks up all three of them. Nobody makes a move, then the smiling German with the machine-gun leaps down and smashes the boy's hand with his rifle-butt. The potatoes tumble to the ground. Fanis bends down to pick them up and the rifle-butt comes smashing down on his fingers over and over again. I'm sure I could hear the bones snapping, but people say I'm being silly whenever I tell the story. The boy is howling now and all together, as one, we move forward. But the other three Germans take aim at us; I hear the click as they cock their rifles. We freeze again. The soldier with the machine-gun has it trained on us again. And in the middle of the square the kid is writhing and flailing around like a chicken with its head cut off. His hand was twisted backwards in the direction of his elbow. Then the Germans go back to work. Three Greek men take a step towards the kid, the Germans bring their rifles to the ready again, and the Greeks step back, while the little boy is still dancing around in the middle of the square.

And then Mrs Kanello steps out of the crowd and heads toward Fanis. My mother is about to faint. Holy Mother of God, his hand, she cries, and I'm trying to keep her upright but half of her is leaning against me and the other half on the ground. I'm doing all I can but she slips out of my hands and

52

falls. The soldiers pick up their guns again and aim at Mrs Kanello but she just keeps on walking towards our little boy as if she was God almighty. She kneels and takes him in her arms, she was wearing long black stockings, before the war the poor people wore them for mourning but come the Occupation who could be bothered with the niceties, bury them fast and get it over with, so the merchants sold off their stockings – nothing but useless surplus it was. As she kneels down to take the boy in her embrace, her stockings tear at the knee and run all the way to her ankle, I recall. A German comes up to her with a pistol, I can remember the dialogue to this very day, word for word.

German: Little boy of you?

Mrs Kanello: Yes. Of me little boy.

German: Him thief. Punish.

And the German turns on his heel and grinds the potatoes into the dirt, one at a time.

Mrs Kanello is kneeling there with one knee in the gravel, the boy's head resting on her other knee. As a matter of fact, you could see the white flesh above her stocking tops. We didn't have proper garters back then, they made their appearance during the Civil War. I remember just like yesterday how white her thighs were, there above her stockings. I wanted to help my brother but I was scared to death, besides, I was holding my mother's head.

Meantime the German crushes the last potato. Slowly Mrs Kanello gets to her feet, begins to drag the boy over towards us as best she can, of course; she was as hungry as everybody else, suckled her kids until they were five when there was no bread to eat. But suddenly rage overwhelms her and she cuts loose at the Germans.

'So he's a thief?' she says. 'Me, I'm a thief too! And all these people, they're nothing but thieves,' and she points to us Greeks. 'We're all thieves. But what're you? You call yourselves a country? Well, you're nothing but a tribe. Your fatherland? I shit on it. Your flag? I spit on it! I dance on the grave that waits for your kids! Us, thieves? Maybe so. But we didn't build Dachau. We didn't build Belsen!'

Mrs Kanello knew what she was talking about, she'd been to party meetings. But the German couldn't have understood Greek much more than those few words of his.

Then she picks up the boy in her arms and strides towards us in a towering rage, turning her back on the German, as if exhausted, and he picks up his rifle and shouts: Halt! And Mrs Kanello never even turns to look at him, just speaks, her eyes on us all the while.

'You want to shoot me?' she says. 'Go ahead, shoot. All you're good for is shootin' women. Screw them you sure as hell can't.'

There she stood motionless. There stood the Germans. And us. Then, fearlessly, she turns back towards him (I was shitting my pants I was so scared, she told me dozens of years later) and lights into him.

'What's wrong? Come on, shoot! Get it over with. No food for three days and my kids are all over me because I can't feed them and Churchill with his baloney over the radio – come on, shoot, I need the rest, I can't take any more. Three days without food in my own house! Your women have enough to eat, I hear, well, may you never be buried in your own soil, may the vultures eat your balls! Your women, all they do is stuff themselves and make lampshades out of human skin! Go on, you son of a bitch, shoot! You too, the rest of you!' and she gestures at the other Germans, their fingers on the trigger. 'Shoot, you assfucking queers, fucking yourselves so you won't dirty yourselves on the Greek girls. Shoot! But one of these days you're gonna pay! The Muscovite is coming – you know the song? You'll puke it all up, every last bit.'

'Unfortunately, Mrs Kanello,' I tell her at Mum's memorial service as we're talking over the past, 'the Germans never paid us back. Not then, and not now. We never even asked them.

54

Look how they're our precious allies today, and oh so politely they let our men go to work for them, and in the United Nations they snap their fingers and we come running. We win the war, and them, they're back on top.'

'Us, win the war, Roubini?' says Mrs Kanello, 'you call that winning the war?' And she broke down and cried. But at Mum's funeral she didn't shed a tear. Only at her husband's funeral, but never mind, I won't say a thing about that.

So Mrs Kanello turns her back on the Kraut and starts towards us.

He didn't shoot. Meantime, Father Dinos had somehow got wind of the situation: there he came, full steam ahead, all decked out in his vestments – he'd left in the middle of a wedding – with his chasuble flapping in the wind. He came to a stop without a word. Mrs Kanello comes over, Get up Asimina, she tells my ma, we got to look after the kid's hand, no time for fainting. Off we go to her house, me following along holding our little boy's crushed hand. Straight up the stairs we go, rip up some old rags, and straighten out Fanis's hand, and he doesn't let out a peep, can you imagine?

I didn't have a clue what was going on outside; I was holding the washbasin while we rinsed off his hand with boric acid and camomile. Seemed like thanks to Father Dinos the Germans were gone. With the potatoes. O thank you so much, holy father, says Aphrodite's ma. Stuff it Mrs Fanny, snaps the reverend father. And he sends out an order for everyone in the parish to turn out for Sunday service; there he reads out a curse and an anathema on the whole Liakopoulos clan. Why, at the Polytechnic Institute during the dictatorship, if even one asshole of a bishop stands up on his own hind feet, you wouldn't have had the tanks breaking into the Polytechnic, Mrs Fanny told me later, back in Athens. But I don't want to get mixed up in politics.

So finally the kid comes around, Run and call the doctor, Mrs Kanello tells me. But as I'm on my way down, who should I see coming up the stairs but Doctor Manolaras. Someone had passed the word. He unwrapped our crude bandage, felt the hand. Nothing serious, he said, quit yelling. A couple of broken bones, that's all. He had gauze bandages and Mum broke off a stick from our garden fence and we set it up as a splint. Now give him something to eat: he shouldn't move his hand for a week, use your other hand when you peepee, he told Fanis, and the boy blushed. He won't lose the hand, but it'll always be crooked.

The doctor gave him an injection, he was always injecting the hind ends of the just and the unjust with that Red Cross surplus of his. Then he said goodbye and left.

And we picked up our little boy to leave. Mother could barely look Mrs Kanello in the eye, I'm so sorry for all the problems we caused you, she said, your stockings are all torn and it's all on account of us.

'And you, you go showing off your thighs so the whole town can see,' pipes up her husband from the next room, as if he was dishonoured. Saw the whole thing from the little window in the toilet, he did. But Mrs Kanello didn't answer back; she always respected him.

We took the boy home.

Time passed and the hand got better but it was twisted for good. Couldn't make a fist. After the Civil War, or was it a little before? Doc Manolaras – by now he was elected to parliament – took him on as a hired hand at his spread on one of the islands. That's where he works to this day, Fanis does, as foreman and quite a spread it is, too; you'll have a job with me for life, the doctor promised, and he kept his promise. So Fanis is doing just fine, even if I never see him. Every year I send him a card on his name day, drop it off at Doc Manolaras' office. I don't have to buy stamps that way. He can't answer, seeing as how his right hand is the twisted hand, but I get all the news from Doc Manolaras, he's been our family MP since way back then, for life

I guess you could say. If only I could latch on with a road show, I'd say to myself, and stop over on his island, so the kid could see me on stage before he dies. What kid? He's past sixty now. And what do you think he asks me to send him, just the other day, the scallywag? Potatoes. And staring up Mrs Kanello's thigh when he came to? A real Greek, what can you do?

Whenever I think back to the episode with the potatoes and the garters, and I see my own suspender belts hanging from the little line over the bathtub (I've got a second pair), I say to myself, Honey pie, when it comes to wrapping a man around your little finger, us modern-day vamps, we've got it all. Take toilet paper. I mean, back then newspaper was all we had for wiping ourselves, and I'm talking about our kind of girls, well-groomed girls with self-respect. Even in the bathrooms of the finest homes in Rampartville you wouldn't find toilet paper. Only newspaper. I should know because I worked in more than a couple of homes like that after the so-called Liberation. Newspaper cut up into little squares with scissors all nice and neat (I did the cutting), but newspaper all the same. It was God's miracle that we got as far as we did with the men, considering we put out and still kept our virginity up front. Ah, the little ditties we used to sing back before toilet paper! Not to mention underarm deodorant. How did we ever manage to turn mens' heads when we had so little to work with I'll never know. And today all the girls want to talk about is solitude and angst and now they've got all the deodorants and creams and I don't know what else for the most confidential uses. Us, we used cotton sheets cut in the shape of a 'T' over and over again until they wore out. Plus we hung out our washing over the balcony or in the yard and everyone in the neighborhood knew our time of the month. Well you can just imagine the gossip, seeing as how some of the local women were keeping track. Why, you heard things like, Did you see, Karatsolias's wife is late with her monthlies? Nothing on the line today, what's going on? maybe she's in a family way?

Today, nobody can tell one way or the other. Sure, sure, no more flowers that bloom in the springtime for me, I know that's what you're thinking. But I still buy the sanitary pads just so I can see the look on you-know-whose face. Still, they're like a little friend sitting there in my handbag, even if I don't use them all that much.

Us modern-day charmers we're spoiled so rotten we don't know what's good for us, all the different creams we can pick and choose between, every drugstore's got at least ten different brands. Plus they've even got European toilet paper, every roll costs as much as a new-release cinema ticket. Saw it in one of those high-class uptown supermarkets. Not that I do my shopping there, but whenever I get over one of my fits I ring up one of my neighbours and we head for the supermarket just to blow off steam; what a sight. We make like we're buying, we load the shopping cart full to overflowing then we just leave it standing there and walk out.

Not to mention all the nice people you run into in the supermarket. Stars even. TV stars. I mean, not real stars of the stage: still, they're stars all the same, though. Furthermore, you can check out the exotic foods; why, they've even got canned goods from Japan; makes you sick to your stomach. Reminds me from the outside of the canned food we used to get from the English when we were in high school; I was back in school by then, for a couple of years. They came driving up in their trucks and handed out the food themselves, because the Prefect went and stole the first load himself, right after the so-called Liberation.

Some of the canned food came from UNRRA, some was army rations. If you were lucky you got UNRRA: they were chock full of food. The army rations had a chocolate bar, a cookie, a razor blade and a condom. Truckloads of English soldiers would drive up and hand out the food in the break, they were all blond and cheerful but they still looked a lot like the Greeks with those low-slung behinds of theirs. We kids blew up the condoms and the whole high school was full of cheery balloons. Our singing teacher managed to snatch one of the good ones out of my hand before I could puff it up. Once in a while we'd even blow them up in class, during the physics and chemistry lessons mostly. One day I went home waving a blown-up condom just as pleased as punch, taking care nobody would pop it and, when Mother saw me, did she ever give me a whipping.

Anyway, a trip to the supermarket makes you feel better than going to the park, where there's nothing but little kids talking dirty and calling you auntie. At the supermarket you can keep in touch with things, social-wise; when I'm going up and down the aisles it makes me feel as if our royal family is still ruling, reminds me just a little of those German operettas at the movies back during the Occupation, the ones with all the food. Plus going up and down the aisles is a lot better than any tranquillizer, which are pretty expensive, still, God bless my medical insurance plan.

One time at the supermarket who should I run into but our MP Doc Manolaras's wife, he's the one who fixed up Daddy's pension for me. Gorgeous woman. I kissed her hand – I know how to show my gratitude, after all – but she blushed. What are you doing, Miss Roubini? she says, I'm young enough to be your daughter. Listen to the old boiling fowl, your daughter! Me, I don't even show my age. But I was determined to respect the social niceties. Because if it wasn't for her husband, Fanis would never be set up for life the way he is, and I would never have my orphan's pension as an Albanian veteran's daughter.

I can still remember her husband as a forty-year-old doctor back in Rampartvillè, in my younger days. Doc Manolaras. Even before the war he was into politics. And generous too. Wouldn't take a thing from a poor patient, But you'd better vote for me when I run for parliament, was his line. But even the better classes of people liked him. I'm the only one in Rampartville who's seen every rear end in town, male and female, from every social class in the whole provincial capital, he used to say. See-ing as how the first thing he did when he visited some sick per-son was give them an injection, even before he examined you, whether it was the runs or peritonitis or the mumps. One day he stuck it into my godmother. Let me alone, you ungodly thing, she screamed, I've got measles, don't! My dear departed hus-band never saw me naked from behind, and now people will start talking, and here I am on my last legs!

Maybe they were goners, but he gave them the injection first, to buck up their spirits and make them feel like science was on their side, was how he put it. Free of charge. Didn't make any difference if you were at death's door, he'd say, You'll repay me with your vote, old boy, when I run for parliament.

Called on poor people for their name day, he did, but instead of sweets he popped them one in the bum. That was back then, before the war. Finally, after the war, they had the first elections and he ran for parliament and what do you know, he won hands down and came first for the whole prefecture. On to minister, we shouted. MP is fine with me, he said from his balcony. Athens, here I come. I can just see the bums just waiting.

He helped me straighten out my pension problems. He remembered the spicy sausages and skewered liver my father used to make. Liked good food and plenty of it, Doc Manolaras did. And when the official returns came through seems like everybody the good doctor ever pricked in the behind came to praise him, and there he was, on the shoulders of the riffraff, swaying back and forth like a flag flapping in the wind. Manolaras, Manolaras, they chanted. Your mother's ass, croaked some dissidents, but they got the stuffings whipped out of them.

Boutsikas the town porter actually did the shoulder-carrying, by the hour. So maybe he was short, but he was all brawn: why, he could unload two horse-carts in a half hour. Boutsikas had a big family and a more solid supporter for our MP you couldn't hope to find. Maybe he wasn't on the same side of the fence as

Doc Manolaras, politics-wise, but who cares; the whole family voted for him, out of respect.

Boutsikas got himself a pension too, thanks to Doc Manolaras. Hauling the doctor from one end of Rampartville to the other on his shoulders he came down with a hernia; that was the end of his portering days, for sure. What a hernia it was, let me tell you; everything just sort of slipped down to his knees; take one look at him below the belt with his pants puffed out right down to the knees and you couldn't keep your eyes off and you'd say, God almighty, now there's a man who's got it all. Why, some women who didn't know he was ill were jealous of his wife's good fortune. Anyway, thanks to the pension he came up to Athens, family-wise, with all the little Boutsikases, eight or nine of them and today they sell lottery tickets at the best locations without a police permit and the mother is a night cleaner in two tax offices; they even built themselves a place, way out in the sticks plus illegal to boot, but they're doing fine for themselves, whatever they take in they drink it away every night, their ma too thanks be to the hernia they all have work and so they always drink to the health of Doc Manolaras: wonderful people, salt of the earth, never forget a good turn.

Asimina old girl, that's how Manolaras talked to Mother (she was the only woman he never managed to puncture with his needle), you're the wife of a hero. And all together you're four votes, he was counting Sotiris, our eldest. Not counting the relatives.

He started procedures a few days after they paraded Mother through town. As widow of a soldier fallen on the field of battle, with three orphan children your mother is entitled to a pension, he tells me. Ma wouldn't admit she was a widow, but you couldn't budge the doctor. You lost him in Albania, he tells me. I'll get you a pension, the lot of you, so shut up.

One thing was certain. My father was lost, literally. After four months of cards, we never had another sign of life from him. Or death, for that matter. Never put down as officially dead, or missing in action, never turned up when our boys withdrew. Never listed as prisoner of the Italians. Mother asked at the police, asked Doc Manolaras, even Signor Vittorio if it could be that somewhere at the front he ran into a man who etc. etc. Not even the Ministry of War knew what to say.

During the Occupation whenever people asked after her husband her answer was, He's gone abroad. Well, she couldn't very well go saying he was dead because it was bad luck, and because she would be obliged to wear black social-wise and religion-wise. So she said, He's gone abroad. When you get right down to it, Albania is abroad after all. Sure, it's not Paris, but still, it's abroad. And she said it with a kind of pride, Mother did. Because back then not everybody and his brother went abroad.

That's when Doc Manolaras gets his bright idea. Asimina old girl, he says, you're entitled to a medal you know. And one of these days I'll get you a pension, for all those spicy liver sausages the dear departed used to make for me.

Mother thanked him, not that she believed him of course; but she did ask him not to call my father dear departed.

Doc Manolaras actually had the grit to come to our place after they publicly humiliated mom. He ignored the public outcry for three votes, that's how Mrs Kanello put it. Finally the pension came through; it took four years, and we were living in Athens by then; but it came through. And after Ma died it stayed in my name, as I was the unwed female child of a heroic soldier of the Albanian campaign, missing in action. From then on, Doc Manolaras kept our voter registration books locked in a drawer in his office, six in all, two for Mother's parents, and our four (he took out a book in Sotiris's name too). Every election time I picked up my book and Mum's along with the ballot. Of course he knew there wasn't any. No, says Mother. But the ballot he fixed for me and filled in a new one where I wrote 'I vote Royal. Raraou.' The boys' books he looked after himself.

After a few years went by I let him look after ours too: Mother had put on weight and we weren't going to queue with all the rabble and the riffraff every four years. After I buried Mum I asked him to give me back her book, I wanted it for a souvenir. But he wouldn't give it back; just leave it to me, Raraou, he said (finally called me by my stage name, you see), leave it to me; your dear departed mother can help us even after her death. I didn't make anything of it, but I was a bit upset, let me tell you; that little photo made Mum look really good.

Truth is, even Mrs Kanello told Ma not to wear mourning. Missing in action is one thing, Asimina, she said, dead's another story. Forget the mourning, you'll only get your kids upset, plus it'll cost you money.

Mourning cost a pretty penny back then, it wasn't just a black dress and that's all. People hung black sashes on all the curtains and put a black ribbon crossways on the tablecloth and covered up the mirror completely or hung it with black tulle for two years. Not to mention the little cakes and sweetmeats. During the Occupation of course, only the upper class could afford that kind of thing; we couldn't even afford the flour.

So that's how Mother didn't go into mourning. Besides, it was the Occupation; how were we supposed to afford black when we had to cut up the flag to make our drawers? Plus it wouldn't have been polite for Signor Alfio to see mourning bands on the curtains. What kind of hospitality would that be? So he was an enemy of our country, but Greek hospitality has to be just so, you can't go upsetting an invited guest even if he's from an occupying army. And all this for what? The mother-land? What's that? Can you see it, touch it? Signor Alfio, he was real flesh and bone; not the motherland.

Some people in the neighbourhood looked down on the Italians because they made passes at the girls and they ate frogs, so people said. But the best families in Rampartville wouldn't hear of it, and I agreed. Nothing but lies! they said. Plus these days we're sophisticated: you can find frozen frog's legs in all the better class of supermarket. But back then if you ate frogs it was as if you were eating filth.

People said the Italians caught them in nets under Deviljohn's bridge just outside town. We kids played a lot near the bridge; the place was crawling with big fat frogs, but we never knew for sure whether they did it or not. During the first years of the Occupation curfew came in at six o'clock. So people who didn't like the Italians claimed they went frog fishing after six: you figure it out. Later on, everybody forgot about it. But back then the rumours were flying thick and fast 'the Italians are eating the tadpoles!' Maybe they didn't have everything they wanted in their canteens? In fact, word got around that some of the families who invited Italians for dinner actually tried frogs in tomato sauce. But that was probably just nasty left-wing gossip.

Anyway, Father Dinos tried his best to protect Ma. That much I found out from Mrs Fanny, Aphrodite's mother, back when we had Plastiras for prime minister. One morning, she told me. Father Dinos comes, pisses out behind the church, shakes off his birdie, pulls down his robes and calls our mother Asimina, come to the church at five o'clock, for confession. Mother kisses his hand and goes back into the house, that was back in the Alfio days.

'Asimina,' he tells her that afternoon in the confessional, 'don't worry about "the other thing", personally speaking I give you my absolution and I take personal responsibility. Of course it's a sin what you're doing, but I take it upon myself. But how in the world can you let people who eat frogs kiss you?'

Mum is upset. 'Now you listen to me, Father,' she says, with all due respect (even though he was younger than her). 'Firstly, I don't believe it that they eat frogs because they're Christians too. But mainly no Italian and nobody else ever kissed me, nobody but my husband. All 'the other thing I admit, he does it.

64

But me, I'll only kiss the husband that married me. When he comes back.'

'Comes back from where, my poor child?'

'When he comes back.'

'Comes back from where? You think he's some kind of ghost? He was just God's little lamb, how could he ever end up a ghost?'

'He can do whatever he wants. He's a man and he doesn't have to answer to me. But me, I'm not going to kiss anybody. I swear it on my wedding wreath.'

Mrs Fanny gave me the whole story, back when Plastiras was prime minister. The reverend just couldn't keep his mouth shut, as you can see; go for confession and you'd end up confessing him. Anyway. God bless him (he's still alive). One thing for sure, Mrs Fanny's no liar. Moved up to Athens too, along with her husband the former partisan but whatever she did, it was her own two hands that did it. That husband of hers, no sooner than they hit town, he goes and gets mixed up in the December uprising and gets his throat slit from ear to ear. It was the royalists from Organization 'X' – 'X-men' we called them – that done it. All that money for the move from Rampartville to Athens, gone to waste. Why didn't they just kill him back in the Resistance; they were going to do it anyway, weren't they? But what can you do? Besides it didn't seem to bother Mrs Fanny one way or the other; after I buried my daughter I got the trick, was how she put it. So she kept on turning out the lace doilies. Being as how she didn't want to sell her place in Rampartville she boarded up the front door and left. That's the way it is to this day. Whenever the boards rot, Mrs Kanello nails up new ones to protect the place. I'll never sell, said Mrs Fanny. And when I die the crows will build their nests and give me forgiveness.

Got a ride to Athens in a truck, You can let us off here, they said a little outside town. The truck belonged to Doc

Manolaras. So the driver drops them off near a little hillock, a barren place with a blockhouse on top. Mrs Fanny had it all picked out from far away; she and her husband climb up to the top and all by herself she moves her household effects into the blockhouse. Then he heads off to Athens to look for his party comrades and they bring him back with his throat slit, he was still breathing. She buries him as quick as she can, ties some dry thistles together to make a broom, sweeps the place clean, plugs up the gun ports with newspapers and turns it into a place to live. Her first night as a widow she shoves the commode over to block the door. A miracle how she ever managed, selling hand-made lace doilies, tatting and needlepoint, and all the time new patterns.

Little by little she settles into the blockhouse, puts in a door, windows, two pots of flowers in front, builds a little wall, fixes up an outhouse and a little kitchen: she was a proper home-maker let me tell you. Later, during some election campaign, the place gets incorporated into the city plan even if it was unauthorized and she gets water and light, just like that. Still keeps up her crocheting, opened a little shop, more like a hole in the wall if you want to get right down to it. Not too long ago she tells me she's putting in for a telephone then all her prayers will be answered.

People are funny that way. First she survives. Then she forgets. Of course, maybe she didn't really forget, deep down, you never can tell. Back then in Rampartville we all had her written off, all alone and helpless; thanks to Doc Manolaras we tracked her down. When her daughter died she locked herself into the house, never lit a lamp even. Only time she showed her face was at Mrs Kanello's evening get-togethers, with her crochet hook and the thread rolled up in a ball at her feet, crocheting to fin-ish the dead girl's dowry, some habits you just can't break.

Never set foot in our house. Only once, the night she knocked at our door just after Signor Vittorio left. Asimina, she calls, open up, quick! We open the door, it was five till, almost curfew; there she stands with this strange woman. She's looking for someone, she tells us. Then she goes off and leaves us with the woman, just like that. Come on in, Ma tells her, what was she supposed to say. The woman comes in; you could tell something was wrong. But she looked like a lady. Who are you? asks Ma. Not a word. Please sit down, I say; we were just sitting down to dinner. Bread and chick peas with olive oil, from Signor Vittorio that was. She takes a seat, but not so much as a glance at the food, nothing. Who are you? Ma asks again; don't you want something to eat? Without a word she gets up from the chair, goes over to the bed, lies down and dies. Just like that. With her purse in her hand. We knew it right away. Dead people we saw every day. Ma stretched her out on the bed, closed her eyes, wrapped her jaw closed with a handkerchief. So get Mrs Kanello, she tells me, but now it was curfew. Mrs Kanello was working that night though so we waited at the window, the three of us, for her to come off shift. And wrapped up the stranger in some old clothes.

Around midnight we hear Mrs Kanello's clogs rattling like a machine-gun; like a home guard she walked. With all due respect, I have to say there was nothing feminine about that woman. But then, I'm comparing her with me, you'll say ... anyway. Mum calls her over, she comes in, looks the woman over. Not from Rampartville, she says. Whereupon I pipe up (where'd I get the idea; I was just a kid) maybe she's some kind of messenger for the partisans. I'll find out in the morning, Kanello says, and leaves.

We kept vigil over the stranger all night, well, all right, so we nodded off a bit before dawn, and little Fanis snored right through the whole thing. To stay awake, I weed the new shoots that were popping up through the floor over in the corner, but Ma snaps at me in a loud whisper, Stop that and bring the lamp over here. So I stop my weeding.

First thing in the morning we go out and start asking around, all hush-hush. Nothing. At noon Kanello comes back from work: not a clue, she says; nobody expecting her, all the contacts got back safe. Seems she even telephoned around, not that I asked where, but however you look at it, we weren't any further ahead than when we started.

Meanwhile our lady neighbours pass on the word to the priest, he'll be having a funeral to do and little Fanis goes running off to the police station. Don't know a thing about it, they tell him, Try the Kommandantur. Can you believe it, the kid's supposed to go ask the Krauts? Finally Father Dinos shows up along with Theofilis the sacristan and the two of them lay her out in one of those church caskets they always kept handy, for the indigent, you know. We took the funeral procession through the whole town on the off-chance maybe somebody recognizes the dead woman, asking people on the sly. Not a clue. Probably somebody from the capital, they said. We ended up giving her a hasty burial seeing as it was just about curfew time, then we all hurried home. Didn't write anything on the grave marker, what were we supposed to put?

I suppose I completely forgot about the incident, all these years. Anyway, just after Ozal gets in, I think it was, I'm back on the stage again, stand-in at some youth movement drama festival and who do you imagine I think of? That's right. The mystery woman; not her face so much as her green coat. Even today, when I visit our plot in the cemetery I light my candle and burn my incense, then I drop an extra lump into the incense burner. For the unknown woman, I whisper. That's what I call her: the 'unknown woman'. Because I performed *The Unknown Woman* with this road company, you know. What I mean is, I played in *The Unknown Woman*, not the role of the unknown woman; had two lines to speak but I'm not complaining. It was prose after all, and besides, it was serious theatre. In the musical reviews they always stick me in the back of the crowd scenes or in the chorus.

The unknown woman, poor thing.

I always say a little prayer for her, I know it's being selfish but I'd like it if someone said a little prayer for me when … anyway, you know what I mean; well. I'm still young at heart and frisky as a filly, why, when I pop backstage after the show the people come up to me and say, Raraou you old fish, where've you been hiding yourself these days? just as nice as can be not how they usually talk to old people and pensioners generally speaking. Of course. I know what you're going to say, I look a lot younger than my age. Don't I know it. Even when I was a little girl I always looked younger than I was, didn't even get a little bump of a chest until after I turned seventeen. When we used to go splashing in the puddles under Deviljohn's bridge in the summertime I wore my drawers without a shift just like our little Fanis and the other boys. But my girl friends from school, they only took their clogs off. Well, really they were former girl friends because in the meantime I quit school; after the so-called Liberation I started going again but by then it was only once in a blue moon.

Still, I went visiting lots of other girls. Afternoons mostly. Always went home plenty early though, back then you had to leave plenty of time to get home before curfew because you couldn't stay overnight at somebody's house, forbidden by the Occupying Powers. If you wanted to put somebody up you had to write a petition and get the authorities to stamp it. They had their ways of checking up, too; every front door had this printed form nailed to it showing how many permanent residents lived in that particular house plus their names and how old they were. Mrs Kanello, well, life was tough and she was hungry but she could always find something to laugh about. So what does she tell us at one of those get-togethers of hers? At most of the better houses (did house cleaning on her days off, what was she supposed to do with all those mouths to feed?) they were correcting the women's ages. Improving them, actually. From forty-eight down to forty-two first, then down to thirty-two.

And Mrs Kanello laughed and laughed, till all of a sudden one day it wasn't funny any more. Seems she dropped by her mother's and what do you think she saw? Her mother's age listed as thirty-seven, that's what! You're nuts, Mum. Thirty-seven? I'm twenty-seven myself. But mother Marika wouldn't budge. I am not nuts, she says. What am I supposed to do, stuck with an unmarried daughter?

Mrs Kanello had this younger sister name of Yannitsa, couldn't unload her on anybody. One big headache, let me tell you. Finally they managed to marry her off though, thanks to party connections. Her other sister's husband, the one in the partisans, he kind of forced one of his comrades to marry the spinster. Party orders, he told the man. Didn't have much choice in the matter, really. So he married the girl, even though she was older by eight years. But they lived happily ever after, had a child even.

The fur really flew over at the Tiritomba's too, age-wise I mean. Mrs Adrianna put down her real age, and that was that; her daughter was eighteen, she was forty-one and a widow, why bother to hide it? But Mlle Salome, who couldn't have been a day under thirty-four, she wouldn't hear of it. I'm not telling anybody my age, she declared. I don't care if they shoot me. And there, beside her name, she writes down fifteen, doing her part for the Resistance, I suppose.

Aphrodite's mother never crossed her dead daughter's name off the list. But in the age column she wrote down 'zero'.

Mlle Salome had her reasons, that's for sure. Back before the war even she joined the old maids' club; she had a swarthy complexion, all skin and bones, her hair was short and curly and she had beady little eyes like a chicken's behind (what I'd give for those lovely eyes of yours, she gushed whenever she saw me) and a shrill voice, like somebody yelling at a deaf-mute. But all the same, she was a good-hearted sort. Not much later, the whole Tiritomba clan went off on tour, mind you. Well 'went off' was hardly the word for it. What really happened is that they cleared out overnight, and all because a goat, if you please. Cleared out lock stock and barrel, in the middle of the great hunger, just as the Year of Our Lord 1942 was coming to an end.

We didn't even have time to say goodbye and before we knew it, they were gone. If I'd have known they were going, I'd have asked them to take me along, I know I was just a little kid, but they were bound to have kid's parts. I could have played boys even; my feminine charms weren't all that developed yet.

That day us kids were snailing down by Deviljohn's bridge bright and early. The snails were up and around at the crack of dawn, so we had to catch them before anybody else did. We used to eat them boiled and salted; in the coffee houses they served them as an appetizer, along with ouzo. Later on, we sold them in little paper cones at the movies, instead of roasted sunflower seeds.

So there we were in the early morning cold, gathering snails under the bridge when all of a sudden we see Tassis' wood-powered jitney go by like a shot – Tassis was Mrs Adrianna's brother. Well not exactly 'like a shot'; the old rattletrap was doing maybe ten miles an hour. And in it, who do I see but Mlle Salome, Mrs Adrianna, her daughter Marina, plus an archangel, which may have been part of some stage set, or maybe it was a plaster statue, I couldn't tell for sure. There were Albanian kilts and medieval costumes flapping in the wind on the side. *Traviata* and the like. Before I knew it, they turned off towards the mountain villages. As soon as the jitney was out of sight we went back to our snailing. We were cold. There was no sun but even with sun we would have been cold. Not enough to eat, that's what it was. But the cold couldn't spoil our fun. What did spoil it, around noon, was the domestic animals from town.

Down by the riverside there were two cats crouching, waiting to pounce on the first frog that popped up. Or staring up at the sky, maybe the poor dumb creatures were waiting for a bird to drop at their feet, so to speak. Dumb animals when you come right down to it.

House cats weren't much good back then, what's a mouse going to do in a hungry man's house? They wouldn't even let us get close enough to pat them, the cats. I mean; they were angry because we couldn't feed them any more. Mrs Kanello had a cat but she had to tell it I don't have anything for you, sweetie-pie, you'll have to look out for yourself.

One day we spotted a mouse in our house. Must have been just passing through, or maybe it just strolled in through the wrong door. Mother almost took it as a compliment. Mice only lived in rich people's houses now. Back in the days before the war we had a few, but for Mother a mouse in the house was a kind of disgrace; cleanliness is next to godliness, she always said. We kept traps with bread fried in olive oil for bait. But when the Albanian front fell apart, well, that was it for the bread in the mouse-trap.

We had a cat too, but she wasn't really ours. More like half a cat. Showed up on the days Father brought the tripe to wash in the yard. I never knew who the cat belonged to. We got ourselves half a cat, Father joked. We always left her a plate outside the back door, along with a little bowl of water. But when we lost our liberty she lost the food on her plate. We still gave her fresh water every day so she would always have plenty to drink at least. At first, she kept on coming around. She came scrambling over the wall, stared at her plate, then leaped down for a closer look, dumb animal. But there was nothing on her plate, nothing but rust spots from the rain, mixed with dust. The last time she showed up on the wall she spotted the empty plate, then turned towards us and glared at us as if she was accusing us of wrong-doing, like the picture in the cathedral where you see the Archangel glaring at Eve, the one where it says The Banishment from the Garden underneath. Took one look at us and disappeared. Disowned us.

72

I didn't even try to find her. Firstly, she wasn't even our cat, and secondly, what was I supposed to say to her, Come back home for some food? I was embarrassed to look her in the face. When she went away she had the same kind of look on her face as my big brother, back then with Signor Alfio. I was lying a while back when I told you my big brother Sotiris called her a whore. When he saw it was Signor Alfio going out the door and saw the basin full of rinsing water under Mother's bed and the food on the table he didn't curse her or call her names, nothing like that. In fact he sat down and ate dinner with us and then he said, I'm going out for a walk. Even though it was curfew we didn't try to stop him. He was gone. For ever. Today he'll be over seventy.

And that's how our half a cat left. I never saw her again, not even down by Deviljohn's bridge where the cats went frog hunting.

But that day, when the jitney with the Tiritomba troupe disappeared over the hill, all us kids heard a strange sound coming from the town, a soft humming sound, like a deaf-mute crying. We stopped our playing and looked up. The road was empty but the sound kept coming closer. So low that it was more like a dream. Then we saw them, the pets of Rampartville.

Lots of them. They filled the road like a silent demonstration, dogs and cats together, marching along with a determined look on their faces. Not so much as turning to look at us. All the pets of Rampartville were deserting the town. And here they were, streaming past us, along the road leading to the villages and the valley. In their eyes you could see it, the look of a mother trying to save her children. And nobody can stop her. They were heading for the countryside, looking for food. A couple of pups were hanging back and sniffing along the roadside, then they dashed along after their parents. The two frog-hunting cats joined the march, alongside a couple of dogs. Not one of them came back again, ever.

73

Fanis and I stopped playing, collected whatever snails we could gather, and went home. We told Ma and I was scared because she said, The animals have turned their backs on our city, animals know when there's danger. Now great tribulations lie in store for us, Mother said, and I was scared; I didn't know what that word meant and that made me even more scared.

We had trouble getting home seeing as the Germans had the neighbourhood sealed off. The Tiritomba family troupe just managed to clear town in their jitney, and all because of a mis-understanding: they thought the army cordon was for them, but that's Mlle Salome for you, always putting on airs. Because the day before she stole a goat from some collaborator, she thought that was why, and they pretended they were going on tour. But the Germans, they knew what they were doing, you think they'd go sealing off a whole district for some Greek goat, which turned out to be a nanny-goat? No, the reason was because they knew Mrs Chrysafis's son was coming. I know who double-crossed him, but I'm not talking. Don't want to lose my pen-sion, the guy's got a top position in both parties, one after the other.

Mrs Chrysafis lived in this narrow two-storey house on the little square, on the opposite corner from Liakopoulos', the collaborator with the potatoes: her son was in the partisans, went by the name of Valiant. The poor kid wasn't all that bright, how many times did Mrs Kanello tell him to be careful, but he wouldn't listen. So every so often he snuck into town to bring his mother food; she was a widow, you know. That son of hers name of Valiant was really a kind of partisan alias, he was a gen-darme before, and the finest-looking man I ever saw or ever hope to see, one look at him and you'd say, Holy Virgin, just let me have him and I'll never look at another man again, I swear. And if they ever build a Paradise just for men, that Paradise would be for him, for his perfect beauty. Mind you he might have been ugly, but for me he was handsome; today I can't really recall what he looked like exactly and if you showed me his picture today I don't think I could recognize him. Tall, like a fine steel blade with that golden hair of his, you'd swear his whole body quivered like the surface of the water in that uniform of his. A handsomer man you couldn't hope to find, just thinking about him was enough to stop your tears and heal your hurt. He was a gendarme. But when the partisans started up he was one of the first to join. It was a former mate of his ratted on him, I won't say who, you think I want to lose my meal ticket on account of a man I can't even remember his face; plus. I may be in hot water for talking too much already.

He dressed up as a priest to sneak into town. But that night they were waiting for him, and at dawn they shot him in an alleyway then dumped his body in the public market, by the fishmongers' stalls.

Mrs Chrysafis was waiting for him, nothing but boiled weeds that's all she had to eat for two days, and she could only think of the food her hero was going to bring her. Mrs Kanello spots him dumped on the ground eyes wide open next to a stack of crates full of eels. She was on her way home from her shift at the TTT – because of her work she had a safe-conduct.

And right through the German lines you go, Kanello; straight home and you get a two-wheeled cart with handles and a bowl of boiled chick-peas with olive oil and you go to Mrs Chrysafis's place. Eat Chrysafina, eat, you tell her. But Mrs Chrysafis turns angry. What for? my son is bringing me food; but it was as though she knew something was wrong, so she took a few bites. And then Kanello, you tell her, Come along Chrysafina and bring the cart, poor woman, you say, Time to bring your son home.

At the public market the two of them loaded him into the cart, arms and legs dangling over the sides; he was a big man, too big for the cart. A handful of small-time black marketeers were standing around, the ones with the eels, but they just looked on, didn't want anybody accusing them of helping. Mrs Chrysafis went first, pulling the cart behind her, and Kanello took up the rear, yanking the ends of the dead man's cassock out from the wheels. Matter of fact an eel ended up on top of him and one of the black marketeers snatched it up and threw it back into the crate. Along they went, with Kanello trying to stuff the dead man's arms and legs back into the cart and Mrs Chrysafis towing until she fell down in a faint. Then some people came out of a store and splashed water over her. She came to, and that's how it was that they brought the fair youth home to prepare him for burial. The Germans let them pass, just like that.

When they get to her front door Mrs Chrysafis lifts the bolt then turns and starts pummelling Kanello. Get out of here, I'll look after him myself, go on, get out. And she hoists the body on to her back and lugs it up the stairs. The neighbourhood was still sealed off, for fear of trouble. But we didn't say a word of protest. We only watched.

For two days and two nights she wailed over the body. Not with words; with sounds like the sea.

She closed her windows and her balcony door, but left the shutters open; staged her mourning just for us, she did. For two days and two nights, hysterically. We couldn't hear a single word, nothing but sounds like the open sea. But we could see her dressed in black with a black kerchief over her head, holding her dead son's cassock in her hands, lashing her body or throwing herself against the walls. Through the windows we could see Mrs Chrysafis appearing and disappearing like someone going by in the street or climbing on top of trunks, or tables as though she wanted to break through the ceiling and fly up to the sky.

The inside walls of her house were whitewashed, and the windows were narrow.

So we could see her clear as day, but bits at a time. Only glimpses of a huge black bat. Desperate to break free from its

76

cage, she pounded against the walls, trying to find a way out. Like a huge, gawky, blind bird she was. But instead of flying towards the window, she kept crashing into the white walls.

At night she looked even larger, as the shadows looked bigger in the light of the acetylene lamp. The house was dark on the outside, and bright on the inside, besides the acetylene lamp, she put the electric lamp and the candles to burn, for her dead son to see better. She just didn't want to close his eyes. We could see her, like a wild blackbird missing the windows, crashing into the walls, backing up and crashing into them yet again; and then she would climb up on to a table or a chair to catch her breath. Then her shadow would cover the whole ceiling, and after that she seemed to swoon and fall, we waited for her to come to, and then we caught sight of her again. Two whole days and nights we watched over her.

The first day we all stood there on the pavement across from her house and that night everybody crowded into our windows. The second night we forgot all about the curfew and, all of us women went out on to the pavement to mourn the fair lad, right outside her door. And inside she kept flitting back and forth like a bird trying to fly towards the light. The inside of her house brightly lit, and the front of it was darkest black. Nobody said a word to us about being out.

At dawn on the second day she came downstairs, opened the door and begged for food, she needed strength to keep up her lament. They gave her food, she ate, bolted the door again, and went back upstairs to mourn her son. We watched over her. Every so often one of us would have to leave for work, or to answer nature's call, or to eat. Then someone else would take his place. Mrs Kanello left all her kids right in the middle of the pavement and went off to work. Don't you budge, she told them, even if the Germans show up.

The Germans showed up. That evening it was. They stared at us, pretending to be puzzled. One of them stopped in front of

77

Mother but before he could say a word she tells him in a soft voice, We're watching over her. And pointed to the bat coming and going in the lighted windows, that was illegal too, the black-out was in force. Maybe he understood, maybe he didn't, but he left, the German did. Laughed and went away.

On the third morning comes Father Dinos, scowling like an icon and all dressed up in his finest vestments, and shouts Chrysafina! Here's where your dominion ends! And he broke down her door and carried the body away for burial. She followed along behind like a little girl, speechless.

There were a lot of us at the funeral. In the front of the church lay the dead man in an uncovered coffin, carefree now, his eyes still open, like a tiny rowing boat cutting its way through the waves without so much as a farewell for us. After the burial mother kissed Mrs Chrysafis's hand and says, Don't waste your tears, you'll never get over it. Until you die. That was when some woman shouted, What's that whore doing here? and Mother said, Forgive me, all of you, and took my hand and we left the cemetery. They didn't put a cross over his grave; just a tiny little flag made from a white sheet of paper, with a blue cross painted on it. Beats me where they found the coloured pencil.

Every day Mrs Chrysafis went to the cemetery and ate a little earth from her son's grave. That's what we heard from Thanassakis, Anagnos's kid, the school master from Vounaxos village. If you can imagine, the yellow-skinned kid would play right there, in the cemetery. Afterwards, we heard the same story from Theofilis the sacristan; saw her with his own eyes and being as he was a bit of a gossip he told Father Dinos, figured he shouldn't be giving her communion. If I was in her shoes, I'd eat dirt, Theofilis, he said, so get the hell out of my sight and go and sweep out the church, tomorrow's Sunday.

Subsequently, after the so-called Liberation it was, some partisans' committee wanted to lay down a marble gravestone, like a kind of monument. But Mrs Chrysafis wouldn't hear of it. All she wanted was to eat the earth from her dead son's grave, a little at a time, just a pinch. Like holy communion, said Mrs Kanello. Kept it up even after UNRRA appeared on the scene. I don't know what happened to her, but she was certainly still alive when we had the Junta; every three days she'd pay a visit to the cemetery, never moved to Athens, did Mrs Chrysafis. Time passed, and I lost track of her. As a matter of fact, it was Mlle Salome who asked after her, years later, when we met in some hick town near Grevena it was, and me on tour at the time. She wasn't a 'Mademoiselle' any more as it turned out; now she was the wife of the biggest butcher in town. When I say 'on tour' you might get the idea I was the star. But at least I got some lines of my own, a whole half page of dialogue, in fact. The actress who was supposed to play the role got knocked up along the way, so they rang me; of course I did it on the cheap, extra pay, but when opportunity knocks, who's going to spoil it by haggling? It was summer anyway; better than spending my holiday in the apartment.

So there we were, playing in Grevena, and nipping up to this nearby town for a quick show. I head for the local coffee-house. Nice town, know what I mean, I tell the owner (some town, the place was a run-down dead-end if I've ever seen one, but me, all my life I've been buttering up people to survive, and believe you me I've survived): anyway, the guy was so flattered – here's an actress from Athens talking to him, after all – he wanted to stand me a spoonful of vanilla treacle, but what I was after was to keep my lipstick in his icebox. It was summertime and the damn thing was melting all over the place. I always let the village coffee-house owners fight it out for my favours; had to protect my lipstick, you know.

So there I am in this hick town near Grevena, back during the Papagos and Purefoy administration it was – you know, the field marshal and the ambassador – just after I nip over to the coffee-house to pick up my lipstick round about midday I say to myself, why not take a peek into the butcher's, right next door, the habit stuck with me from the Occupation, butcher shops were romantic places back then. Across the street some men were taunting me in a highly unseemly fashion; forget them, I say to myself. In fact I'll just hang around at bit longer, let them tease me; give my stock in the company a boost. So I turn my back on them – I was always more spectacular from behind – by then they were howling Hey look, it's Raraou! they must have seen my name on the poster under my picture. I'm pretending to be eyeing some ox liver when all of a sudden I hear a woman's voice from inside.

'Why if it isn't Roubini! Roubini? You are Roubini, aren't you?'

It was Mlle Salome, of all people. Last time I saw her was that day during the Occupation when we were gathering snails under Deviljohn's bridge and she drove by in the wood-burning jitney clutching a caryatid.

Lo and behold, there she sat at the cashier's window in the butcher's shop looking like Cleopatra sitting on the Sphinx, and behind her on the walls were pictures of the royal couple (the late and former, these days), and Christ. Next to them was a picture of an Alpine meadow full of woolly Merino sheep, an ad of some sort.

Mlle Salome was sleek and portly now, but I recognized her right off. Just imagine the hugs and kisses and the tears, why she even gave me two pounds of mince meat, plus she ran over to the coffee-house, got my lipstick and put it in the refrigerator where they kept the best cuts.

Remember, they were the ones who went on the lam from Rampartville just before the Germans sealed off the neighbourhood. Actually stole a goat with her own two hands, she did; they thought that was the reason. There was only one way to save themselves: take to the road. But Mlle Salome abandoned the troupe when they hit this particular town, eight months after the premiere. That was where the town butcher asked for her hand in marriage. What swept me away were his thigh cuts, that's how she put it, and so I bade farewell to Art, she said, waving at the joints of meat hanging all around her.

She looked wonderful, even if she did have varicose veins. The butcher turned out to be the ideal husband, worshipped her like a goddess, gave her two kiddies. Just in the nick of time, dear, she tells me, I was over thirty-eight but in the maternity hospital I gave my age as thirty-four, I know I was taking a chance, I say to myself, but I never told the invaders my age and I'm not about to change now. Better die in childbirth. But I made it! Two kids after forty. As she talked she kneaded the mince meat, her fingers were full of rings, she was a real princess now, thanks to that butcher of hers. That night they came to the show. Darling, you were born for the stage, she told me afterwards. Remember I always said so, back before the war even? Who gave you your first role, back then in Rampartville remember? Remember how hungry we were? I still miss it a little bit to tell you the sinful truth; my waist was as slim as a wasp's, remember how I used to look?

Listen to that, Salome missing the hunger! I asked her about the rest of the Tiritomba family.

Well, to tell the truth, their last name wasn't really Tiritomba. And they weren't real stage people either. Salome was from Rampartville on her father's side, the place across from ours was her family's, she was even engaged, before the war that is. It just happened that her sister Mrs Adrianna married an entertainer, still, deep down she was a housewife. The guy was from Salonica, name of Zambakis Karakapitsalas. Married for love, mutually. He had a troupe of travelling players, even acted himself. People said he even used to have a dancing bear in the troupe, before Adrianna, that is.

81

So, this guy Zambakis Karakapitsalas had the most lavish sets and costumes of any road show.

Anyway, this opera company from Sicily goes bust in Salonica and Zambakis, who was a young man at the time, somehow scrapes together enough to buy the whole show, lock stock and barrel, even though it's all opera leftovers. That's how he made his name, putting on *Cavalleria Rusticana* or *The Intrepid Albanian Maid* with the same stage settings; in the *Unknown Woman* – get this – the chambermaid making her entrance in a broad-brimmed hat and petticoats. And the female lead in the *Shepherd Lass of Granada* appeared in Greek national costume along with lace gloves and parasol from *La Dame aux Camélias* (which he changed the title to *Consumptive for Love*). Well, you make do with what you got.

He and Mrs Adrianna made a perfect match from day one, except he was the jealous kind, wouldn't let her out of his sight, even dragged her along on tour, the man was a bit of a hot-blood. If you're not here when I want you, I'll do it with somebody else, he said, just as barefaced as that. But they lived happily, seeing as how Adrianna had a bit of the wanderlust herself, liked new places. Before the war in Albania (fight over a country like that? Big deal!) she visited 570 villages and towns on all her various tours, picked up some wonderful home-made dessert recipes along the way; Mrs Adrianna was just wild about cooking. Me on the stage and you at the stove. Zambakis was always telling her tenderly. They had a daughter, too. Fortunately for them, on account of two plays in their repertoire had little orphan girl roles, and Mrs Adrianna always blessed her child before she went on stage to play the orphan.

Hubby wouldn't let her set foot on stage though, except to sweep up after the show. I want my wife to be an honest woman, the poor guy tells her. So she ran the wardrobe department: she was the one who mended Tosca's or Marguerite the consumptive's evening gowns, glued the sets for Nero's palace back together when it got ripped in transit, and minded her husband in the bargain, particularly when he was playing a role where he had to wear a fustanella, she would un-eye him as a precautionary measure, and double-check to make sure he was wearing his drawers. Because one night the rogue slipped by her and suddenly there he was, dancing a folk dance in his fustanella with no drawers on, wanted to impress some young lady in the audience so it seems. That was when Mrs Adrianna whipped him for the first time. The first time, and the last time. No wonder, you'll say, never gave her cause, never went on stage bare-bottomed again.

They reached Rampartville in October of 1940, late in the month, just a little before 'No' day, as luck would have it. They only had one work lined up. *The Orphan's Daughter*. The daughter in question had to be five or six years old, so they announced a contest: all families with daughters were invited.

All the high-class mums with daughters took on seamstresses to get ready for the audition. But talk about good luck, that very same day Mlle Salome drops by to order tripe for her fiancé, takes one look at me. Diomedes, she says to my father, your daughter's a natural for the role, let the kid do it – and pick up a few drachmas while she's at it.

Next day she takes me to the cinema herself, the 'Olympian' it was called, and they picked me, unanimously; have to thank Mlle Salome, she was the first one to unearth my natural talents. They didn't pick me just because I happened to be the tripe merchant's daughter, no, they saw that inner spark of mine and that's the story of how I got started on my future career.

So I played the part which put the high-society mums in one fine dither because some gutwasher's kid beat out their precious little darlings, not to mention all the seamstress money. My part only lasted two minutes, no lines to speak either; I played this little girl whose mother was always beating her and sending her to her illegitimate mother-in-law and she, the mother-in-law, would send her right back again, anyway, generally speaking, they made a football out of me, right up to the final curtain.

The premiere, which took place on October 26th 1940, was my triumph. The audience, all high-society people, was relieved when they saw the kid getting slapped around and tossed to and fro like an old rag doll; that's what my part was. And on account of how back then nobody played expressionistic, all the slaps were real naturalistic and my head was spinning and I was seeing double, not to mention them pitching me back and forth across the stage, but the leading lady wasn't all that strong so I fell plop on to the floor like a ripe watermelon, and a cement floor it was too. But even then I didn't let out a peep, not a tear; from that moment on, I was in it for the glory. Got paid, too, three drachmas for the premiere: probably to make sure I'd show up for the next performance. Of course I played the second night, got another three drachs, which I handed over to my mother, and that was how I entered the world of the Theatre.

On the twenty-sixth was the premiere, my moment of glory as the motherless child, and on the twenty-eighth the war breaks out, you'd have sworn somebody was out to sabotage me, artistically speaking. Zambakis, he's called up on the spot and gets himself killed even before he reaches the front, kicked in the head by a mule and that was curtains, so to speak; end of career. And us, as a nation, we have to go and say that cursed 'No', just to spoil my future. Anyway, fatherland comes first, even if you can't see it.

Mlle Salome's future was futzed with that 'No' of Mr Metaxas', he was prime minister back then, God curse the ground that covers him: there. I'll say it, even though I am a nationalist. That's when her fiancé leaves for the front. Scared out of his wits and miserable, but her fiancé all the same. Not that she really wanted him; the whole thing was Mrs Kanello's doing, August 15th it was the day they torpedoed the armoured cruiser *Elli*. The wedding date was set for October 28th, after the last performance. Mrs Kanello liked playing the matchmaker; even today she's always harping on the matter, but you won't catch me getting involved in any love match, not on your life.

So the moment he hears the declaration of war on the coffeehouse radio, Mr Fiancé dashes off to enlist, primarily he was deserting, actually, running out on love. Snuck out of town, he did, so not even his fiancée could catch a glimpse of him. Actually, it was really Mrs Kanello he was afraid of, afraid she would beat him and force him to get married, right then and there, at the railway station.

Not too much later Mlle Salome gets a card from the front and shows it all around, just as proud as she can be. Loaned him to the nation, was how she put it. What are you so proud of? says Mrs Kanello, believe you me, I have to crawl on all fours to set you up and now you go lending him out, the nation is better than you, that's what you're saying?

Kept his picture on her dresser, Mlle Salome did; during the Occupation she would kind of look sideways at it and say, His face reminds me of somebody, but who? Us too, his face reminded us of somebody, impossible to say who.

Until one fine day during the Occupation, Mrs Adrianna's daughter Marina goes and draws a moustache on the fiancé's photo, just to annoy Salome. Mrs Adrianna takes one look and goes, Holy Christ and Blessed Virgin! She shows the photo to Mrs Kanello and she goes, Holy Christ and Blessed Virgin! all this time, and we never noticed! They muster all their courage and show Salome the photo, but just as she's about to sigh with longing, she gets a good look at it and goes, Holy Christ and Blessed Virgin, why, he's the spitting image of Hitler.

That's when we realized just who the fiancé reminded us of. Aye, so that's why the Germans show you all so much respect when they search your house, says Mrs Kanello.

85

From that moment on Mlle Salome put him out of her heart once and for all, like a true patriot. Recovered from the complex she got when her fiancé stopped writing after the first postcard (we never found out whether he ever came back, nobody ever heard a word about him, down to this day). But she goes over to Kanello's and says, Pay me back for the engagement rings, dear. That's how we found out Mlle Salome bought the rings out of her own pocket. And she went back to her knitting, making sweaters for the partisans.

After Mrs Adrianna's husband died – by then the Occupation was settling in for the long haul – she says to herself, That's all for the artist's life and the tour we'll live and die right here in Rampartville, in our family home. Now she was a forty-year-old housewife with an eighteen-year-old daughter and her sister Salome unmarried and almost-married, and the main thing in her mind was how would they survive and what would they have to eat. So Mrs Adrianna calls all her relatives, meaning her brother Tassis. He's the one who had the little jitney, before the war he did the run between Rampartville and a couple of villages up in the mountains, full of scrub oak, goats and now partisans. He converted the jitney to a wood-burner. But business was slow; real slow.

They were fine for clothes though: still had the late lamented Zambakis' stage wardrobe. All their artistic accessories were stored on the first floor, in memory of him; they lived on the second floor. Managed just fine what with bits and pieces from this heroine or that, especially Mlle Salome, she was always dressing up in cloaks and lace shawls and pill-box hats. Mrs Adrianna had a knack with the needle and thread, so she would model the costumes a bit, Madame Butterfly, Lady Frosini at Ali Pasha's Court, the Unknown Woman, you name it. But Mlle Salome would wear the evening gowns as is, all she had to do was take them up a bit at the hem. Why, even the German patrols stopped to look, like the time she went out in a three-quarter cape, just like Errol Flynn in *Elizabeth and Essex*.

One time she even took the parrot along for a stroll. The bird was an engagement present from her former suitor and now it was all hers. When we took Korce, in Albania. Mrs Kanello taught the parrot to sing 'Mussolini, macaroni', you'd swear it was Sophia Bembo, the singer, even if he only learned one line. Come the Occupation, they locked him in the house and tied his beak shut on account of how he would pipe up with the song; even the parrots in our neighbourhood are in the Resistance, Mlle Salome used to needle us, back when we had Signor Alfio.

Come the second winter of the Occupation Mrs Adrianna took pity on me with that thin cotton skirt of mine; she brought me over to her place and fitted me in a fustanella. That's when she found out I was wearing drawers made out of a flag. I tried it on. Looks great, she said. A bit long, but you'll keep warm, poor kid. Wear it, and as soon as we're liberated bring it back.

I liked it fine, even if fustanellas were men's skirts and it was way too big for me. It came to below my knees and I held it up with a trouser belt just under my arms. Mother didn't like it one bit but no way I was going to take it off, not when my bottom finally warmed up a bit.

But when it came to shoes the Tiritomba family truly suffered. Had to wear clogs, same as everybody else. All they had in the wardrobe was men's clodhoppers with tufted toes. At first they sold off some of the small stuff for food, but then Mrs Adrianna put her foot down, It's profanation of our dear departed, she said.

Back then we made the rounds of the villages, selling dowry supplies to the local yokels. Me, personally, I couldn't sell eyes to a blind man, but I went along with Adrianna, to keep up her spirits. We traded hand-knitted goods and jersey underwear for a sack of wheat ... Father Dinos' wife even managed to sell off some of the priest's vestments. And on the way back we gathered kindling for the charcoal brazier. Those outings of ours were pretty well organized affairs. I can tell you, several women all together, because if the peasants ran into a lone woman, they'd grab all her food, Even if they don't rape us, Mlle Salome joked one time. Who could even think about rape back then?

But we went on other outings too, the sneaky kind. Mrs Kanello, Mrs Adrianna and her daughter Marina. Mlle Salome and me and our little Fanis – the two of us they dragged along as a kind of alibi, who was going to suspect a couple of little kids? Plus, seeing as we were so small it was easier for us to squeeze through the holes in fences. We set out fully loaded. That loony lady Kanello had us draped with hand-grenades and ammunitions of all kinds; we pretended we were off to pick dandelion greens, but what we really did was deliver the stuff to the contact who was that pipsqueak Thanassakis, the schoolmaster's son from Vounaxos village. The man who took final delivery of all the weapons. Today he's a top man on the nationalist side, but I'm not naming names, might cause him embarrassment.

Mrs Kanello took us down to the ground floor at her place, tucked our shifts into our drawers, the ones made from the national flag, pulled our belts tight to get the shifts to puff out, and then stuffed them with grenades. But before that she made us pee, whether we wanted to or not, so we wouldn't have to untie our belts before we got where we were going. And as we walked along she hissed at me, Don't you go leaning over forward, or so help me you'll never know what hit you.

Mlle Salome hid bullets in her turban and a hand grenade in each cup of her brassiere (she didn't have much in the way of a bust either, always wore puffy, pinch-waist blouses). But she wouldn't tote ammunition in her drawers. Makes me itch, she said, I'll give myself away. Keep your head high or so help me I'll whip you within an inch of your life, hissed Kanello as they strolled through the German lines. If you drop so much as one

cartridge and the Germans catch us, I'll rip you in half like a
sardine; a team of wild horses couldn't tear you out of my
clutches, I swear to God.

That was the way Mrs Kanello talked. Even rubbed off on
me whenever we met. She may live in Athens and her kids may
be studying in Europe, but she still talks like a provincial. Me, I
always make a point of speaking like a real Athenian in all my
social encounters.

So Mlle Salome had to walk head high with those pointy
breasts of hers and a tall turban like Ali Pasha in *Ali Pasha and
Lady Frosini Dishonoured*. I acted in that too, with a travelling
company. Played the role of drowned woman number two.

Mrs Kanello – she was as scatterbrained as she was daring –
carried her grenades in a basket. When we got to our destina-
tion we met that other dimwit Thanassakis. Anagnos' son, and
handed over the stuff, for which we hid in a country chapel to
undo our underwear. On the way back we gathered wild greens
and onions.

Whenever we came across a roadside shrine we had a race to
see who would get there first. If we found the little lamp burning we pinched out the flame and stole the oil: poured it into a
little bottle we kept with us. Mrs Adrianna always begged forgiveness from the holy icon; she was a devout woman. I have
sinned blessed Saint Barbara, she would say, for instance: Forgive my sins, don't be angry at me, a martyr like you should
know what it means to go without, don't be quick to punish me.
Yes, I'm taking olive oil from you, but I'll make it up to you in
sheep's-milk butter once our nation is restored, she said.

Mlle Salome sang the same tune, but grimmer, turning to the
icon and saying, You saints, what do you need? you can get along
just fine without olive oil, particularly you. Saint Paraskevi, for
instance, since you're such a big name and number one in the
heavens at that (Salome was always the one for compliments).
But our kids can't live without it. Besides, you've gotta keep the

89

saints in line, piped up Mrs Kanello. If you don't put your foot down, they won't listen. Still, she said it with a fearful look in her eye, stealing a sidelong glance at the icon.

That was when we hit a shrine with a lamp that was still operating. We divided up the oil. And that night we enjoyed a tasty meal of greens, porridge and olive oil to top the whole thing off nice. So what if the food tasted of burned wick; better, claimed Mlle Salome, this way we're eating blessed food. So she was a Communist – still, every now and again she got religious.

You figure it out. Today she's up to her eyeballs in roasts and chops in that hick town with that butcher of hers. Sent me a double string of sausages for Mother's memorial service though, how did she find out about it? Still, God bless her.

Anyway, Mrs Kanello was scared of anything that had to do with religion, even if she called herself a left-winger. After the meal with the stolen olive oil she would recite an act of contrition.

One time we filched some eggs from this chicken coop; the mother hen turned mean and put up a fight – she had one mean beak, let me tell you – but finally she backed off. Fortunately the eggs were fresh-laid. That evening, as each of us was eating an egg, we heard a dreadful ruckus from the Tiritombas's place. Mrs Adrianna caught Salome with this strange beauty cream on her face. Her, instead of boiling her egg, she smeared it all over her skin. Not that you could call that skin, God forgive me. Still, I should be more tolerant. Because nature has endowed me with skin and with other qualities, I shouldn't be so critical of my neighbour's little shortcomings, should I?

Sundays, mostly, was when we would make our ammunition deliveries; it was Mrs Kanello's day off and the schoolmaster's kid from Vounaxos wasn't in school. How'd he do it, the poor freak, said Kanello with that provincial twang of hers, a job like that in the partisans? Had a streak of ambition, she did. Can you imagine? Actually wanted the Occupation to last so her son could become a messenger for the partisans too.

Thanassakis was a little shrimp of a kid, twelve years old. Of course, you'll say, it was all because he had a donkey. He was in his father's class at the Vounaxos school house. When he finished primary school – had a bent for book learning even then, the kid – his father rented him a room in Rampartville, out past the railway station; you couldn't really call it a room, it was more like a shed with a low ceiling, a bed, a window with no glass, only shutters, and a wash-basin and water jug just outside the door. He used the place to rest at noon and study for afternoon classes. We had school mornings and afternoons back in those days.

Besides the guns and bullets Thanassakis carried messages for the partisans from a couple of school teachers. Mr Pavlopoulos, who was kind of partial to me, and a tall, handsome man called Mr Vassilopoulos, Alexander the Great we nicknamed him in class, died young, poor fellow. Everybody trusted Thanassakis, first because he was so dumb nothing scared him, second because he could carry things. His father knew exactly what he was doing. What's more, seeing he was such a tiny little squirt, with such innocent blue eyes, who could ever be suspicious of anyone with blue eyes? He knew all the minefields, learned them from his father, a devout man he was all the same.

The fields outside Rampartville were thick with German mines, but fortunately for us, nobody got hurt. Because the numbskull Germans told the Italians, and any Italian who had connections with a Greek family told them what places to avoid when they went out looking for greens. I suspect the Italians did that because the Germans treated them like second-class allies, people said, so they turned right around and passed on the information to us; what better chance to show how gallant they were, plus get back at the Germans.

Signor Alfio let Mother know where not to go for greens 'under any circumstances'. And Thanassakis discovered two mine-fields all by himself. When classes were over in the morning he went back to his room to study. And when school got out in the afternoon he and the other village kids would go back to their village. It was only three-quarters of an hour by foot but they had to make it fast, because after seven it was forbidden to cross the German lines which were just the other side of Deviljohn's bridge. But you expect kids to worry about things like that? So they were always stopping along the way, to spin their top, which was really an empty English hand-grenade. Anyway, by the time they got to the German lines, the hour was late and the barrier was down. In wintertime the kids would just duck under the bar and go on their way: because of the cold the Germans stayed crowded into the little brick hut they used as a guard house. (Thanassakis blew it up on them with a real grenade not long before the English arrived, wanted to blow off steam.) But come springtime the Germans would be standing there at the barrier like tenpins, firing off shots every time they heard footsteps.

Thanassakis watched where the Occupation forces would go to answer nature's call, and where they wouldn't. That's how he discovered the two mine-fields – 'turd fields' is what he called them – and so, from then on, they could come and go as they pleased.

In the adjacent mine-field there was a kind of round mine planted, roasters, we called them. Thanassakis, that crazy kid, danced around right on top of the mines, couldn't have weighed more than fifty pounds dripping wet, besides, you'll say, those mines were built for heavy vehicles, nothing for the kids to be afraid of. Only one time one of them blew up when a cow stepped on it and all the nearby trees were full of chops; our little Fanis got there in time to grab an armful of meat, for two days we had enough to eat.

There was the other mine explosion too, the one that blew Thanassakis sky high, but we're talking about the Tiritomba family right now, and for what reason they so hastily went on the road.

Mrs Adrianna fought it as hard as she could but hunger was closing in on them, no matter how many roadside shrines they busted into. One Sunday she went and fainted on one of our outings and we just about panicked because she was loaded to the teeth with grenades. Had to drag her back to town.

Her brother Tassis was in love with that rattletrap bus of his. He was always saying, Boy, I can't wait for the English to get here, get me some spare parts and some petrol. In the meantime he converted the thing to wood-fuel. But finding wood was another story, as you can imagine. The hills were crawling with partisans. So he stole grapevine stumps from the nearby villages. His sister would send him out to scare up an ear of corn or two, but he would always come back toting a bag of vine stumps. That dingbat Kanello even got Adrianna's daughter Marina – she was a bit older than me – mixed up in resistance stuff. Mlle Salome, you say? Out of resistance to that fiancé of hers who goes off to Albania – now there's a man for you – to escape the marriage and who turns out to have a face like Hitler in the bargain, Mlle Salome spent all her time getting dressed up to the nines or knitting underpants for the partisans. Occasionally we had little soirées at their place, what I mean is we had to stay over seeing that with all our chit-chat we lost track of the hour and by then it was curfew time, in which case we'd all cat-nap together. Other times we had to spend the night whenever we got word from Thanassakis that the Germans were going to seal off the town, just in time for Father Dinos to signal Mrs Chrysafis's son Valiant not to come home, that was before his ma hauled him home shot dead in the two-wheeled cart, of course, at which time we had one less job to do. Father Dinos sent messages with the church bells. Sometimes, out of the blue, the bells of Saint Kyriaki's would start ringing mournfully, as if for a funeral, or joyfully; at first we didn't know what to think. That's it, the priest's lost his marbles, we said, but finally we figured out that he used the church bells the way we use the telephone today, some even said that he had a special way of ringing the bells to let Madam Rita know she should wash up and expect him that evening.

Those overnight stays, Mrs Adrianna would brew up hot herbal tea, and throw in a dried fig or some grape juice molasses if she had it, for sweetening. Showed me how to weave rag rugs, she did. We tore the rags into narrow strips, rolled 'em up and I stitched 'em to a piece of matting with a darning needle, each colour – the red, the green – in its own place; Mlle Salome did the design.

We couldn't get by without those rag rugs at our place, because the earth floor was always damp and slippery; not to mention the shoots that were always sprouting up in the corners and under the bed right on top of the pullet's grave which kept getting deeper, by now the fowl must have worked her way as far down as dead people do, I said to little Fanis. That means our pullet is as good as any human, he said. We liked the idea.

The wool for the vests the women were weaving on those long dark evenings came from Mrs Kanello, but where she got it was a mystery. Except for all the old woollen stuff we unravelled. Plus somewhere she'd picked up a teach-yourself Italian book and she studied it so she could listen in on what the Italians were saying over the telegraph, that explains why they gave her the medal when the Republic came in. Why, she can still talk some broken Italian to this day.

Mlle Salome's speciality was underpants, Well, each to her own, piped up Mrs Kanello. Salome's knitted underpants were enormous; when she tried them on her brother Tassis, they came up to his ears. Must be starving, poor girl; why knit them so big, you're wasting all the wool, shouted her sister. What'll they use that crotch sack for, bombs? You don't know what you're talking about, says Mlle Salome. I may be a royalist, but I respect the partisans. What d'you take them for, pedigreed freak halfbreeds like the king of England? (I guess you'd have to call her a localist; no way she'd insult anything Greek.) They're all tall, like Captain Courageous. Me, I knew the partisans were small, mostly, and badly fed, that much I knew, ever since the Germans started dumping dead partisans in the town square.

The Tiritombas were weak from lack of food; what could we give them? it was all we could do to get by on what Signor Vittorio brought us, not to mention Mrs Adrianna wouldn't accept help from collaborators. One day, three Italians brought Mlle Salome home, unconscious. Panic. That's it, we whispered, she's blown the whistle on us. But no, we were wrong. Salome had gone out for a stroll (which wore her down all the faster) just as all Rampartville polite society would do every afternoon, come hell or high water, right up and down the main street. Still do the same thing today. I found out. Hunger was one thing, cutting off the evening promenade was another, even girls from the lower social classes would join in, putting on like people were bothering them or following them around. Anyway. Mlle Salome insisted on doing the afternoon stroll to demonstrate that she belonged to polite society, but wearing those high-heeled wooden clogs of hers and faint from hunger, she keeled over, twisted her ankle, and collapsed right in front of the Carabineria. The three Italian soldiers carried her back in a dead faint, as stiff as an Easter lamb on the spit. What really happened was that halfway back she came to, that much she confessed when I ran into her in that hick town of hers, but when she realizes she's in the embrace of three men, she told me, is she so stupid as to come to? Officers would have been better, of course, but when times are tough, you have to make do with what you've got, even if it's only soldiers.

So the foreign lads carry her home, all I've got is water, Mrs Adrianna says. Plus who should the Italians bump into on their way out but Mrs Kanello who's just sailed in with a straw basket full of wild herbs. Marina, all she was hoping was for Kanello to show up with some edibles, so when she spies the basket she pipes up, right in front of the Italians, Sweet Jesus, more hand grenades!? What happened to the corn meal? Shut up, idiot, hisses her mam. Fortunately the Italians were making eyes at the girl, they didn't notice a thing. All this time, Tassis was out scouring the valley and when he came back he brought some vine stumps and an inner tube, stole it from a stalled Italian truck.

Meantime the New Year was approaching. Better Black Year, I should say. The Year of Our Lord 1943. They had one head of cauliflower to their name, plus ten hand grenades in the ice-box, as well as the three Mausers stashed in the ceiling. Keep up your spirits, said Mlle Salome. The British are coming, and we'll all be eating pudding. She didn't have the faintest what pudding was but she was quite the Anglophile, because she liked the King of England, now there's a real man, she would say. If he were to ask for my hand, how could I refuse?

She said as she hammered a long nail into her heel to keep it in place, then stepped out to finish her promenade; you can never be too careful; people will talk.

'Won't be long before New Year,' goes Mrs Adrianna cattily. 'Think your Englishmen will get here in time for the pudding? Weren't they supposed to be here in 41?'

Still. At New Years dinner they had meat on their table. It was boiled, and there wasn't much of it. But it was meat, and there was plenty of broth.

'Can't even chew the stuff,' grumbled Mlle Salome, 'what kind of meat is this, anyway? it's purple. What is it, ferret?'

'It's as fine and tender as you could wish,' her sister shot back, 'just chew it; your teeth aren't used to meat, drink some broth and you won't go fainting away in the arms of the Occupation troops.'

Mlle Salome gets up from the table in a huff, without so much as crossing herself, doesn't even undo the napkin from around her neck. Whenever she's in a huff she goes and complains to her parrot. Into her room she goes; no parrot. Then she realizes what's happened; like divine revelation almost. Back into the dining room she storms, napkin dangling from her neck. Cannibals, she screams! Fortunately the others had gobbled up the parrot in the meantime; in fact, Marina snatched the half-eaten portion from her aunt's plate.

Salome let loose a torrent of invective; her sister listened silently with head bowed, what I mean to say is she couldn't speak because she was still chewing her last mouthful of the parrot's thigh. Mlle Salome was devastated. You don't respect my engagement present? You went and cooked your little sister's love? and such like. But when she called her Medea to her face, and man-eater, Mrs Adrianna burst out:

'You listen to me little lady,' she says. 'As if I wasn't sorry enough I had to kill the poor innocent bird, it just about bit my finger off! What am I supposed to do? Let my kids starve?'

'One kid, that's all you've got. And barely, at that,' Salome says sarcastically, seems as though Mrs Adrianna never managed a second one, at least that was Father Dinos's version, the one the whole neighbourhood knew.

No holding back Adrianna now.

'Three. I've got three kids,' she says. 'That good-for-nothing daughter of mine who all she can do is hand out leaflets, my good-for-nothing brother who I send for wheat and what does he come back with? Inner-tubes for a bus that won't even run …'

'Well excuse me,' Tassis cuts in, stung to the quick. 'You want me to steal? With pleasure. Just tell me where to go. But you won't catch me gleaning, a grown man of thirty-two, never!'

But Adrianna wasn't about to be stopped.

'And my third kid is you, my precious little lady! My good-for-nothing sister. We do a warehouse break-in but you, it never occurs to you to pick up some food, to help out a bit. Nothing but Tokalon powder. And lipstick for that mouth of yours that looks like a chicken's behind. The only reason we can still remember what a chicken's behind looks like is because we've got your mouth to look at. Snotty-nosed Brit-lover!'

She had a point there. Those were the days when people broke into bakeries, grocery stores, warehouses, 'busts' we called them. When we found out somebody was hiding food, our self-respect just evaporated. Even Mrs Adrianna – she was such a respectable woman back in the pre-war days and the Albanian war – let herself go, didn't miss a single break-in. Last time around she brought Mlle Salome along all dolled up in her high heels and her turban, although she didn't have any make-up on. In the confusion they lost track of each other. But everybody got back safe and sound. Mrs Adrianna with two loaves of bread, Marina with a half-empty sack of raisins, Tassis with a pocketful of feta cheese and a carburettor. Back comes Mlle Salome in triumph like the Empress Napoleon, with a lipstick, some rouge and a jar of face powder, some domestic brand it was, still … One of her high heels had snapped off.

For Mlle Salome death by firing-squad was better than going out without her makeup on, which she considered indecent. When they announced our surrender to the Germans over the radio she ran straight out and bought ten lipsticks, five rouges and five pounds of talcum powder, the kind they put on babies' rear ends; that was all she had to spend. So that's how she faced the Occupation, fully equipped. How long could it last? Five or six months? The English are such gentlemen, they'll set us free in no time. She was so blinded by her pro-English sentiments that she ran out of cosmetic supplies, which is why now she began stealing herself. Cosmetics only, though. Which was how come her sister was giving her hell.

Her sister was right, Mlle Salome had to admit it, the King of England was a little late for his date with Greece. But she wouldn't budge on one thing, they had to give her back the parrot's feathers. So she washes the feathers, and hangs them out to dry on the balcony, one clothes-peg each (that she did on purpose so all the neighbours could see how cruelly her own family betrayed her), then she sews the feathers on to her turban. Later she even wore the contraption on stage when she played Angela in *A Priest's Daughter*, it was a role for a seventeen year old, God forfend.

From that day on, the day she ate her own parrot, Salome vowed on his memory to make a liar out of her sister, who accused her of being a good-for-nothing Brit-lover right in front of the whole family. Meantime, she spotted a few domestic sheep grazing on the Zafiris family pasture; not far from Thanassakis' first mine-field. The Zafirises weren't concerned about thievery; they were German collaborators so their animals grazed unguarded except at night when they herded them into the living room.

Never even crossed their minds they should guard against us, Kanello and her friends that is, seeing as how due to our cowardice and our pride they never suspected us, didn't even pelt us with rocks if we picked greens on their land.

The day after the boiled parrot, Hey, Roubini, Mlle Salome says, let's go digging wild onions and get some fresh air. She was dressed to kill, complete with her niece's shoulder-pads, which were all the rage back then, even Mussolini wore them they say, one thing for sure, all the German charmers of the silver screen wore shoulder-pads, Jenny Jugo and Marika Rökk especially. Mrs Kanello didn't approve of shoulder-pads, mostly on account of the German connection.

'What're you doing walking around in shoulder-pads in broad daylight,' she says to Salome. 'You look like that fiancée of Hitler's.'

'Well, no accounting for tastes,' goes Mlle Salome. And with a yank on the arm off we went. But the remark really stung, as she didn't respect Hitler one bit, she knew he had this relationship but never married the girl. The no-good brute, she always said, playing her along all these years, when is he going to make an honest woman out of her? If it was me I'd hand him his marching orders.

We were on our way to dig wild onions; the sun was out, a good source of calories, is what they said. I was carrying my little trowel, you've got to dig to get the onions out of the ground.

By the time we reached Thanassakis' first mine-field I was starting to get suspicious. Mlle Salome, I ask, are we going for Resistance again? No, she says; you wait here and pretend you're digging for onions and don't say a thing no matter what happens.

'See those sheep?' she says.

'Goats,' I tell her. 'They're the Zafirises' goats.'

But even that couldn't hold her back. She's carrying a sack, and a shoulder bag. I watch as she steps into the minefield, leaping this way and that like Imperio Argentina when she sang in the film of Antonio Vargas Herredia, back before the war.

The livestock were grazing contentedly. All the time looking back over her shoulder she gradually steered them into this deep ravine. Then she leaps in after them like a Souliot woman and I lose sight of her. All the while I pretend I'm hunting for wild onions. But it's not long before I see her climb out of the ravine dragging the sack behind her, stuffed to bursting. To this day I still can't figure out how she steered it through that mine-field with those high heels of hers, the turban and the shoulder bag. She comes up to me. Give me a hand, she says, and don't let out a peep if it drips blood a bit. I do as she asks and what do I see? A bloody knife sticking out of her bag. In the sack is a butchered goat. Let's be on our way, she says, you go on ahead with a big smile on your face and without a care in the world, now get moving.

Now just picture us, walking along without a care in the world, two starving women with a load like that. Truth is, it was all we could do to drag the dead goat along behind us.

When we finally get to Deviljohn's bridge she says to me, You go on ahead, we don't want to attract attention. She sees the other kids waving at me, besides, it was almost curfew time and I had to pick Fanis up. I found him of course; but in the meantime Mlle Salome sets out for home hauling the goat along behind, anyway, it was a paved road for the rest of the way to town.

When we got home Salome still hadn't shown up. Every couple of minutes Adrianna popped out on to the balcony, looking up and down the street and what does the woman see: on the wall of Aphrodite's place Mrs Kanello is teaching Marina Italian. They were using the wall as a blackboard, and Marina had written REDICOLO MUSSOLINI without a mistake, and underneath HITLER EPYLEPTIK, which she didn't get quite right. As she's watching the spelling lesson all of a sudden she sees a short, stocky Italian soldier with a rifle slung over his shoulder come round the corner, probably on his way to his girlfriend's, with a big grin on his face. He says hello to them, then spots the writing on the wall, and comes to a stop. Mrs Adrianna rushes downstairs and what does she see? The Italian with his gun lying on the ground arresting Marina, trying to be courtly and chivalrous and patriotic all at the same time; wanting to take her off to the Carabineria. So there's Kanello looking for a way out of the mess, there's Marina, yelling, Get your filthy hands off me, and there's Mrs Adrianna falling over in a faint – at a time like that, yet! – when, all of sudden, they hear a sound like a burst of machine-gun fire. They turn; it's Salome's high-heeled wooden clogs on the cobblestones. Like in a dream, and faint from fear and hunger, Adrianna sees her sister let the bag drop and march right up to the Italian, frothing at the mouth.

'Let the kid go, scum!' she goes. 'She's a Greek! Hands off the Greek lass, you scum!' She goes.

The Italian mumbles something, tries to get out a few words, even Kanello can't understand him, but all the while he keeps dragging Marina in the direction of the Carabineria.

By this time curfew is in force and Mrs Adrianna has come to, but when she sees blood dripping from the sack she's just about to faint again, fortunately at that very moment we hear a faraway gunshot, from a patrol. Kanello is chasing after her five kids who came running outside to see what all the fuss was about and Mlle Salome is tugging on Marina's other hand, Let go my niece, you nincompoop, you'll pull her arm out of its socket! she yells at the Italian who's starting to look worried by this time. Then comes a second gunshot and Salome is really fuming.

'You can take your firecrackers and go to hell!' she yells in the direction of the gunshots, just like Leonidas before Thermopylae.

She yanks her niece's arm with all her strength; nothing. That pipsqueak of an Italian wouldn't let go. Suddenly Mlle Salome lets go Marina's hand, she falls over and so does the Italian, the poor sucker, which is when Salome lands him a swift kick in the shin, he doubles over in pain, weeping and begging, 'No, no signorina.' Salome hears that signorina of his (she was just dying for people to call her Madame Salome) and grabs the rifle, the young Italian is weeping and clutching his shin and Mrs Kanello is screeching from her balcony Adrianna, Tassis, hold on to that overgrown tomboy or she'll make mincemeat of the poor kid.

Meantime Marina slaps her mother to bring her around and she comes to, sees her sister with a gun in her hand, the foreign occupant weeping, hopping around on one leg like a stork, and cuts loose at her.

'Hey, leave the guy alone, give him his rifle back; we've already got three hidden in the ceiling,' says Adrianna. 'Mama, shut your big mouth, you're giving us away', squeals Marina.

Fortunately the Italian didn't understand a word of Greek plus with his shinbone hurting like that I bet he couldn't even understand his mother tongue.

At that very moment we hear gunshots, machine-gun fire this time it was and the gr-gr-gr of treads. A German armoured car heading in our direction. No time to get back upstairs, we all crowd into our house: lucky for us it was a single-storey place: first went Salome with the Mauser, Kanello's kiddies hid behind a homespun blanket hanging over their balcony. No sooner do we lock the door behind us than we hear knocking and whimpering, *Aprite, aprite per pietà, belle signore!*

Kanello opens the door for a split second and we let the Italian in; saved him just in the nick of time. Can you imagine what the Germans would do to him if they found him without his gun? The armoured car whirls around angrily, pointing its cannon at one house after another, and me, I'm staring out through the keyhole. Finally it roars off; fortunately it completely misses the sack with the goat.

'Go to hell', yells Kanello after it, with impunity, of course, the Germans were long gone. We make double sure, then push the foreign kid out on to the street, give him back his gun, dust off his trousers even, he was all gratitude, *Grazie, grazie mille, belle signore*. Out he goes, wipes the slogans off the wall with his sleeve and goes about his business.

Then the Tiritombas left. You, Salome orders Adrianna, you haul the trophy upstairs. And up the stairs she goes, just like Aida (I never performed that particular play).

Meantime Mrs Adrianna opens the sack, sees the big game, her eyes start to glaze over again. Hey, she shouts, where'd you steal this from?

'I killed that goat myself. That'll teach you to call me shirker and Brit-lover,' she said as she swept up the stairs without so much as a backward glance. 'One leg's for you Mrs Asimina,' she calls out to my mom, 'for little Roubini's help.' And all the while Kanello was looking on wide-eyed from her upstairs balcony, jealous probably.

'You imbecile,' goes Mrs Adrianna. 'If they catch us they'll eat us alive.'

'Let them eat our shit,' shoots back Mlle Salome haughtily, from the balcony.

'Don't you go using foul language in front of my children,' yells Mrs Kanello from her balcony.

'Have Tassis skin the goat,' Salome says from high up, as Marina tries to heave the sack on to her back.

'It's not even a billy goat, it's a nanny', says Mrs Adrianna as she looks closely at the trophy.

Here Mlle Salome just about comes unstuck.

'Whatever I do it's not enough! As far as you're concerned, my whole life is nothing!' she said, stung to the quick, and went inside whimpering.

Adrianna was right, though. It was a nanny goat.

Anyway, they brought their prize upstairs and we closed our windows, hoping for some boiled goat to eat the next day; I got some macaroni put aside, Ma tells us. First time she ever mentioned Signor Vittorio's little gifts.

But that was the night the Germans sealed off the neighbourhood, the night they shot Valiant. What really happened is, they executed him right in front of his mother's then dumped his body in the marketplace (I know who ratted on him, guy's big in frozen food today, so be it, you won't get another peep more out of me, these are evil times). The whole neighbourhood, it was crawling with Germans all night long, even broke into the church; we couldn't sleep a wink, lying there in bed awake, listening. Every now and then we heard gunshots. Ma tucked us under the big quilt, right up to our chins. Now go to sleep, she said, tomorrow we'll have goat to eat. What worried us was maybe we couldn't go snailing next morning at Deviljohn's bridge.

Tassis wanted to skin the goat right there in the courtyard but his sisters wouldn't hear of it. Everybody in the neighbourhood will know, said Salome, plus we'll catch the evil eye. So he ended up skinning and gutting the carcass in the dining room; strung it right from the chandelier and slid a roasting pan underneath to catch the innards, and there was Mrs Adrianna, watching the Germans through the balcony-door curtains, all on tenterhooks. And all this time Salome was hacking up the meat as the big cook-pot was heating over the brazier. Around three in the morning the Germans withdrew and we all breathed easier.

Come daybreak, as the cooking was in full swing, they hear Kanello hammering on Mrs Chrysafis's door, her shouting something and then they catch a glimpse of the two of them rushing off God knows where with a two-wheeled cart which immediately makes Salome think Kanello is trying to make a break for it, leaving her kids behind. Meantime, Germans start appearing again.

'That's all it was, a misunderstanding, but it changed my life; and I met the butcher of my dreams,' was how Mlle Salome described it to me years later in that hick town near Grevena when I was passing through with the travelling players. They invited me over for dinner; after all, it's not your everyday backwoods butcher's wife who can boast she's had a true artist at her table. Still, she always had a liking for me, since back when she was a maiden lady. After the meal, over coffee and cupcakes – her husband went off to open the shop – she brought me up to date on everything that happened.

The Tiritombas didn't have a clue about Valiant; no idea where Kanello and Mrs Chrysafis ran off to either. They heard the shots in the night, saw the tanks at dawn; all Salome could think of was her own crime. She confessed to her brother and sister that the goat she murdered belonged to the Zafiris clan, the same people who worked as stool pigeons and providers for the Occupation forces. Must be us they're after, says Tassis, and rightly so. How are we going to get out of this one? So Mrs Adrianna gets one of her brilliant ideas: head for the hills.

Take the show on the road, in other words. What else were they supposed to do?

All night long they packed the dear departed's costumes, rolled up the stage settings with their Sicilian-style castles oil-painted on canvas. Salome supervised the cooking of the goat. Not one of them was a real actor, of course; Adrianna was a housewife by birth, but she knew a bit about travelling shows; ticket sales, schedules, that kind of thing. Now really, can you call that a 'travelling company'? A handful of amateurs, that's all they were, so I discovered later, after the war. Oh well.

Tassis, Marina and the two sisters, the whole family divvied up the roles. Tassis, he handled the dramaturgical side of things: rummaged through the dog-eared old portfolio where Zambakis Karakapitsalas the impresario kept the scripts; some of them were printed, some were hand-written in pencil, and everything on loose pages. Plus, Tassis was in such a dither that he stuck the final act of one play to the first act of another. Take *Tosca*, for instance, which had a happy ending off Cape Matapan. But staying alive, that was their main problem, to be honest, who gave a damn about what happened at Cape Matapan. Take care of your life and art will look after itself, Mrs Salome told me, over our second cupcake.

Round about noon the troupe managed to get all their stuff crammed into the jitney, including Salome's valuables: she was in fine spirits, in the search they unearthed a whole boxful of make-up accessories.

And so it was we saw them turn, right after they crossed the bridge, like a stage coach straight out of a cowboy movie, except there were no Indians chasing after it, and no Germans. Still, you can't say they weren't decent people; fact is, they left a big plate of boiled goat on our window ledge, and one on Mrs Kanello's front steps too, which her kids polished it off before their Ma got home from work. But their leaving was a blow for me; Tassis came and asked Ma for the fustanella I got from Mrs Adrianna as a gift.

We reached this village called Pelopion after six hours on the road, the now-Mrs-at-last Salome relates (takes you less than an hour to get there today) wiping some crumbs from her lipstick. We were safe. Three days we stayed there, to pull ourselves together. The village was way up in the hills, crawling with partisans, tall and handsome too, every one of them. We said we'd suffered at the hands of the Germans. And we used Mrs Kanello's name every way we could; you remember her? (That's rich! Me, remember Kanello? Me?) Everybody who was anybody in the partisans knew her. They let us stay in the schoolhouse, we drew up our programmes, planned our route, got letters of recommendation to other villages controlled by the partisans, and some messages to pass on. We even held rehearsals. Of course, we had some disagreements over who would play what part, Mrs Salome admitted (over a third cookie, with a shot of brandy to wash it down), my dear elder sister insisted her daughter should play all the little girl's roles, and I did the grown women, not to mention the time I played a man, a baron he was, can't recall the play, name of Javert – wait a second; no, it was another play where I played Javert, anyway, here, have another cupcake.

I took one, my fourth: no danger for my silhouette.

'That tour of ours, the one that started back in Pelopion, in the Peloponese, ended almost a year and a half later, halfway between Albania and Romania, or was it Yugoslavia? Don't ask me. Not bad, the cupcakes, eh? Homemade. In the meantime, we learned how to act and generally how to run a road company, travelling in partisan territory, and in occupied territory too. I deserted right here, in this town. My butcher was making eyes at me, and I said to myself, Salome, when's the next time somebody's going to fall for you head over heels? So I gave in. You can't imagine what it cost me, she says, tossing back a glass of brandy to help down the last mouthful of cupcake, her fifth I think it was. You know, I was really beginning to get the knack, more than any of the others, she said. Maybe she was just being catty about my success with that last crack of hers.

'Every time we had a new young woman's role to play, we just about scratched each other's eyes out to see who would get first shot at it, Adrianna or me, I mean to say. My niece? If she so much as hinted she wanted the part (the ingenue or charming maiden as the stage directions put it), we'd put her in her place and then we'd jump all over her. You're still young, you've got all the time in the world to play young women; wait till you're grown up, her mother said one day. If we don't play these roles now, the two of us, when will we? As you can see, Adrianna had developed a taste for the footlights, even if she was a widow. The sad truth is I paid the price; sold out my art for a bed and a life-time of meat; still, it was all lamb-chops, filet mignon and sweetbreads.'

But Mrs Salome needn't have worried about the troupe. One day, as they're pushing the jitney up a steep hill, an Italian sol-dier, a long tall drink of water he was, leaps out in front of them rifle and all. They all surrender at once, of course, after block-ing the back wheels with rocks to keep the whole contraption from rolling back down the hill. But as they're standing there, hands over their heads facing the occupying troops, what should they see? The Italian was just a blond-headed kid, throws down his gun at their feet, starts blubbering and surrenders to them.

Finally they figured it out; it was a deserter (than really could have used Mrs Kanello and her Italian right then). A fine kid, name of Marcello. Heard the Germans were about to ship them off to the Russian front, at which point he turns tail, trying to find somebody to surrender to. But instead of partisans, he hap-pens on the troupe, so he surrenders to Mrs Adrianna, and later on, to Marina, especially her.

Turned out to be really useful. Had a knack for just about everything, he did; a born joker and comedian. What's more he could dance, do impersonations, and sing too, so they put him on stage. Certainly he was in no position to replace Mlle Salome, but they dreamed up a number just for him 'And now, ladies and gentleman, the great impersonator, Michael and his Italians!', Michael they named him. And Marcello sang his canzonettas and danced his tarantellas. At the same time, Marina gave him Greek lessons. But the lessons came to a halt, due to extenuating circumstances: one morning Mrs Adrianna nabs them in bed together. Him without a stitch on and Marina wearing only her undies, and smoking a cigarette! The sky just about falls on Adrianna's head; last time she saw a naked man was before the Albanian war. (And what a man, let me tell you, she told Mrs Kanello when they met at Mum's memorial service, my eyes just about popped out.) Long-suffering mother Adrianna unleashes a string of curses, eyes riveted all the time on the poor boy's private parts. Hussy, she screeches at Marina, just what do you think you're doing? Don't you fear God? Smoking?

The racket brings Tassis on the run. What's the big fuss about? he says to his sister, they make a fine couple. Still, even he objected to his niece smoking. So he snatches the cigarette out of her mouth, puts the Italian's clothes back on, and pronounces them engaged then and there. Today Marina and Marcello are married and living in Rimini, with three kids, all boys. May you grow up to be strong and inherit your father's best attributes, Mrs Adrianna writes to her grandchildren every New Year, that's what I heard back during the Renegades' government, from Mrs Kanello it was.

Well, after they took leave of Pelopion – the only things they staged there were some Resistance sketches to build up their courage – Mrs Adrianna steered the troupe back to all the places they did so well before while her dear late husband was still alive, they'll remember us here, she said. Even got up kind of a poster for every occasion:

Adrianna (widow of Zambakis Karakapitsalas, hero of
Albania) and her travelling players
A new production every day
Starring: the ever lovely Salome Papia
(couldn't live without her own stage name)
Featuring the ever-alluring Marina Kara
(lopped off the rest of her father's name).
The side-splitting Tassis.
Admission in kind.
Costume and evening-gown rentals for weddings and
baptisms.

In villages they played the coffee-houses mostly. Admission was in kind: eggs, bread, sausage, liver, whatever people happened to have.

Didn't always play to sell-out crowds, either. Sometimes they performed for five spectators, or for the proprietor only. Interpretation wasn't really a big problem; in less than a month they'd learned all the plays and all about the public as well: whatever you played, they ate it up. No problem about critics of mixed-up pages.

Tosca was their big success. They presented it as a British play, about the Allies, and the Resistance.

Anyhow, there was this one coffee-house proprietor who takes pity on Adrianna, seeing as how in the last act of *Tosca*, she has to jump off a wall. So one night, to keep her behind from taking a pounding with every fall into the wings, he sets up two inflated inner-tubes. So, with all the flare of a true artiste, Adrianna leaps from the wall on to the inner tubes, and comes bouncing right back on to the stage and ends up straddling the wall, which is how they improvised the perfect happy ending.

Lighting was no problem; they had acetylene lamps. Main problem was commercial success. Artistic success we had, in our hip pocket, says the now-Mrs Salome as she gobbles up cupcake number six (I was keeping pace with her, with brandy though). In lots of villages we couldn't even put on one performance: had to spend the night hungry in the jitney. Way she described it, it made me think of the time we went hungry for three days, Signor Vittorio was on guard duty; all we had was a cup of rice, and Ma boiled it up, and mixed in some sawdust to make it look like more.

One performance, Salome goes and keels over right on stage from sheer hunger. But Tassis – he was a whizz at improvising by this time – simply slings her over his shoulder and carries her offstage like a swooning lover, and gives her a raw egg; she pulls herself together and goes back to her role.

But there were some villages where they took in extra, because they rented out costumes and evening gowns to the local rich people, for weddings or baptisms, or for memorial services; in some places memorial services were more like parties, with boiled wheat and a big cauldron of barley soup full of chopped-up innards. We ate all the barley soup we could stuff into ourselves and forgave souls for all we were worth, Mrs Adrianna confessed one time, when Greece had its first beauty pageant I think it was. Our best season was the springtime; had more spectators.

With Adrianna there was a hitch; she didn't always remember which lines went with which play, plus she was impetuous by nature, she was always forgetting the prompter's box and letting herself go. In this medieval costume drama, just to give you one example, she drops the sock she's darning and enters stage right, but instead of saying to the lead, 'It's I, the guilty one!' she blurts out, 'My son! It is I, your adulterous mother!' At which point the audience breaks in and corrects her – the play was one of our most popular ones, so most of them had already seen it the night before. In another drama, in a more patriotic vein, a Turk appears (we had him dressed up as a Nazi SS-man) and starts stealing children. And Adrianna, she's supposed to come rushing out as a mother who they're going to turn her children into Janissaries. This time she's busy cooking something backstage. Adrianna, you're on, they call her. She's confused. What do I say? she asks. Your child, they tell her. Fine, she says, don't let the food burn. And she comes rushing on stage full of passion, embraces the Turk SS-man and cries, My child. It is I, your long-lost mother! Well, what was the Turk supposed to do? (Tassis was playing the role.) He kneels at her feet and cries Mama! And the crowd goes wild with applause.

'Little snags like that we had plenty of, but everything we did was a big success. Another cupcake?'

They had their bad days too, like any normal company. One time they come into this village, not a soul to be seen. They start shouting their pitch, not a window opens. When they reach the square they see five people, hanging. They hear a commotion, and down the cobblestones comes a little boy, maybe eight years old, with his mother in a push-cart, how he ever managed to cut her down, a little tyke like that? It's enough to make you wonder. It was the Germans killed her. Partisans ambushed them down on the highways, at which point the Germans trooped into the village and hanged the civilians to set an example.

'Everyone that could make it fled for the hills; and they weren't coming back. We could see them there, up among the rocks, motionless as tree-stumps. We helped the little boy get his ma to the graveyard, Tassis pulled the cart', Salome went on, now she wasn't eating. 'Buried her, the boy knew which was the family plot. Afterwards we cut down the others, loaded the bodies into the jitney and carted them off to the cemetery too. We nearly busted our rear ends from all the digging, but we looked after the lot. The boy gave us each one's name, and we stuck a little marker with the name on it on top of each grave, so their families could find them when they returned to their homes. After, the boy drummed up a loaf of bread and kills two chickens for us, and we left.

112

'There was this other village we didn't even go near, even if it was on our schedule: from far away we saw it was burning. The place was crawling with Germans, no show here tonight, we say to ourselves; so we hide the jitney in a sheep-fold until they've disappeared and then go on our way. We ran into the villagers a bit further on, bent double under their belongings, the girls were carrying their dowries on their backs but you can't very well put on a show in the open air, can you?

'If you take away a few episodes like that, we did pretty well, I've got no complaints,' goes Salome, and pulls out a cigarette. Smokes now, she does, even though it's a small town. I gave her some of mine, filter-tips, and that really impressed her.

'If you really want to know,' she goes on, 'I was the star of the show, thanks to my mandolin-playing. Before the war, back in Rampartville, I always got invitations to certain homes for name-day parties, I played tangos or fox-trots on my mandolin while they danced. Not that they were anything special, socially speaking, as they didn't even have no phonograph, mostly teachers or bank-clerks' houses it was, dear. On tour, whenever I'd forget my lines, I grabbed my mandolin and came out with a barcarole, and my partner exited stage rear with a look of ecstasy on his face, they whispered him my lines, and the show went on. Only one time, in a royalist town it was, some sonofabitch in the audience makes me sing "Son of the eagle" in honour of the king, while we're performing *The Adultress of Sicily*. What could I do? I break off the love scene and do the song, but I throw in some risqué bits such as "from in front and from behind".

'Another time, this merchant takes a shine to Mrs Adrianna and in the interval he sends her a message with the coffee-house owner: If she desires to make his acquaintance and a half-sack of flour to please drop by his store after the performance. Adrianna sends back her answer: We may play kept women consumptives with camelias but we're honest housewives; in fact, I'm going to tell my brother.

113

'But in comes Tassis – didn't have an idea what was going on – as they were discussing the matter, so they disclose the immoral proposition so as to, you know, such and such local wants Adrianna to come by his store to give her flour, but she won't go.

'Tassis didn't have an immoral thought in his head, in fact, generally speaking, he was an easy-going kind of guy and a bit slow on the uptake; so he goes up to the merchant. Holy Virgin, now they're going to kill each other, thinks Adrianna. But Tassis says to the man, Thank you very much, but my sister is indisposed and can't come, maybe you'd like me to drop by your store?

'Later we tried to tell him,' goes Salome, 'why the merchant cursed him like a dog, called him a rotten limp-wristed artiste and kicked him in the bargain. As it happens, it wasn't really Adrianna he wanted,' Salome says, busting out laughing. 'It was me, but the coffee-house owner mixed up the roles (the guy had told him, the one who plays the mother). But I never breathed a word of it to my sister. Go on, let her think someone has the hots for her, I say to myself.'

Other places, further north – this was after Salome dropped out and Marcello the Italian joined the troupe – it just so happened they invited the whole audience (six people it was) up on stage, because during the first act interval word got around the Krauts were about to surround the village and take reprisals. That story I heard from Mrs Adrianna. When was it? Must've been when we had the National Rally government.

The coffee-house proprietor got wind of it, and herded them all up on stage as a kind of chorus; fitted them out with costumes of sorts and they escaped certain death, the poor devils. Can you believe it, those uncultured Krauts, interrupting an artistic performance? says Mrs Adrianna as she gives me a light; she was smoking too, took herself for a veteran of the footlights, if you can imagine!

'That's why I just don't have any respect for German artists, they've got a nerve, coming here to our various festivals after the war and all. Playing their roles as if they're still wearing their Wehrmacht helmets, men and women, it's all the same! You want to know what I think? After the Liberation there should be one big mud puddle where Germany is, insisted Mrs Adrianna.

What she never told me was how once she executed a German while he was doing a caca. They were just leaving a village in the jitney, she spots him from the window, grabs Marcello's rifle and fires. Gets him with the first shot and everybody congratulates her, first time she ever touches a gun and bang, scores a bull's-eye on her first shot, that bit of information I got from Mrs Marika, Kanello's mother, she was past seventy by then and everything seemed funny to her, her daughter especially.

Still, Adrianna was a kind soul. Lots of times she hid partisans in the jitney or drove them right through the German lines all wrapped up in the scenery or hidden in the troupe's wardrobe.

'People ought to learn Geography, really,' Mrs Adrianna goes on, we're still back in National Rally days if I'm not mistaken, just before Karamanlis. Came to see me when I was playing in Athens with a road company, a musical it was; just paid the apartment off. She was all for Geography, seeing as how one day while they're on tour, about a year after they started out from Pelopion village, they come into this village and Marcello goes out to drum up an audience for the night's show (learned Greek really well, he had; you'd swear he was from the Peloponese), people just stared at him and laughed. At which point the players realized what was going on: they crossed the border, now they were Abroad. First they thought they were in Yugoslav territory. But somehow it turned out they were in Albania. Mrs Adrianna, she gets all emotional remembering Zambakis, this is the place where my hero heroically left his bones, she says. And – I mean, was she crazy or wasn't she? – she starts asking around, maybe her late husband's grave is somewhere close by. Always was a simple-minded woman. Anyway, they put everything in reverse and turn back towards Greece. The border was wide open, the Albanians, they didn't ask for passports, nothing. But before they leave Albanian soil, Mrs Adrianna plants a cross. Nothing much really, just a couple of boards as kind of a cenotaph for her spouse. She never found out that he was killed by a kick in the head from a mule even before he could contribute to the combat against the invader. Later Mrs Salome learned what really happened, from the Ministry of the Army, but she never breathed a word to her sister, if she wants to make out she's a hero's widow, let her. And so she collects her pension every month, just as proud as you please.

Once they were back on Greek soil they kept up the tour for a couple months more. Things had got quieter, the Italians and partisans were nowhere to be seen, not even the Germans. But they were so involved in the artiste's life it never occurred to them to ask why. Until one day some guy asks Tassis, Hey mister, how come you're still burning wood to power that thing? Why not use petrol?

Only then they noticed: across the street, above the door to the municipal office, he sees a Greek flag and rushes off to tell the rest of the troupe. As it turns out, Liberation had come to pass three months earlier but they were so taken up with the life of the artiste, and the youthful couple Marina-Marcello with their love life, that they never heard a word about it. Found out three months after the fact, celebrated the occasion retroactively, and turned back towards Rampartville, not in too much of a hurry of course; along the way they staged a show or two. Changing the titles of the plays to match the new victorious situation, of course.

MUST BE NEAR ON two years since the Tiritomba family upped and left. Autumn or thereabouts, there I was playing on Mrs Kanello's upstairs balcony with her six kids and she's telling me, It's high time your ma makes up her mind, Roubini; she's got to get out of the house, everybody's forgotten the whole thing. I was saying, Not yet, wait till her hair get a little longer. Her hair just wouldn't grow any more after they sheared it off; she maybe had an inch left.

All of a sudden, what do we see coming round the corner by the church but the Tiritombas' jitney, only now it was running on petrol, and pulling up in front of their house, with the flag on the front bumper flying.

'Well I never ... it's Adrianna,' goes Mrs Kanello. We run over, hugs and kisses and tears all around; the Tiritombas were back, without Salome but with a fine-looking blond lad who talked Greek like a country boy. The whole neighbourhood gathered around, we helped them open up the house, and stayed up the whole night listening; everybody just adored Marcello, and after I gave Mother the whole story. Didn't come to the overnight though; ever since the public humiliation she wouldn't even stick her nose out of doors. Fortunately by then I was working, in three houses; I was a grown-up girl now, why, the year after I got my period for the first time and Ma made me halvah.

That night we got all caught up on the adventures of the troupe. Mrs Adrianna was a changed woman; used to be a plump little housewife but now she looked like some partisan band leader. Asked us to forgive them for missing the Liberation, can you beat that. Marina and Marcello got married in Saint Kyriaki church and we all attended, Mother even sent a wedding present, six hand-embroidered napkins from her dowry it was. After the wedding they left for Rimini, Italy, where they lived happily ever after.

Mrs Adrianna was completely liberated now, as a woman I mean. Did more than become a feminist, even went and remarried, an Athenian would you believe. Lives in Athens, she does, with her brother Tassis; I run into her now and then, her second husband is buried in the same cemetery as Ma, she even managed to get her Albanian war widow's pension activated again, thanks to this politician she knows. So we talk it over, the two of us, waiting for the priest to show up and read the prayers.

Yes indeed.

Meantime, we're so-called Liberated once and for all. In my family we were all Collaborators because of Signor Vittorio. Only Mrs Kanello, poor dear Aphrodite's mother Mrs Fanny and now the Tiritombas would talk to us. Valiant's mother wouldn't say a word to anybody in any case, talked to herself, that's all she did, or to her son's grave.

The work started picking up. Doc Manolaras found me the three house-cleaning jobs, and to show my gratitude I did his place for free. One day Anagnos' boy Thanassakis comes calling. Grown up now, he is. Comes with his father the schoolmaster, their donkey's loaded down with things to eat. Thanassakis unloads the lot of it, brings it right in without so much as a how-do-you-do; Ma's sitting at the table. It's no fault of yours, Asimina, says the schoolmaster. Our first duty is to our children and to our own lives, then to our honour. Your choice was the right one and I respect it, you knew the price you'd have to pay. Never regret your decision: be patient, things will calm down, people can't keep on being vicious for ever, they'll leave you be.

A saintly man, the schoolmaster. But Mother didn't so much as give him a glance, and pulled the kerchief tighter over her head so her sheared-off hair wouldn't show. Thanassakis was struggling not to look at her, making out he was stacking up the

118

victuals or nipping outside to check the donkey or chitchatting with our little Fanis. Couldn't keep his eyes off her though. Never once looked at me, mind you. Not once.

His father, he sees how awkward a situation it is, so he goes into this description of the exploits of his boy wonder in the Occupation, mostly with mines and minefields. But what with Ma not saying a word and us too embarrassed to talk, the visit didn't last long. I almost didn't thank the people, I can't remember, did I kiss the schoolmaster's hand? Or was it Ma kissed his hand? Can't remember. All I can remember is how hard I laughed when I remembered Thanassakis stark naked, back when the mine blew him sky high.

Come the so-called Liberation lots of people made good money thanks to the mines. The big landowners, they paid real good money to clear the explosives out of their fields and olive groves and vineyards, rush rush, seed, plough and cash in. But plenty of poor people put bread on their table digging up mines. See, there's one good thing the Germans did for us. Nobody died, only the odd arm or leg got blown off.

Thanassakis, he did it for free, his father wouldn't let him take money. Knew just where the mines were, all he had to do was point to the spot. Left Greece long ago, he did; no way was he going to stay and rot. He's in America now, a professor; got his own university, so Mrs Adrianna tells me when we meet at some demonstration or other, can't for the life of me remember what about.

One time I spotted Thanassakis, a little before Ma died, outside a bookshop it was, but how was he supposed to know who I was? I didn't say a word. He comes back every summer to visit his father's grave. Now he's moved up the ladder, socially speaking: why, over there, in Boston, he's quite something. I hear: me he's going to remember forty years later. What I mean is that there, as he's window-shopping at the bookshop. I wanted to walk right up to him and say, hey, roly-poly, remember the time I saw you with your bum showing? Just getting hairy, you were!

Happened a little before the Germans fled the scene. There I am, out hunting wild artichokes, and who do I run into but him and his gang; our little Fanis was with them. Come on, Thanassakis says, I'll show you where there's all the artichokes you want, only be sure you step right where I do. He takes me through his minefield. Don't be scared, he says, look, look at this! And he starts hopping up and down right on top of this mine like some kind of dare-devil. So we get to a fence thick with artichokes, and I start picking. Hey kids, shouts Fanis, look here, pears! At the edge of the field is a pear tree covered with ripe fruit. Nobody makes a move; all around it are mines.

'I'll climb it,' says Thanassakis.

Up he shimmies, but when he reaches the second branch he kind of slips and falls, smack on top of a mine, roasters we called them, the flat, round kind. In the twinkling of an eye I see the other kids playing further off, a flash of fire and Thanassakis shooting up like the Prophet Elijah headed straight for heaven, I barely have time to tell myself No time for jokes, you dingbat. Everything he's got on, the mine burns it to a crisp and the shreds are hanging like dead birds from the tree, and there's Thanassakis, hanging from one of the branches like a bat, stark naked. He drops to the ground like a ripe fig, fortunately the ground was wet, his hind end goes plop like a busted water-melon, but all things considered he's still alive. As naked as the day he was born though, and there I am, tittering; I drop all my artichokes, prick my fingers, and his pals, a bit further away, are standing there dumbstruck, yelling, hey, Thanassakis got hairy, Thanassakis got hairy! As if they were jealous or something.

In spite of everything, he stays cool, the little rascal. With his bum almost split in two and bleeding, he dashes off, picks up his school cap and hides his private parts, but not before I get an eyeful.

Meantime, the others come over, Fanis gives him his school-bag to hide his behind, and yells at me, Don't you dare look or I'll tell our ma.

They plaster his posterior with mud to stop the bleeding and we escort him back to the village in a kind of human ring so people won't see his nakedness. His mother gets one look at him and gives him a whipping, Why you good-for-nothing little ... she sputters, didn't I tell you not to play around with mines, and now look at you, your underwear's all gone.

While she's cleaning off his behind in the water-trough where the pigs and cattle drink Fanis is hissing in my ear, Don't look at naked men, you hear! (man, ha! he was just a runt), then we went home.

That's why he wouldn't dare look me in the eye when they show up at our place with their donkey, seeing as how I saw him humiliated and naked. His behind was cured by then, but still, he had to walk around with bandages for one whole year. Wasn't so much bringing us food as giving us moral support against the rest of society, his father was like a kind of judge, wherever he went, he took away the shame of the house whatever the wrongdoing was.

They made a nice stack of the victuals, said their goodbyes, untied the donkey's reins from our window and left. Mother didn't even turn her head, didn't so much as glance in his direction. But the schoolmaster knew. And Thanassakis knew, because of how he followed along for the whole parade, and he saw everything. I'm saying to myself, he came to see you, to keep you company from a distance, but you know me. I get the strangest ideas sometimes, I just get carried away.

I could tell the situation was different three months before the partisans marched into Rampartville. The Italians vanished into thin air; Signor Vittorio didn't even come to say goodbye. You know some of the higher class families, the ones who were so friendly with the Italians? Well, they left town. A couple of others took on seamstresses to sew them up British flags. The Germans got meaner, gave the Italians the boot as allies, and set up the Security Battalions, a kind of home guard, nothing but a bunch of starving Greeks was what they were, dressed in short little khaki-coloured fustanellas Secbats we called them. Them Shitbats, they scare me sweetie, Mrs Kanello tells me one day, can you imagine a Bouboulina like her admitting she's scared. She heard something about the Russian front – it had broken.

From the departure of Signor Vittorio onwards we weren't all that hungry, I must confess. We had the public soup kitchen. Got four servings, because we never told a living soul that Sotiris, our big brother, was missing; in fact, we still had his coupons. Even had food in reserve. we did: a whole crate of chick peas left over from distributions. And we had Mrs Adrianna's ration book, the one she let us borrow when she left and when she came back we returned, as a souvenir.

And one night in September it would've been, we hear lorries. Next morning the Germans are nowhere to be seen. We kids run downtown for a look-see; the Kommandantur is empty, the door hanging open. Mrs Kanello didn't go to work that day, the Shitbats (that's what she called the Secbats, called them Rallis' roughnecks too) will make mincemeat of us, she said. She stayed home from work, bolted the door and herded her whole family down to the cellar. The whole city was waiting. For something. The shops were closed but the Secbats broke down doors, stole whatever they wanted, killed people to settle personal differences; later on they put them on trial but most of them got let off scot-free.

Three days we laid low; we only stuck our heads out into our back yard, the one with the wall around it, had a few vegetables growing there, a couple of sick-looking tomatoes, that kind of thing.

At daybreak we hear gunfire. And far away, the sound of voices. They're burning police headquarters, the partisans are here, brayed Kanello from her balcony, waving a bedsheet in jubilation. Now was she waving it like a flag, or to show that she surrendered, I haven't the faintest idea. Lie low a bit longer, we'll soon be liberated, she shouted. A voice like a foghorn, nothing feminine about that woman I swear. But good as gold all the same.

'Hide', says Ma. But we didn't have any place to hide. We close the door, put the cross-bar in place, not far away we hear a machine-gun chirping, The bullets sound like kisses, Ma, says Fanis. And a voice yelling though a megaphone, This is the People's Government speaking! Holy Mother of God, I go, they captured the bell tower. I peep out of the window and see this tiny partisan waving his machine-gun from side to side, dancing. Duck, idiot, I hear Mrs Kanello yelling, that woman wanted to direct everybody and everything. I swear. It was all her kids could do to pull her back inside, finally they managed to drag her back in, the six of them plus her husband, first time he set foot on the balcony since before the war. At which point a shell rings the church bell and the whole neighbourhood echoes, and the little partisan ducks down behind the parapet.

That very instant we hear a mortar. I didn't have any idea what a mortar was, Mrs Adrianna explained it to me later; it's a sort of small war tool, like a manual meat-mincer. But dangerous too, shoots a shell way high up so if some ham-handed Secbat aims at the bell tower the shell could just as soon drop right smack on our roof, seeing as it's right next door to the church, and only one floor at that.

So Ma drags our table out into the back yard and around it we set the crate of chick-peas and broad beans and a trunk full of clothing from her dowry, and on top we pile all our mattresses and quilts; then we crawl into our shelter, Go on, now shoot all you want, says little Fanis. Three whole days the bullets flew back and forth overhead. And there we were, huddled under the table for three days; bread we had, plus water from a bucket we used for watering the vegetables. It had a thin film of kerosene on the surface to keep the mosquitoes away which we pushed aside with our hands to drink; it smelled. Don't worry about it, says Ma, paraffin's good for your hair. Besides, we survived.

On the third day the shooting stopped. But the smell of smoke was in the air. Scraps of charred paper were fluttering by in the air over our yard. They burned down the town hall.

It was a Godsend for the nationalist or leftist women with files on them. Seeing as the town registrar's records went up in flames they all took out new birth certificates with whatever birthdate they wanted; swear an oath, that's all you had to do. So every female in Rampartville, women and ladies alike, go and swear a false oath – even the best families. Mrs Adrianna even, she swore she was only about twelve years older than her daughter, not because she needed the certificate. but, she said, everybody else was doing it. What's more she took out a fresh birth certificate for Salome, knocked thirteen whole years off her age just like that, and sent it off to her as a wedding present, a bit late but a terrific present all the same. Only Mrs Kanello refused to play along. Even today she'll tell you her real age, nothing feminine about the woman!

Doc Manolaras our member of parliament got me a new birth certificate; two, to be exact. The eight years less one, Keep it, he says, you'll be needing it one of these days. The other one he adds on nine years, but he holds on to it himself, to get my voter registration book. This was in Athens.

At any rate, that first certificate came in handy twenty years down the line, it shut up plenty of my co-workers. God bless the partisans for burning the damn thing to the ground, I wish them all the best even if it's a sin to say so, a nationalist gal like me. Many's the time I prayed to God to look after them, later on when they shipped them all off to some island for some kind of exile; what did they call the place, Long Island, Little Island, can't recall. But it didn't make much difference that I could see,

124

I was wasting my time, plenty of them died on that island. Ever since then I just don't approve of tourism on islands even though it's all the rage these days; no way you'll catch me galli-vanting around the Aegean and such disgusting things, so what if they advertise, what with all those people dying there, why, maybe they're vampires now.

So, as I was saying, these scraps of burned paper were flut-tering over our house, and me, I was as curious as a cat. Out of our shelter I crawl and go over to open the front door; in the street I see a handful of corpses and I see Mrs Kanello, that woman's curiosity was something else, let me tell you! The whole family was there, poking their noses up from the cellar. How're you all doing, Roubini? Did you all survive? We made it, we did.

Further off, from the town centre, you could hear noise. It was a human voice, calling through a megaphone. I couldn't make out the words, was it partisans talking, or Secbats? But before long I see Kanello starting to jump around like Indians in a John Wayne movie.

'We're free, neighbours!' she shouted.

'You hear? We won!'

The voice with the megaphone was coming from a partisan. Now I could make out a few words: people's government, free-dom, stuff like that. Then a hubbub from downtown, the peo-ple were coming out into the streets. Ma came to drag me back inside but in the meantime little Fanis scooted off; the two of us wanted to get a look at liberty. The little partisan was hanging from the bell tower like a bunch of grapes. Further off, smoke was rising.

Mrs Kanello lined up her kids and they marched off to greet the people's government. And there was her husband, watching from the upstairs gallery; fortunately it was Liberation and he could enjoy a bit of sunlight, said his wife. Holed up inside all this time, poor man, ever since the night spirits bewitched him.

He looked at us for a moment, My, how you've all grown, he said, and went inside again.

Smoke everywhere, lots of smoke. The Music Conservatory was on fire too, try and figure out why they'd burn that; the Secbats did it, people said. The Police Station also burned to the ground but things kept on exploding there in the ashes; probably ammunition, is what our Fanis told me.

People were sort of numb, mostly staring out windows or standing in doorways. A few of the most notorious collaborators had British flags hanging from their balconies, or hammer and sickles. Now the voices from the megaphones were louder and clearer. And to top it all off, people from all the nearby villages were streaming into town.

Peasants, that's who it was, with donkeys or mules carrying empty sacks and pickaxes, come to town for plunder and for looting the shops. You figure out who told them. Let's go take a look, goes Fanis, he spotted a real nice fire. But all of a sudden we hear voices from a back alley shouting Freedom! and stones hitting our roof, and shouts of Burn the Collaborators, burn the whores! The two of us turn on our heels and run. Fanis, they're going to burn Ma, I say, let's get out of here.

What with all the hullabaloo, and what with our curiosity to see just what kind of thing it was, this freedom, we forgot all about Ma. We went down the back alleys so we wouldn't get trampled by the peasants pouring towards the town centre, finally we reached the cemetery. They had about a dozen Secbats nailed up against the wall – I think they were nailed there anyway, I was too shocked to tell. They were stripped bare from their throats to their thighs. We went closer; they were all dead, slaughtered, two long crisscross slashes. After, people said, they dumped pickling salt into the wounds. I was just about to puke and I turned around and ran home with the kid.

Meantime the peasants were heading back to their villages. On donkey back, furious. The partisans wouldn't let them loot the shops. So they went off cursing and throwing rocks at windows as they left. But we never promised they could loot anything, Mrs Kanello's sister the partisan told us, when she came down from the hills, family in tow. We never told anybody in the villages that we'd let them wreck the shops in Rampartville. That's what she declared, back when we had Archbishop Damaskinos as regent. A little later, was it when Maximos was the prime minister, or was it Poulitsas, I forget which, how am I supposed to remember them all, politicians, you can have them, that's all I need now, to remember their names, they were just a bunch of political walk-ons anyway, back then all the peasants voted the monarchy. And after that, which prime minister was it? some ugly short guy it was, Mrs Kanello's sister and her family, they sent them off to exile to the whatever island they send those people to, Little Island, Long Island, never could remember which; what can I do?

One thing's for sure, we felt a little bit of a let-down that first day. That's all there was to Liberation? We were nothing but kids, of course, what were we supposed to understand. So we took the water jug and went off for water, we weren't going to let Ma out of the house, seeing as how they called her collaborator. Water had been cut off to all the houses; the Germans blew up the town reservoir on their way out.

So we take the jug and head off for the Canals, a kind of irrigation ditch just down the hill from Saint Rosolym church. But we kept slipping and sliding going down the hill, because there was blood all over the street. The dead bodies were stacked up neatly off the roadside but the pavement had blood all over it. So we had to watch where we were going, we didn't want to slip and crack the jug or else Daddy will give us a whipping, says Fanis.

I turn and stare at him.

'What daddy, Fanis?'

'When he comes back from the war,' he says, with downcast eyes.

'What daddy, Fanis?' I ask again. 'Daddy's dead, killed in Albania years ago.'

'When he comes back from the war he'll give us a whipping if we bust the jug,' the boy kept repeating, with downcast eyes. 'And besides, Ma won't let us say he's dead,' he went on. 'So people will think we've got someone to look after us. So they won't burn our house down.'

Finally we got back home with a full jug and safe and sound, and had ourselves a nice drink of fresh water. And that's the way Liberation came, and that's the way it began.

A few days later I started my job cleaning floors and dusting houses, Doc Manolaras our future member of parliament put in a good word for me. I didn't let on to Mrs Kanello how I wasn't getting paid for working at Doc Manolaras's place. Our Fanis would hang around the burned-out houses and wherever he saw the owners rummaging around trying to save whatever was left, he helped out as best he could, poor kid, that crushed hand of his you know.

Mother, she stayed inside the house; we couldn't open the shutters because they'd throw stones at us, twice it happened, and shout dirty collaborating whore. And generally speaking things were worse for us than the so-called Occupation. It's time Mrs Kanello and Aphrodite's mother Mrs Fanny took our side, it's a sin, they shouted from their windows, the poor woman. Me, I went to work with a kerchief over my head like a pretend peasant woman, for fear somebody would recognize me on the street.

Seeing as how in the meantime reprisals against the collaborators had started. Some of the well-to-do homes, the ones who invited the Italians into their living rooms, plus they had eligible daughters, well people went and nailed horns above their front doors, got them from the public abattoir. And we all went and laughed and stared, me and little Fanis, until one day Mrs Kanello talked some sense into us.

128

A couple of families, the ones that engaged their daughters to Italians, went and locked and double-bolted their doors, but those kind of people didn't have any food problem, their pantries were full, only the evening stroll with the rest of the town's high society, that's all they were deprived of. And the ones that were quick enough to hang an allied flag from their balcony, nobody even disturbed them: they opened their French doors and windows wide and threw flowers on the partisans' heads. When the English came ashore and the so-called Liberation was complete they put up signs that read 'Welcome Liberators' right next to the flags. The signs were in Greek and Italian; nobody knew any English yet. When the British arrived people started learning English with the Xavier de Bouges Teach-Yourself method. Chocolates reappeared too. Foreign-made, better than our own chocolates before the war.

Doc Manolaras's wife – I was working at their place – she wanted her husband to send me back to school, to complete my education. Fine, I said, and they put me one class higher than the one I never finished. But I was worried, the rocks kept on hitting our roof tiles. Though now they only threw rocks at night. Mrs Kanello heard the noise – she heard everything that went on in the street – and came out on her gallery shouting, That's all your people's courts are good for, going after poor people? What's the matter, you don't know where the big whores are? She had a point there, nobody wanted to mess with the collaborators from the best families, not even the leftest of all the Communists.

I was the man of the house now, a woman just about almost sixteen years old. Mother sewed up pads for me expecting my period would come any day now but I had plenty else on my mind, how was I going to manage with school and four houses to clean. What's more we were all waiting for the Allies. To bring us what I don't know. But all of us, we were waiting, every house was waiting, personally. We imagined they would be much more dashing than our own local partisans, they were foreigners after all. In fact, back then everybody was talking about the modern movies we were going to be getting soon and they would all be in colour, people said. Every home was expecting the Allies, it was like a formal dinner invitation where first they would eat our food and then give us all gifts. What kind of gifts? At school they handed out allied rations – that was the main reason that I decided to go back to school for a couple of weeks, but I kept right on cutting class – powdered milk and a little individual ration can. Thanassakis Anagnos gave me his, probably trying to tell me something he was, but I never got to enjoy it. I open it up and what do I see? a condom and some razor blades. Mrs Kanello snatched the condom before I had a chance to blow it up like a balloon. Give me that, harebrain, quick, just once in my life I'm going to enjoy myself, I'm sick of the poor man pulling out just when. In the meantime, she had her seventh kid.

Me, I knew what condoms were. I saw them back when Signor Alfio used to come by, used ones; threw them out along with the rinsing water before my little brother could spot them and ask Ma, What's this thing? And besides the fresh ones I saw under the beds in the houses where I worked, they hung one all bulged out and half-full of water just outside our front door. Our little Fanis asks Mum what's that balloon? and Ma smacks him one on the head.

When they gave me a can with a condom inside I traded it with Mrs Kanello, her son got one with chocolate. The little fart wouldn't let go of it for nothing, but Kanello, her mind was made up, I ain't having no kid number eight, she said. And she yanked it out of his hand.

So that was how I got to eat chocolate again. Used to eat it before the Albanian war, and now after the so-called Liberation finally I could eat it again. Whole Occupation long all I ever dreamed about was chocolates and sweets. Me, there's two things I never could figure out: God, and how come in some homes, they don't keep the sweets under lock and key. At our place Ma always kept the jar with the preserves locked up tight, for visitors, this was before the war of course. Never could get enough sweets to eat. When I was a little girl we didn't have any. And when I became an artiste I couldn't eat them, I was afraid I'd get fat, plus when I was on a diet I felt a little like a real leading lady. Now I'm just about ready to retire I've come down with diabetes. Can you believe it!

Ma never really ever enjoyed chocolate either. Whenever we came across one in a ration tin she saved it for Fanis. He'll forget his hand that way, was what she told me. She was always making plans how she would eat a whole bar all by herself. But the public humiliation came instead, and the bitterness, and from then on she never wanted to taste chocolate. Until the day she died.

The first collaborators to pay the price were Madame Rita and Siloam.

Madame Rita was a whore by profession. Rita was a pseudonym, Vassiliki was her real name. Madame Rita was the most respectable whore in Rampartville. A real star she was, I copied a lot of her tricks later on in my acting career. She had her own brothel, but she did call-out work too. For the Germans mostly, at the Crystal Fountain restaurant where I took her the holy bread from Father Dinos that time during the Occupation. The rumour was they had relations, that Father Dinos, he was a real skirt-chaser, plus his wife was super-religious. Plan too.

When Rita went by in the street all the honest women crossed themselves. Holy Virgin protect us from such a fall, Ma said one time, right in front of Mrs Kanello. That was back in the Signor Alfio days. No smart remarks from Mrs Kanello, though; she never looked down on Ma because she was seeing two Italians.

Madame Rita was a public official. Swished around like a church bishop, she did. Everybody greeted her in the street, even the judges, and as she walked along she was glancing right and left and making a mental note when someone didn't say hello. A man ignored her at his risks and perils, and if he did. Madame Rita tore into him right there in public, in the middle of the market with curses to make your hair stand on end, reminded him how many times he visited her girls, at half price even. Only accepted high-ranking civil servants, she did. And military men, from captain up.

Me, back before the war, I got goose bumps when I saw her, how grand she was. Only two people gave me goose bumps as a kid, Madame Rita and the queen, when I saw her for the first time. Unfortunately, we never met again. She came to Rampartville on the royal tour, still only the wife of the heir to the throne she was, so the little people would fall in love with her. There was such a huge crowd at the welcoming ceremony, we lost track of Ma. The crowd kept pushing us back until we ended up in the very last row, Daddy hoisted me on to his shoulders, Look at the queen, he was shouting, look at the queen. There was a big crowd and we were all the way to the back, and Daddy never even saw her in the end, being so short as he was, but he was weeping with devotion. Madame Rita was there too, even though she wasn't with the dignitaries. Greeted the Prefect even; smart man, he returns the greeting, How are you, Madame Rita, and how is business?

After Liberation they demolished half her brothel to make an example of her, and took away her permit for a whole year. But she opened right up again when the Allies arrived, thanks to our member of parliament Doc Manolaras; he was still a doctor back then. In fact later on she added three extra rooms on to the main brothel with money from the Marshall Plan people said, from the budget for war reparations, claimed it was destroyed in the bombing, all of that during the Tsaldaris administration.

That was how Madame Rita was punished for collaborating with the Enemy.

Siloam was the other one.

Siloam was a tailor. He only went with men and didn't even hide it. Stelios was his real name, I didn't know what it meant, 'going with men', or why they gave him a woman's name (Picked it out myself, dear, he tells Mrs Adrianna latterly; everybody who comes up to me, I want them to know what I fancy, not going around afterwards saying I lied to them. Like a sign in a shop window so people know what they're getting and who they're getting it from. You've got to tell the truth.)

Siloam was nowhere near as grand as Madame Rita. But he was good natured and a bit of a sad sack, nobody was scared of him, or should I say her? Everybody who went by he greeted with deep bows, as if he was begging their pardon and they were obliging him by saying hello. Orphaned from age thirty, he was, and he kept his hair combed into a pompadour.

A first-class tailor though, took pride in his work and if he wanted to swear on something, he said 'by my scissors'. Just how good a tailor, Doc Manolaras told my father, back before the war. And a useful man to have around; he was the one who made men out of most of the boys of Rampartville, on top of him was where our young men learned their lessons. Seeing as the girls were all honest and they never went with a man before marriage, first they got married and then they took a lover.

Anyway, nobody bothered him. Seems he knew plenty of secrets; many of the worthiest married men of Rampartville served their apprenticeship with Siloam. God forfend I should ever say a word! he used to say, Ass may not have bones but it surely can break bones.

Collaborated with the Occupiers too. Come the Liberation they arrested him but in jail he cooperated with the partisans so they let him go. After, the X-men arrested him but in jail he cooperated with the X-men so they didn't ship him away.

When you come right down to it we never did figure out what Siloam's real political beliefs were, if he was left wing or royalist maybe. They were influenced by his emotions of the moment. He was in love with a partisan? Well, you got a lecture about Marx and a little embroidered hammer and sickles. He was head over heels with an X-man? You'd find him wearing a little crown pinned to his lapel. But he was no double-dealer, he stood up for his beliefs every time. Once during the Occupation he even gave me an egg. And when our whole family left town after the public humiliation, he stopped by to pay Mother his respects.

Siloam stayed on in Rampartville. But after the partisans, the X-men and even the Brits (they took the bread out of my mouth, he always said) let him down, so people say, he finally put his foot down, cut his hair and went and got married. Today he's faithful to his wife and his scissors, turned out fine children. So I heard. Of course, it did happen that he fouled his wedding wreath from time to time. They say he used to tell his wife: listen here woman, society is society, family is family, and ass is ass.

Siloam and Madame Rita may have been the first of the traitors to be punished, but the other women collaborators weren't far behind.

We were liberated a good three weeks by then, cleared away all the dead bodies from the city streets. The burned stench just wouldn't go away, but we were used to it by then. The only thing we couldn't stand was this particular stink, right in our neighbourhood it was. Wouldn't be coming from your house, by any chance, said this woman cattily as she went by; from a couple of streets over she was, dead now.

One morning we were playing with Mrs Kanello's seven kids in front of our houses and I lean against the wall of the church and I feel a kind of dampness on my back. I turn around, there's a thread of green slime oozing down the wall, from the top of the bell tower all the way down to the ground. And that's how we discovered that the little partisan's dead body was still there, all those weeks. Some people climb up to the top, covering their noses with hankies. He's decomposed, they yell down. Mrs Kanello hands a sheet of muslin up to them, and they haul him down. The body was dripping, nothing was left but this sodden shapeless thing like crushed grapes in the muslin. How can you bury this, this … thing? somebody said. Day after day we scrubbed the street, sprinkled quicklime, nothing doing. The stink was still there when we left Rampartville, probably still there in fact.

They took him to the graveyard; I didn't take part because at that very moment the truck came to take Mother away. Mother didn't put up any resistance. I can't even remember where our little Fanis disappeared to, but I wanted to follow along, only the vehicle was moving too fast and I couldn't keep up with it.

Maybe an hour later it was, I spotted her in the main street, you know, where the nice folks take their evening promenade, she was standing there in the back of the open truck. The sun was hot. The truck was an open truck and the women collaborators were standing there, thirsty, hanging on to each other so they wouldn't fall over. But they didn't have to worry; the truck was moving really really slow now, at a slow walking pace so everybody in town could enjoy the public humiliation. All the women's hair was gone, cut off with sheep shears. Mother's hair too was cut off. There she was, standing at the back of the truck, not even trying to hide, she wasn't. Was she looking at something? Don't know.

The truck was just crawling along, the driver had his instructions, but there were people everywhere, in front of the vehicle, behind, on all sides, and so the driver was creeping forward, had to be careful not to run down any of the citizens, laughing merrily as he went. The whole crowd was enjoying itself in fact, everybody was laughing and all the windows were full of onlookers and the proper gentlemen stepped out of the coffeehouses to stare at the passing truck. Most of the people in the crowd were carrying goat horns or full animal guts cut open, all free from the municipal slaughterhouse, some others were ringing sheep or goat bells, where did they find all that stuff? Some were carrying flags, and waving them patriotically over their heads. And the goat horns they were waving them in the air too and dancing around and sticking them to the sides of the truck like votive offerings and some people were throwing the guts against the truck. What I mean is, they were trying to hit the sheared women but they were missing mostly and only spattering them with bits of green filth, plus a few of the honourable people standing around, but nobody seemed to mind what with the general Liberation high spirits and they just kept on dancing around and around.

I got my hands all smeared with the stuff, I was hanging on to the truck like a bunch of grapes, but when the second slug of guts hit me I fell off, and now I had to run, run to catch up, Ma was all the way to the side of the truck now, as if she wanted to climb off and guts were smeared all over her, up climbs another guy, hangs a pair of horns tied together with animal innards around her neck, and a sheep's bell, and everyone is clapping and cheering and there I was, following along behind in slow march step.

That went on from ten in the morning till maybe six in the evening, up and down every street we went, downtown and uptown, but I wasn't going to leave. And lots of people were hammering on empty tin cans with stones. And church bells were ringing. Not at Saint Kyriaki's, though; Father Dinos refused, locked the church doors tight.

Come afternoon we passed by the Venice pastry shop, the place where the better families of (Rampartville, used to go for French pastries before the war. During the Occupation, of course, all they served was diluted grape marmalade on tiny little plates. Fortunately for me I fell off right in front of the Venice, seeing as Doc Manolaras's wife was sitting with some friends of hers right there at one of the tables, and she shouted, Don't trample the kid! Waiter! And when I came to, the waiter poured a pitcher of water over my head. Mrs Manolaras had a name with a big reputation. So she says, Go home little girl, what are you doing here? Go on home, you shouldn't be seeing this, you'll only remember it all your life, go on home and don't worry, it's just one day and it will be over soon, this evening they'll let them go.

I felt better already. Then I remembered something Mrs Kanello told my mother, So maybe you were a whore for a while, but it was for Christian and moral reasons. Mother never did admit she was a whore because she had two Italians. But she was an illiterate woman and she respected Mrs Kanello's opinion and since Mrs Kanello said she was a whore, that got Mother really upset, but she accepted it. So when the truck stopped outside our house to pick her up for the public humiliation, Ma climbed right up almost eagerly, never crossed her mind they were wronging her, punishing her the way they did.

I grab the pitcher out of the waiter's hands and run off to catch up again and scramble up the side of the truck and pour water over my Ma, standing there all day in the hot sun with her hair cut off, can't let anything happen to her, I was saying to myself. And the sun was getting hotter even though it was almost afternoon, the sun was getting hotter and I don't remember anything more.

Of course she remembers but she won't talk about it, was what a common street walker told Dr Manolaras about a month after; the woman, who had also been publicly humiliated in the same vehicle, had a certificate as a 'lewd common woman', what else did she have to lose?

Then a virtuous man with a flag in one hand climbed up on to the truck bed and he began cracking rotten eggs on the heads of each of the humiliated women and the crowd was applauding, they hadn't seen a movie or a travelling theatre company for so long, the whole thing was more like some kind of entertainment. The virtuous man was bowing like a lecturer before his audience, or like a mayor, each time he cracked an egg on a shorn woman's head. Hey, you been robbing the hen-houses, have you? shouted someone admiringly, and the crowd burst out laughing and, by and large, a good time was had by all at our Liberation: one man was shouting Hurrah! The young girl Meskaris Roubini was running along behind the truck, it was moving faster now, and her mother was standing bolt upright in the back. Roubini was holding the pitcher high over her head, trying to hand it to her mother to drink. Then her mother took the pitcher but instead of drinking of it, she moistened her face and neck daintily to clean off the filth and the ashes. Then the virtuous man grabbed it from her and showered the crowd with water and people roared with laughter and shouted, Hurrah, hurrah, the church bells were chiming, now the virtuous man stood beside the mother of Meskaris Roubini and broke a rotten egg over her head, and the raw egg dribbled down her neck and the people were laughing and then the young Meskaris Roubini caught hold of the truck and tried to climb aboard. And then the virtuous man leaped to the ground and the crowd roared out its approval with a burst of happy applause. Then Meskaris Roubini had a seizure. She started to applaud with great ceremony and then proclaimed solemnly to the crowd, Long live my Mother Meskaris Asimina, Long Live my Mother Asimina. And the crowd applauded with gales of laughter, it was like something from a variety show. Meskaris Roubini wasn't crying; there was a kind of froth coming from her eyes.

That was when the mother of Meskaris Roubini started to cry out, but it was only a sound, a shriek. Then some citizen threw a wet rag dipped in soot at her and it hit her right in the eyes. And Meskaris Roubini was hanging there from the back of the truck and she turned towards the crowd to speak, but she could not speak and she began to howl like a beaten dog. And then her mother went berserk and started to scream 'Get that Dog out of here, get that Dog

away from me, get it away – what's that Dog doing here, I'm not its
mother,' she screamed deliriously, deadly serious.

... that's all I remember, nothing else. When you come right
down to it people are real wild beasts, there's nothing they can't
forget, nothing. But that's not what I mean to say: in the end they
let the women go, right in front of Rampartville cathedral, and we
went home, and along the way I remember how proudly I held my
mother by the hand, as if I was carrying a church banner and
nobody tried to stop us. And I said to myself, I'll always remember this day. And now look, I went and forgot the half of it ...

And when we got home I sat her down at the table and heated
some water and washed my mother, first time I ever washed her,
it was. The second time was about forty-two years later, right
here in our apartment in Athens, when she died.

After that I put on some soup to warm. There came a knock,
it was Mrs Kanello. Ma ran over and threw her body in front of
the door, she wasn't going to open it, and Mrs Kanello was calling to her, Open up. Asimina. Darling, open the door I tell you!
She was in a rage, and sobbing at the same time. Ma threw all
her weight against the door. Then Mrs Kanello kicked it open
and barged in.

'Brought you some chicken stew with potatoes,' she said.

And that's all she said. The tears were running down her
cheeks. She left us the pot full of food and gave Ma a kerchief
for her head, a flowered head-scarf, you know the kind that was
in fashion before the war. And went off without a word, still
furious.

After, her and me sat down and we ate the chicken stew and
the potatoes and I even remembered the pullet buried under my
bed, if the pullet had been a dog and if it was still alive today it
would be gnawing the bones.

Our little Fanis didn't come home that night. Or the next
night. We went to bed early, slept in her bed the both of us,

didn't even wonder what happened to the kid. Had to turn in early, because I had to be up early to do the laundry at Mrs Manolaras's place.

And so that's how we had our first chicken come the Liberation. The last time was before the Occupation.

Next morning we had milk to drink, with cocoa and real sugar, dear departed Aphrodite's mother Mrs Fanny brought it, her and Mrs Kanello. Hailed us from across the street as if nothing had ever happened. This time Mother opened the door, hurried over to open it in fact. The two women came rushing in, and Mrs Fanny had a smile on her face for the first time since her daughter died, the two of them were all bright and cheery as if they were ready for an outing, as if life was going to go on.

Mother drank the milk and cocoa, dipped her bread in it what's more. And the two women went off feeling better, Mrs Kanello to her job and Mrs Fanny to her knitting. Me too, I went off to work feeling better, and when I got home that afternoon there was Ma sitting by the window, with the curtain drawn back. The house was clean and spotless, the blue wrapping paper the occupying forces made us use for the blackout was gone from the window panes, the sink was whitewashed, everything in its place and neat as a pin.

The day after that our Fanis showed up. No questions. I had no idea where he spent the night and I didn't ask. Years later, at Ma's funeral it was, he finally told me how Kostis, the son of Mr Kozilis, who worked at the Prefecture, took him home. The first night our little one slept outdoors, down near the ditch at the Canal. Further along, behind the church of Saint Rosolym, was where Mr Kozilis lived, they were left-wingers but respectable people all the same. So his son Kostis took Fanis in. He had a meal and left, and spent the next night sleeping down by the Canal. Kostis didn't say a word to him about the matter of our mother. (Today he's quite an impresario in Athens, he has the loveliest wife, she's an actress too, but not quite as talented as me, name of Eugenia.)

Fanis didn't say a word to Mother, didn't ask a single question, just looked at her sitting by the window with the flowered scarf Mrs Kanello gave her tied under her chin. The scarf suits you just fine Ma, he said and broke into tears. Ma didn't say a word. Just then Kostis's mother Mrs Kozilis appears outside the window, a tall, dignified woman. She glances through the window, sees us, breathes a sigh of relief, leaves us a plate of walnuts on the windowsill and goes off.

But we didn't talk about Mother's matter even when it was just the three of us. Even today when we're grown up, we never talk about that day that happened to Ma. Not even the day of her funeral, which Fanis came for especially; all he told me was where he slept those two nights when he left home for the first time.

Mother, she wasn't talking. Not about her matter, not about anything.

Four whole days after the public humiliation it was, when I noticed Mother had not said one single word, not even when we asked her a question like did she want me to cook the meal, and such. At night she wouldn't sleep. I just dropped right off to sleep I was so worn out from work and all, but I was worried about her and every so often I opened my eyes and there I saw her, right beside me, we left a small candle burning at night and I could see her eyes staring at the ceiling. After, I fell sound asleep again, I was still just a kid after all, with all those floors to scrub, all those buckets of water to empty, all that laundry to do.

Fanis didn't notice it either, he was always slipping out to play with that kid Kostis, the son of Kozilis who worked at the Prefecture, how was our little fellow supposed to know his playmate was going to be even more famous as an actor than his sister. I

141

see around a lot these days. Doesn't remember me, so I don't let on I know him. But once it happened I was temporarily out of a job, so I was took on with his company as an extra. Picked me out himself, he did. I'll take that one there, the cute little brunette, he said. Doesn't know who I am, I say to myself, forget it. And today he looks right at me, can't even remember how we used to play together for goodness sake.

After the first week I say to Mrs Fanny, Mrs Fanny, still not a word. Her and Mrs Kanello come by, as if it's a casual call, and strike up a conversation, but nothing from Mother. The eighth day Mrs Kanello pricks her on the arm with a safety pin, not a peep. We call Father Dinos to say a prayer, free of charge he did it, the poor man, then good old Doc Manolaras passes by and before he does anything else he gives her a shot in the arm, then he examines her.

'I just don't understand,' he says. All of a sudden he slaps her on the face, to surprise her, result nil. Father Dinos's wife sends over a woman to break the spell but she makes us swear not to say a word to the reverend or he'll beat her within an inch of her life. Finally we had to admit it. Your Ma's struck dumb and that's all there is to it, said Mrs Kanello. Doc Manolaras said the same thing, of course. Asimina seems to have suffered an attack of catalepsy, it is impossible to say if she will ever recover. You'll just have to accept it.

And so we accepted it.

Mother was perfectly normal in every other way. Why, she even smiled too, what's more. Not that we halted our efforts: we took her to see healing women, Mrs Kanello's brother-in-law, the husband of her sister with the marriage troubles, he took Ma to a tiny chapel up in the hills with his buggy, but all in vain. Just imagine how word got around the neighbourhood, and afterwards all Rampartville knew about it. Seems that's the reason why people stopped throwing stones at us. Hardly even bothered her any more when she left the house for work. Because after the public humiliation I found her two houses to do, ironing and minding kids, that kind of thing. In fact people liked having her work for them because she was dumb. Life got better, and finally we managed to save up some money. One lady told me right to my face, Roubini, better a deaf-mute cleaning lady, you can be sure she won't go around talking to the other ladies where she works. Seeing as all the respectable families of Rampartville were scared to death of gossip, what would their cleaning lady tell her other customers about their patched sheets and their trinkets and such like.

One day Kanello comes by with a primary-school reader, belonged to one of her kids. Here Roubini, she says, seeing as how she got no voice, you ought to teach her to read, that way at least you can communicate.

Ma agreed. I taught her the alphabet and slowly she learned to write words. She couldn't spell all that great, but she could write at least. One Sunday I remember how, way back before Albania, my big brother Sotiris asked her, Let me read you my lesson Ma. And I asked her the same thing, to help make her feel good. She liked it. So we sat her down, gave her our school books and recited our lessons by heart. One day I read her my essay, How I spent my Sunday. I wrote how we went looking for artichokes, about the purple sunset and about a cartful of sheep we met on the road.

Later, on, doing the dishes, she asks me, Why didn't you write how you met a hare?

'Hare?'

'Yes, in your school composition.'

'But Ma, we didn't meet any hares.'

'Doesn't matter.'

'But we didn't see a hare.'

'It would make your composition nicer.'

'Imagine seeing a hare just two steps away from the Zafiris' fields. Am I supposed to write a lie and say that we saw one?'

'It wouldn't be a lie. It's a composition.'

To this day, now that I've passed the sixty mark (I'll never say when, it's enough to admit I passed it, so don't expect me to say by how many years), I never did figure out why she wanted me to put a hare in my fifth-grade essay.

In the end, she warmed to reading, and even learned a little arithmetic. Fanis started back to school again in the meantime, and I was going to night classes, although I missed more than I made. Our school books we got from Thanassakis' father, the ones his son had finished with. So on Sundays Ma would sit down and read a book, mostly History and Geography it was, from the sixth grade. All about the Trojans, King Priam, the Twelve Gods, the Hellenes. That's when we found out, Mum and me, that we are also called Hellenes, in addition to Meskaris. Later she learned where to find Andaluca on the map. She read from the Modern Greek reader too, stories with a plot were her favourites. By the time she died she could read an entire novel.

Meanwhile, Doc Manolaras was getting set to go into politics, which is the reason why he was pulling strings to get us a pension. Politics was starting up again, you see, and the politicians were beating the bushes for votes. From us he stood to collect six, two from my father's parents and four from us, counting our big brother Sotiris. Why, Doc Manolaras even promised to find him, saying, Asimina, I'll leave no stone unturned to find your eldest and bring him back to you, no vote can escape me. Never did find our Sotiris though, but he did get a voter's registration book issued in his name, which he used himself.

Still, the X-men didn't give us trouble, even though plenty of families started leaving Rampartville due to their beliefs. Rampartville was a nationalist town, and everybody knew just who the left-wingers were. And when the X-men started their beatings and breaking down doors, plenty of people made up their minds to move to Athens once and for all, for shelter. That's when Aphrodite's ma left. Fortunately for her, because she got ahead. If you take away that they slaughtered her husband in those December Events, or whatever they call them, she's doing just fine today with her lace doilies. Really has the knack, she does.

Funny thing, back then, there was this X-man, the sentimental type and a travelling greengrocer by trade, and he goes and falls in love with Ma. Her hair was a bit longer, styled it à la garçon I did, looked real good on her. So, late at night on his donkey he came by, most likely on his way back from the countryside where he went to buy his vegetables, he hung around behind the church singing songs full of meaning, like If you turn your back on the past or the hit of the day, I'll take you away with me, only he changed the words to say he would take her away to other lands where they had a king and queen. Other times he sang patriotic hymns, things like Sofia-Moscow is our dream, but they came out sounding like a hesitation waltz.

This same greengrocer, he even put in a good word for Mrs Chrysafis. Another X-man comes right up to her door and tells her to her face that they're going to dig up her son's corpse, they're not going to give that stinking commie a moment's peace. But the greengrocer had a word with him and he left her alone. Not that Mrs Chrysafis cared a hoot: Go on, dig him up, she tells the X-man, and give me a call so I can see what he looks like now. Everybody's nerves were pretty much on edge.

People in the neighbourhood were starting to talk about the love-sick greengrocer, but it was all a big misunderstanding. One day Mrs Fanny comes up to me and says, Roubini, get it over with, girl, either tell him Yes, or get rid of him. I was speechless. Mrs Kanello was telling me the same thing, got it all wrong for the first time in her life. No, I tell them, the greengrocer's making eyes at my ma, what could he see in me? But I said it without really believing it, seeing as by then my breasts were coming out and I was getting taller.

145

But the greengrocer wouldn't give up. One evening, in fact, while he's serenading right beside our window, the donkey starts braying, and his master starts kicking the poor creature. Shut up, he hisses; my heart sank to see him tormenting the animal. It was a neat and tidy little donkey, come to think of it, with a little crown hung right under its forelock. Finally Mrs Kanello takes matters into her own hands, she buttonholes the guy and asks him what are his intentions towards the orphan, meaning me, the dimwit. That's when everybody realized that it was Ma the royalist greengrocer was after. But soon after Mrs Kanello's efforts he disappeared for good, and I could only think about what would become of the donkey, maybe he would beat it again.

She was always sticking her nose into everything and standing up to everybody, Mrs Kanello was. And nobody dared lay a finger on her even if everybody and his brother knew by now how thick she was with the Resistance and the partisans all along. Meanwhile we got our first letter from Mrs Fanny; it was addressed to Mrs Kanello, but it was for all of us. Didn't ask a soul to tend the little candle on her daughter's grave. All she said was there were plenty of empty – or emptied – houses in Athens. Also that there were blockhouses and they were all made from a new kind of material, concrete it was called, never wore out, and if you moved into one nobody asked any questions, particularly after the uprising. Didn't make it clear what uprising she was talking about or if she was living in a blockhouse herself, sent us all her best and announced that her husband had been killed. The details we learned later, when we made it to Athens ourselves.

That letter of hers, it gave me inspiration: I made up my mind to head for Athens. In fact, the minute Doc Manolaras gives me his word he'll look after Fanis for the rest of his life I say to myself, Roubini, I say, time to spread your wings.

Seeing as even from before the war, from back when the Tiritombas used me as a kick-ball on stage, I had this dream of the artiste's life, of being an actress. That's my main quarrel with the Axis and the Occupation, the main reason I condemn them is because I wanted to take off as an artist and they wouldn't let me. And now it was starting to look as though my dreams would come true.

Artistic dreams, they can't flower in the provinces. Put together the public humiliation, Ma's condition, the encouraging housing news, plus Doc Manolaras who would be looking after Fanis, everything seemed to be pushing me to see myself as a future Athenian.

Ma's condition gave me this problem. I mean, how are you supposed to enjoy yourself evenings keeping company with somebody who can't talk? A couple of times I put on a little stage number for her, something I picked up from Mrs Adrianna, but Mother, she didn't laugh. Plus in addition people made nasty remarks about her, even if they didn't throw stones any more. I found out about it later from Mrs Adrianna, but what was I supposed to do? Take her out for a stroll or go to the movies? Impossible, after the public humiliation. Now it wasn't only honest women made fun of her; even the other collaborators, women from good families who could pay to get out of the public humiliation, they started throwing things at her. Even one of the houses I fixed up work for her, they kicked her out, saying she was a collaborator.

That particular house, it had three daughters, the Xiroudis family it was. The place was always swarming with Italians, seeing as the father couldn't budge from his chair since before the war and the mother had a taste for social climbing. When he heard Italians coming up the wooden stairs (really squeaky, they were) from his room, the father shouted, Sluts, that's all you are, don't you have any respect for your country? to hell with the lot of you. And you, what do you want with these whores of mine, you Italian bastards? And the mother stepped out on to the landing and said, Now now dear, calm down, the girls need a little amusement.

The Xiroudis family owned olive trees, lots of them; big money. Their cellar was full of jars of olive oil, big as a man. When I was working at their place, lots of times Mrs Xiroudis gave me the oil can and a funnel and sent me off to the cellar for a refill. I climbed up on a stool, uncovered the jar and ladled out the oil. More than once I fished a drowned mouse out of the jar along with the oil. Don't breathe a word to the girls, Mrs Xiroudis told me. They're so touchy, they'll turn their noses up at the food.

When the people's government committee started rounding up collaborators for the public humiliation, Mrs Xiroudis hustled her daughters down to the basement and stuck them into full oil jars, covered the top of each jar with a lambskin with holes punched in it so the girls wouldn't die of asphyxiation, and tied down the lambskins with a rope around the neck of the jar. And that's how she saved her daughters from the public humiliation; the committee came to take them away, searched the house top to bottom but couldn't find them, so the truck went away empty-handed, my mother was already standing there on the truck-bed with a handful of other women, they started with the lower-class women. At night she tiptoed down and gave them water through a funnel.

Three days and three nights the three Xiroudis daughters stayed there, up to their necks in olive oil. How that affected the olive oil, it revolts me to say. Still, they escaped the public humiliation. And as for the oil, well, later their father, the old fart, he sold it to the army, not to mention what he donated to the Partisan Fund, nearly fifty kilos of the stuff. Just think what our brave soldiers on the field of battle were eating mixed in with their olive oil, so be it, nobody ever died of polluted food, no matter what the scientists say.

The whole story we got from Victoria their housemaid a couple weeks later: they were beating her, so she happily told us everything. Victoria was no stranger to the Italians either; her mistresses handled the officers, she looked after the stable-boys. The day the British landed she packed all her belongings into a little satchel and at ten o'clock one morning she stood outside her master's front door and began insulting them, Rotten traitors, bitches. That's when she brought up the oil jars, how they made her eat food cooked with pissy oil (what else she said, even more gross, I won't say: might make me sick to my stomach). After she said her piece she set off on foot for the port, how she got it into her head that Liberation equals marriage proposal and the Brits would take her away on their ships to their country and marry her, I'll never know.

Three whole days Victoria waited there on the pier (beats me where she relieved herself) and singing 'It's a long way to Tipperary'. Finally, when she gave up on the Brits she hiked back to Rampartville beating her breasts and braying, No good double-crossing allies. Finally, with some help from Mrs Adrianna, they sent her back to her village with a truckload of unsheared lambs. I haven't heard a word on the subject of Victoria ever since.

When the dust settled a bit, Mrs Xiroudis hung out a British flag like everyone else and fired my mother as housekeeper. Unfortunately you're a collaborator Mrs Asimina, she told her. And those cold-fish daughters of hers had already taken up with Brits, fortunately the old man had croaked meanwhile, so he couldn't keep up his raving against the Allies too.

Me, I never held a grudge against the Xiroudis daughters, just thinking of them doing their business in the olive oil three days and nights, I forgave them. But the other houses started telling Mother they really didn't need her, seeing as now everybody was against the Italians and praising the Allies and liberty. So I had to drop out of night school so we could get by, now that Mother was out of work.

One evening I come home and I see the table set and beside my plate I see our big brother Sotiris's ration book. Mother put it there. Now our ration books were nothing but souvenirs, there was no more soup kitchen, soup kitchens were for enslaved nations and now we were free and supreme among the victorious.

Next night when we sat down to eat there were four table settings, the fourth plate was at Sotiris' place. She puts a serving on the plate, with bread and all. Fanis and I look at each other but we don't say a word. Who was I supposed to talk to, anyway? Mother was learning to live with her dumbness. Fanis, the only thing he was worried about was that crushed hand of his, and me, I didn't want to discuss it with the lady neighbours. I was head of the household now.

The routine with Sotiris's plate lasted for almost a month, complete with a chair and everything. Then finally one night before dinner I get up, take the plate and empty it into the sink, quite a luxury you'll say, but for me, it was waste I had to make. I wash the plate, put it back in the plate-rack, and after we finish our meal Fanis looks Ma in the eye and says, pure coincidence it was. He's probably in Athens by now, Sotiris is. And goes outside to play.

That was his first hint that maybe we should be moving out.

Then came the trouble with the roof. In one corner the tiles were cracked from a couple of near misses from mortar shells, but we only noticed it when the first rains came. Adrianna's brother Tassis brought his ladder over, climbed up and laid a sheet of muslin over the split tiles and set rocks at each corner to keep the whole contraption in place, a fine job he did, hardly leaked at all inside any more.

Besides the hole in the roof, the other thing that was pushing me towards Athens was Fanis. Everybody called him 'The mute's boy' or 'Fanis the whore's boy'. Not that they meant any harm. That's just what they called him, kind of a last name, just like Venus de Milo, for example. But our little boy was almost grown up now – has hair on his face the rascal – and now he was just wasting away, because of his hand. He made out it didn't matter, and kept smiling though. Say he tried to show some temper when people called him names, or wanted to fight back, well, he always took it right on the chin and everybody knocked him down.

Plus in addition, I thought to myself, maybe in Athens we can find doctors to look at Mother, maybe scientists in the capital can bring her voice back. But my dream never came true. Those Athenian doctors, they never did find a cure.

We had to make up our minds, the roof was leaking again, Mrs Adrianna was always giving me encouragement: You were born for the stage; Kotopouli might be a half-decent actress but is she any prettier? I'll give you letters of recommendation for theatrical companies, you'll see all of Greece, she said.

Meantime Doc Manolaras, bless his soul, took on Fanis to work his country estate. It was land he bought on one of the Aegean islands. Later people said the land used to belong to a big Collaborator then the Allies confiscated it and Doc Manolaras bought it for a crust of bread, with title deeds and all. I don't know a thing about titles and deeds but there's one thing I do know, our Fanis is still working there, to this very day, and that's where he'll end his days, fortunately.

Once I didn't have the boy to worry about, I made my decision. My ally was Doc Manolaras; moved up to Athens for good in the meantime, he had, and now he was hard at work bringing his voters to the capital, had to get elected in another district, you see, in Athens. Set up a kind of private moving agency, was what he did, when you come right down to it. Got Tassis appointed to the Anglo-Hellenic Information Service, and rented this half-car half-truck for him. This particular vehicle was always heading back to Athens empty, and returning with a load of material for the Service. So Doc Manolaras made sure it was loaded with voters who wanted to move to Athens, along with all their furniture, free of charge. That's the way we went ourselves, finally. What's more, Doc Manolaras made the rounds of his supporters' homes in the evenings, it was all unofficial of course, promising a free house if a family had more than five votes. On account of those troubles, those December events, Athens was full of empty houses. Every family with less than five votes he set up up in an empty blockhouse, there were blockhouses to spare and no taxes to pay. Appears he also looked after Mrs Fanny, even if she wouldn't admit she lived in a blockhouse; but later on all she could do was boast how she took over the place all by herself. She was a proud woman and she didn't want to admit she gave him her voter's book, or that Manolaras took out a book in the name of her slaughtered husband and now the late lamented partisan was voting for the nationalist slate ten years after they slaughtered him like a heifer that December in Athens.

Goodbye provinces, for everybody. That much good we got out of the Liberation and the hunt for lefties. Seeing as now they were lumping us lower-class collaborators in with the lefties, and the nationalist X-men would go after the both of us. For me, getting dumped in the same category as the lefties was as big a disgrace as Ma's public humiliation. Whether I used to knit sweaters for the partisans or not. I always respected the partisans, but I never knew they were leftists, too.

It wasn't long before we got our first letter from Fanis. He was doing just fine, the estate was full of fruit he could pick and eat to his heart's content and he didn't even have to ask permission, plus there was a beach not far away. He was supervisor, had a shotgun even. His advice was that we should leave. And he wrote he was only going to write to us again if he got sick; so long as he's healthy he won't be writing and if we don't hear from him not to worry but if anything happened to us we should write him. And in the meantime, he'll send us his best every time our member of parliament Doc Manolaras would go to the island on business. And we should send him our best the same way and keep him posted if we change our address, if we move to Athens was what he really meant.

I discussed it with Ma, I mean, what was there to discuss; me talking and her listening, didn't even shake her head yes or no. Had to arrange for all our belongings, sell the house, part of her dowry it was. Some house, you'll say, with a dirt floor and a scrap of muslin over the hole in the roof; who wants to buy the place?

What I mean is, that's how it looked to me back then. Just imagine what it looks like today! Now there's this huge apartment house, makes the church look like a chicken coop. So I hear, that is. And I'm thinking, My poor little pullet, how can you bear it with a huge building sitting right on top of you, my poor baby.

That's how I bought my apartment. Back then I couldn't even dream of such comfort. Anyway. I'll see that it gets sold, Doc Manolaras tells me, in a couple of years it'll be worth more bless his soul. We gave him power of attorney, picked us up in his car, drove us over to the notary and Ma put down her signature See, I say to her, good thing we taught you to write, look how handy it comes in.

We said our farewells to the neighbours, to Mrs Kanello, to the Tiritombas: I stopped off at the houses where I used to work and paid my respects and a couple of them gave me a tip, then Tassis and Mrs Kanello's kids all pitched in and we packed our household belongings into bundles and loaded everything into Tassis's vehicle, the bundles, the furniture, and Mother sat down right in the middle, with Mrs Kanello's scarf over her head, didn't shed a tear or blink an eye. Didn't even turn her head as the car turned the corner and she left Rampartville for ever. And when we were clear of town, she tossed her head, undid the scarf and tossed it out the window, a pricy item like that! and let her hair blow free in the wind.

A little before we left I went into the house; it was stark naked and spotless. All swept and dusted, top to bottom, it was my way of showing my respect for all these years that house respected us, after all. I went over to the corner where my little garden used to be, my little pullet's grave was nothing but a hole in the ground now. I spoke to her, I'm leaving, I said. But I won't forget you. But you listen to me, do your best to melt into the ground, because it won't be long before the machines come to dig you up. Now farewell; I will never forget you.

I didn't keep my word. Forgot all about her, what with all the excitement of the life in Athens, what with settling down, moving in with people, me entering into the theatrical realm, all those tours, almost 2,000 little towns, I forgot my little pullet. Now, when I'm having some difficulty finding work, now I remember her. What I mean to say is, I'm not having any difficulty finding work, I'm in fine form in fact and I have this psychiatrist's certificate to prove it, but the impresarios seem to like the rabble better, what can you do? In any case, I'm thinking a lot about my pullet these days, not so much her face though, if you know what I mean. A few days ago I dreamed about her, I'm having some weird dreams recently.

What I mean is, it was Mum I dreamed about. It was as if I could see her in my sleep. We were in this green field, full of tall grass, no earth to be seen. And there was a gentle breeze blowing from somewhere, the tips of the grass were bending over as if a little brook was flowing over them. In the distance of my dream picture was a factory with a tall smokestack, but it hadn't worked for years. Mother was sitting there in the grass. It was me who put her out to pasture, to scratch for worms with her fingernails. She's looking at someone, but it's not me. She's looking right through me, as if I was never born. She's sprouted feathers. Coloured ones. So that's it, I say to myself, she didn't starve to death in the Occupation after all. There's a ring of fine white downy feathers around her neck, like a beard fluttering in the breeze. And I'm sitting there beside her on the grass, all ready to enjoy her company and to

154

look after her at the same time just in case somebody tries to steal her. But I'm not in my dream picture, I'm in the audience like a spectator. Mum is calm, it's late in the afternoon and she has everything she needs, she's doesn't see anything, doesn't need her eyes, staring straight ahead with a kindly look on her face, not even scratching for food. I'm feeling sad that she doesn't even need me. There's a sun in my dream, but it's far away. The downy white feathers on her neck are fluttering like a kind of thin beard.

Don't ask me how it was I had that dream. It didn't make me the least bit happy. Not sad either.

Anyhow, that trip of ours was kind of a festival for me, because it was the first time I ever left Rampartville, not counting our school excursions before the war and our hike down to the seaside. We drove through cities and towns; places I would get to know better after I turned twenty, on my many various tours.

And so I was on my way towards Athens, light-hearted and without a worry in the world. The youngest of the family was taken care of, he had a job, a place to live, a wage. Ma's hair was uncovered. The moment we crossed the Isthmus I decided from now on I would call her Mum, no more Ma or Mother. All of a sudden I had a past which I was leaving behind me, all nice and tidy, clear of the cobwebs and the dust.

We disembarked in the capital, but it was a month before I got a good look at it. Seeing as Doc Manolaras gave Tassis instructions to drop us off at the outskirts, not far from Mrs Fanny's blockhouse. We hugged and kissed, she was obliging but kind of distant, without a smile on her face. She climbed into the van and showed Tassis the way, Doc Manolaras already sent her the instructions.

'Stop here,' goes Mrs Fanny when we get to this open field. We climb down, there's a low hill with what looked like a country chapel on top. That's your blockhouse, Mrs Fanny says.

It wasn't exactly the kind of place I was expecting; what I was expecting was more like an uninhabited, furnished one-storey house, but I didn't say a word. We unloaded our worldly goods with Tassis and Mrs Fanny lending a hand, and we moved in.

'Why it's just fine,' I said, 'got lots of room'.

'There's water down the hill, the public fountain,' said Mrs Fanny pointing. 'If you don't have your own can I'll lend you one.' But we had our own. She showed us the way, we filled our can and a jug besides, and climbed back up the hill, Mrs Fanny right beside us like a guide, and I felt like an explorer as she pointed out different things to us, I liked feeling like a tourist, even though I didn't know that particular word yet. She even offered us a broom made from dried thistle stalks, but we had our own, from Rampartville. Still, her gift came in handy, particularly outside the blockhouse. I got out a chair for Mum because she was getting in the way, standing there like a dressmaker's dummy, still couldn't get it through her head that we were living in the capital now. I sort of throw things together go off and buy some paraffin for the stove and the lamp and when I get back Mrs Fanny says, Well, I've got to be going, it's almost dark. When they bring you the cripple tonight, don't be frightened. He's entitled to half the space. And off she goes. I show her to the door, and from the top of our little hillock I could see Athens off in the distance, for the first time. After, I went inside to cook supper, we ate and then we waited to see just who was this cripple and why he was coming to visit us.

ROUBINI AND HER MOTHER were in bed when they brought the cripple. It was their only bed, Ma's double bed; the other one they'd left with a neighbour of theirs, a woman named Kanello.

First Roubini swept out the blockhouse; the cement floor was littered with garbage. Then the two women laid out a rag mat on the doorstep. The cripple who had been first to claim it had left the place in a mess; all his possessions – a pillow, a blanket, a water jug and a cup – were piled in a heap at the back, out of the draught from the entrance and the gun ports. The earth was banked up at the entrance to make a kind of ramp for his cart.

Roubini plugged up the gun ports with wadding and scrap paper and hung a blanket across the entrance, for a door. Their dining table did double duty as a kitchen: on it she set up the gas burner, the tin water can with the spigot at the bottom, and the plates. On second thoughts she moved the water can outside, next to the entrance. Tomorrow she would look after a toilet.

Then she whipped up a quick meal, they ate, turned down the wick until the oil lamp only glowed faintly, and the two of them turned in.

When a kid brought the cripple; the two women woke up and stared. He was a half-man, his legs were missing, cut off at the roots, and there he sat, bolt upright and top-heavy, like a statue of some Latin American dictator, on a hand-made wooden cart with four castors, two handles at the back for pushing, and a rope in front like a bridle, for pulling. He was maybe forty, with a muscular back and sinewy arms, he'd lost his legs three years ago and his arms had grown strong from pushing. He looked like a wrestler. Every morning he would go down to the main road. The kid was from a nearby group of houses, he would come for the cripple and help him out of the blockhouse. At night the same kid would sling the rope over his shoulder and drag him back up the hill, for money. And every night when they got back the cripple paid him. First the kid would lift him out of his cart so he could do his business, then plop him back on and pull him inside, right up to his bed. Then the man would give him the money, the kid would say goodnight, and the next morning he would be there, ready to go.

The cripple begged for a living. If he handled his cart carefully, avoided going uphills and took all the short cuts, he could reach the main road on his own. When he begged he would vilify anyone who passed him by without making an offering, he was a war amputee, he shouted in a demanding voice, and people had an obligation to support him. He put money aside, socked away all he could from whatever he collected – mostly loose change – and every so often, every three months or so, he would go to a woman, a common street whore, and plonk his savings down on her table.

Sharing living quarters with the two women was perfect for him. Two frightened provincials, a mute mother and that skinny, plain, feeble-minded daughter of hers, now things were beginning to look up. Now he had partners, he could expand, start soliciting in Athens, find himself a good location.

The first thing he did was declare that the blockhouse belonged to him, but he would let them stay. They would settle the rent later, he said. But it was a bluff, to keep them in a state of permanent insecurity.

At first he thought to himself, 'now I've got me a whore of my own, free for nothing' whichever of the two happened to suit him. But when he saw how terrified and wild-eyed they were, he said to himself, Forget it, some other time.

Finding his living space tidied up and his meals ready was something he hadn't expected, he was accustomed to his way of life. He didn't mind having someone to take him outside for his bodily needs, of course. His main concern was business, though, the begging business. But now, in exchange for rent, he had two partners; the older woman to push and pull the cart, and the girl as a crier, to pass the cup. Now it was on to greater things. Part of the take he'd pass on to them, for their food.

The girl bridled at first. Our member of parliament put us here, she said. Better watch yourself, because us, we got legs. But finally she went up to him and announced they'd be happy to work together, what a wonderful idea, she would get to know Athens better plus get the feel of the stage, their MP was going to arrange a pension for her Mum and he was advising her to make a career in the theatre. Well, until all the appropriate arrangements had been completed the girl agreed that they would work together. On condition he call her mother Mrs Mina and her Miss Roubini. What d'you mean 'miss', he says. For the life of him he couldn't remember her name, kept getting it upside down, backwards, inside out. In fact, one day he came out with Raraou. She was so delighted she adopted the name. That would be her stage name, she told him. Raraou. Or, Mademoiselle Raraou.

And so they set up shop. Only for a little while Mum, said feeble-minded Raraou to the mute. Till our member of parliament fixes us up, she said.

They would set out at dawn. Took a good two hours' slogging to reach downtown Athens with the mute hauling the cart, harnessed like a draft horse. Her daughter had made her some pads out of old rags for her armpits, so the rope wouldn't cut into her flesh. Behind came the girl, holding on to the handles, and atop the cart sat the cripple like a totem pole, shouting at them all the while to mind the potholes, the bouncing irritated his private parts. Raraou would giggle, just hearing him say it gave her the itch, she had to be a virgin, for sure. Sleep together? she wouldn't hear of it.

They strung up a kind of curtain between them, with a sheet on a string, so they could undress at night. He liked to ogle them. The mother sat upright in her chair like a dressmaker's dummy while the daughter washed her face and combed her hair. When they wanted to take a bath, they hauled in water by the bucketful, heated it, poured it into the wash tub, and moved the cripple out.

Nights, when he couldn't sleep, he looked them over in the dim light of the lamp. The two of them lay there sound asleep, dead tired after a whole day of walking or harnessed to the cart. In her sleep the daughter was embracing the mother, protecting her head and running her fingers through her hair, sound asleep, the both of them. Mostly he couldn't sleep. He would masturbate in the hope it would tire him out and he could get some sleep.

Come daybreak they would set out again. And when they reached their location they made up their minds exactly where they would beg, at the public market, or over where they unloaded vegetables. The daughter steadied the cart with four chocks which they always kept on hand. Then she swept off a space in front of the cart with a little broom, laid down a piece of carpet, smoothed it out, set out the contribution plate, and beside it a pot with a sweet-smelling herb like marjoram or basil, depending on the season, which Raraou filched from windowsills or first-floor balconies. When customers would see the little pot, they knew they were dealing with nice, clean, neat people, down-on-their-luck people, and not some kind of riffraff or something. The cripple had them buy a little paper flag and stick it in the pot, to make the whole thing more nationalistic. And so, with the broom and the little flower pot, it was the next best thing to being at home, like being in their own front yard in fact, and anybody who noticed all that tender loving care would think maybe they were really the owners of the swept-off space, and would show them something like respect. Raraou felt just like the lady of the house. Going through the cripple's junk she'd even turned up some high-heeled pumps with tinselled bows. She would keep them on his cart, hike the whole distance in her normal shoes and when they started work, slip on her pumps and wait for the customers to arrive, then launch into her begging number. That's how she imagined it, as a number in a review, as her theatrical debut.

Her mother sat off to the side to catch her breath, after two hours in harness. She would sip from her water bottle and eat some bread and cheese at the appointed hour, after the shops had closed for the midday break and before they opened again later in the afternoon. Bold as brass, Raraou would cry, 'Help the cripple who gave his legs for the nation'. She liked the job. Sometimes she would sing the message, even dance it. At first the cripple would lose his temper. You're makin' me look like a jerk, dimwit, he growled, me, I'm a pro. But as time went by Raraou stopped paying attention to him, stopped fearing him, began talking back to him. Even threatened to hit him one time, right there in front of the audience, Come on, get up! Get up and catch me, hit me! And at the same time she howled, 'Have mercy on the crippled soldier!' And the cripple was shouting, 'A drachma for the deaf-mute and her starving daughter, a drachma for the poor refugee deaf-mute!'

For Raraou that was an insult, He'd better stop, she told him, or they would dump him on the spot. But her mother didn't seem upset and so, over time, Raraou got used to it too, in fact she started using the line herself, wailing, Have pity on the crippled hero and his deaf-mute wife. From then on she used it continuously, her mother didn't seem to mind in the slightest. In fact, the cripple got the idea they should learn how to say, 'Have mercy on the heroic crippled warrior, have mercy on the deaf-mute refugee' in European. The take would go up for sure, he explained: there were more and more foreign tourists in the bazaar he'd noticed; they were kind of simple-minded people, good for a handout. But they didn't know anybody who could talk in foreign languages. The cripple kept reminding her, Hey, Raraou, how come your member of parliament doesn't translate

161

it for you? But Raraou didn't want her protector to know she'd turned her mother into a beggar. And as time went by the cripple forgot the idea, the deaf-mute hauled the cart and while the other two were begging she would sit there staring off into the distance. Nothing could bother her. Only one day this passerby made a remark that riled her. The man, a weird-looking sort, dropped his contribution on to the plate and turned to Raraou, Tell me, miss, just how does the couple here manage, technically speaking, I mean? Then the deaf-mute jumped to her feet, but Raraou reached him first and leaped at him, hanging from his jacket lapels until they were just about ripped off. Police! Police! he shouted, and the trio quickly gathered up their belongings and moved to another location for three days.

Once every two weeks Raraou would set the cripple back on to his cart, prop two boards against his back and wedge them into the corners; his movements were abrupt and he had a tendency to topple over on to his back. Afterwards she whispered something in her mother's ear and went off, without telling him where she was going. It was to the office of her member of parliament, name of Manolaras, a sleazy tin-pot operator from the provinces, nobody knew just what strings he'd pulled to drag her all this way, right to his electoral district.

Manolaras always greeted her with a smile, treated her to Turkish delight, and assured her that the pension was on the way; he would also pass on the latest news from her brother, who was working on his farm doing general upkeep, and as soon as the foreman died, Raraou's brother would get the job. She asked him to pass on her greetings to her brother Fanis, kissed Manolaras' hand and then went back to the cripple feeling relieved, particularly now that she had some spending money and a pocketful of Turkish delight.

He was still looking after their house in the provinces, he told her, but the best thing was to wait a while, property prices were going up, people from the villages were moving into town. looking for places to buy. And as far as the theatre was concerned, You're still too young, he told her, first let me get your pension looked after, then I'll introduce you to the right people.

Yeah, he was just a small-time operator, but open-handed and kind-hearted, and besides, he had a soft spot in his heart for Raraou. So off she went, as happy as she could be, holding tight to the Turkish delight, and later she would insist her mother eat it. You have to, Mum, she said. And she waited until she was sure her mother had really swallowed it.

In less than six months she'd learned all the streets, Mum, I feel just like an Athenian, she said. Coming back from Manolaras' office she went down streets where there were the-atres, musical reviews mostly. She stopped in front of the posters with the names of the stars, pretending to read. But when nobody was looking she would reach into her pocket, pull out a stub of chalk she always carried with her and scrawl, at the bottom of the poster: 'And Mademoiselle Raraou'. Then she would step back, admire her handiwork, and go back to work. No worries about leaving her mother alone with the cripple in the bazaar any more; she was used to it now, begging didn't bother her. In fact, her hair had grown and she'd put on some weight, the weather here in Athens seems to agree with her, thought Raraou.

Of course the cripple was always trying to feel her up but it seemed normal to her, a kind of status symbol. Her mind was made up, all men are destined to lust after me, because there's no other ticket for me to get ahead as an actress. Certainly, it never occurred to her to actually do it with him, not even for an instant. Firstly, she felt shame for her mother: if my mother became a sin-ner by performing that act, I will never in my life perform that act. To honour my mum. Furthermore, it would have been a mockery of her ideals to experience love with a man who was missing half his body, he was just a flesh-and-blood chest-of-drawers sitting there bolt upright, until they bundled him up in his blankets. Besides, he was a beggar. A beggar by choice and by conviction. While her goal in life was to become a princess.

When you get right down to it, the main reason she didn't want to go with the cripple was because when she heard people talking about 'love' or 'bed' it meant nothing to her. Used to titillate her when she was a little girl. But after she was twelve or thirteen, she had never known the desires of the flesh. And when she happened to think to herself, which didn't happen all that often, why she had no taste for this thing, why she had no urge, no desire, up from her memory would rise the image of herself as a little girl standing there outside the church of Saint Kyriaki along with Fanis, her brother, playing games, the two of them, hide-and-seek mostly, to keep warm and to dry the rain on their clothes, until Signor Alfio had finished and left the house, then little Roubini could scurry back home and shake off the raindrops. And mostly help her mother empty the basin and set the table for dinner, the Italian was an interruption in their daily schedule, a delay.

And so it was that never once did the desire to touch a man's body overcome her.

But that hardly worried her. She kept it hidden in any event, considering it ill-suited for a future star of the stage. Not that she didn't have opportunities, but she never once had the desire to caress a man's body. Sleeping with her mother at night, that gave her pleasure. The only thing that disturbed her was the lack of a toilet. She had arranged a crude, temporary one outside the back wall of the blockhouse; she dug a hole, set up a wooden crate upside down over it, cut a circular opening in the top and surrounded it with a cardboard partition; that was where they looked after their daily needs. In fact, she trained her body so she only needed to use it at night, after dark, even though there were no neighbours to spy on her.

She felt no humiliation in begging, first because she had neither approved the idea or even chosen it. Second, it was only a temporary solution, until the pension came through, until they could sell their house in the provinces. What's more, she found out all about Athens, learned how to sing and handle tough situations in front of the public, learned how to bow; in fact, she had lots to show from begging.

Won't come across, the little bag of bones, mused the cripple. But he wasn't hot for her. Still, if she did put out, at least it would be free. He liked the mute more. But one morning when he tried to reach his hand under her dress when the two women were getting him dressed, the girl tipped the cart on its side, the cripple toppled over and fell on his side on to the cement floor. The mother stood there staring straight ahead. The cripple lay there on one arm, like a stump. Then the girl grabbed the bridle rope from the cart and lashed him across the face. Then she took yesterday's earnings and walked over to the corner where the cripple hid his money, he had no idea the girl knew his hiding place. Right before his very eyes, staring straight at him, she took his savings, dressed her mother and out they walked, the two of them.

First they dropped by a woman's from their home town, lived in a blockhouse just like they did, but she'd fixed up her place. This woman crocheted lace, which she sold from door to door. When Raraou and her mum came calling, she brewed them a cup of coffee. Then mother and daughter went off.

They took the bus downtown, first stop was their MP's office. Then the daughter took her mother sightseeing, to all the attractions, the royal palace, the works. Afterwards she treated her to a French pastry. And while they were at the pastry shop, they nipped down to the toilets to primp themselves like human beings for a change. The mother didn't want to go at first, Raraou almost had to drag her, Don't be afraid, she said, we paid good money. After that she bought shoes for her mother, a butcher's knife, a dog chain and a small sack of cement. And that was how Raraou spent the cripple's stash. Then they went home (that's what they called their blockhouse now) on the bus. They found the cripple as they'd left him, lying on his side atop his arm, in a puddle of piss.

They cleaned him up, covered him with blankets and prepared him a meal. When Raraou took him his plate she said, Listen, no-legs. I spent your money, every last drachma. Don't you ever touch my mother again, see. Bought me a butcher's knife and some cement. And she showed him them. If you ever try and touch her again I'll mix up the cement and I'll stick the knife in your belly, and as soon as you open your mouth to yell I'll plug it full of cement. And we'll walk out. And the cement will set right in your mouth and you won't be able to yell and you'll die alone, you'll rot right there where you sit. It's not us who need you, it's you who need us. So if you know what's good for you, you'd better mind your p's and q's and show us some respect.

From then on the cripple treated them respectfully. Still, every night before they turned in Raraou would lock one end of the chain around the legless man's wrist and the other to a leg of their bed. And she slept peacefully, there beside her mother. In the morning, she would release him. He didn't like it of course, but what was he supposed to do? She threatened to have her MP call the police to throw him out. But the cripple didn't want to have anything to do with the police, especially since he claimed to be a hero of the Albanian campaign, in addition to begging without a government permit. He'd lost his legs in an accident, poaching fish with dynamite. So he let Raraou have her way. When you get right down to it, he was pretty well off; he had two slaves, and he'd begun to salt his profits away again, things couldn't be better.

He didn't try to touch the two women again. Better share the living space and work together, he reasoned.

What really impressed him was how strong the mother was going up hill. She wrapped the rope around her chest, lunged into the harness, and towed him along like a mare threshing wheat. At night the daughter massaged her shoulders, and rubbed fat into the rope burns on her chest and arms. One day, the mother stole a wad of cotton batting from a shop where they'd gone to beg for money for the disabled hero, and that night she took the batting and some old rags and made a kind of harness which she wore right next to her skin, under her dress, when she towed the cripple's cart. The daughter was delighted, What a wonderful mum I have, Mum, what a great idea! she shouted.

Not far from their place was a graveyard. Raraou jumped over the wall and pulled out a couple of wooden crosses and loaded them on to the cart beside the cripple, and that solved the problem of firewood for the brazier. It got a bit smoky of course, but the warmth helped cut down on the dampness.

Raraou hid the butcher's knife and the bag of cement where the cripple would never find them. And come summer, after she finished cleaning him up, helped him on to his pallet and brought him his meal, Raraou went off for her first acting lessons. On the way she dropped her mother off at their neighbour's, the lady with the lace doilies, and strolled on down the hill, to the group of houses which was getting larger all the time, why, they even had an outdoor cinema. Raraou would scramble up the wall, or up a nearby tree and watch the stars gliding to and fro across the silver screen. Those were her acting lessons. Greek films, those were her favourites. Afterwards, she would pick up her mother and the two of them would stroll home. Her mother enjoyed those little social calls, since her neighbour was so busy with her knitting she hardly said a word. The mute woman helped her with the household chores, did the sweeping, you name it, and then sat there and listened as the lady of the house talked about her house back in the provinces, about her neighbours. She'd managed to get electricity which meant they had plenty of light, and the time passed pleasantly. One day, on their way back home, Raraou told her mother, See, mum, Mrs Fanny hasn't put up one photo of Aphrodite. Not of her husband either.

The take was good, at public markets mainly. There were always lots of people in a hurry, housewives for the most part. Raraou set up the cart so that it blocked their way, what were the good ladies to do? How could anyone who was a true Christian, a believer in the Last Judgment, walk past a half-man and a deaf-mute woman without giving something, some money or a piece of fruit from her shopping basket.

Later on, when Roubini began her theatrical career as Raraou, she came to know almost every small town in Greece with travelling theatrical companies. Gigs were always easy for her to find, since she worked at half-price; in addition to on-stage extra, she would also do odd jobs and run errands for the impresario, which meant she got lots of work. The other actors considered her a petty stool pigeon. Later, when she'd finally bought her own apartment, she told her mother that the time they'd spent begging with the cripple had given her the inner strength she needed to face an audience. More important, she learned not to let people hurt her, not to feel shame, shame is for provincials, she told her mum. But she also respected her obligations. There was this certain Mrs Salome in Grevena she always sent her best wishes to. Mum, she said, Salome's the one that discovered my talent. Salome showed me how to live, thanks to her I know how to live, theatre-wise. But begging taught me how to live better. That saying I remember from school, she said.

From fellow actors to stage directors, everybody admitted she had a kind of presence, even if she always seemed to end up in a nervous collapse which meant she wouldn't be hired for the next season. Plus she had a reputation for being trouble, not to mention her two fits on stage, on tour, how did she expect an impresario to go running off at night to find the village doctor, it wasn't his obligation, and furthermore, he was of no mind to pay the doctor bills; so they gave her two or three brandies to calm her down, and the show would go on. But come the following season she wouldn't get the call. By then, of course, she had her father's pension, her own apartment, her radio, stereo, records and, when you get right down to it, she was proud of her condition. It was sort of aristocratic, nerves, none of those tumours and gynaecological things any woman can come down with. The kind of illness that made her feel like a big city girl.

Her performance really picked up when the cripple bought a radio. It was the kind that fitted into your hand, ran on batteries. That meant Raraou could do musical numbers; she began to enjoy her begging act even more.

Summer was their toughest season. The cripple had put on weight thanks to all the good treatment, now he really weighed a ton. Pushing the cart was humiliating, too, how were two women drenched in sweat supposed to beg cheerfully, all soaking wet? Especially Raraou who had to perform her number before they brought out the tin cup. What's more, the customers began to thin out.

Summer was hard on Raraou, she'd got into the habit of fainting at noon in the bazaar, and the cripple had to whip her with a green stick to bring her around. Twice her mother collapsed, also.

One day in July, at two o'clock, the cripple fell asleep in the sun, with his hand stretched out. Raraou propped up his back with the two boards and pulled her mother over into the shade to rest. The market place was empty, it might as well have been the desert.

I'll just rest for a bit and then I'll try and find an ice-cream man, she told her mother. And she leaned back against the wall and fell into a deep sleep. Before her eyes closed they looked at the cripple sitting there plump and sleek, sweating in the heat of the sun, his hand stretched out for alms, fast asleep, and suddenly she hated him, and wished for his death. But at that exact moment sleep overcame her and she began to dream. She dreamed the cripple was dead.

The burial was in progress. It was late afternoon, the light was soft and diffuse, the heat of the day had abated. Flowers were blooming in neat little rows on a green-grassy hillock. The sky was a deep blue. And Raraou was looking at the funeral as if it were a brightly coloured picture, with a blue-sky background. The cripple was laid out on a wooden pallet, without a mattress; candles burned at each corner, but the flames were invisible in the sunlight. The cripple's hands were folded in the proper fashion, a wedding wreath on his head; he was wearing a jacket. And he was whole, his legs joined to his body, patent leather shoes on his feet. The funeral psalm droned on. At his head stood the Gypsy who begged alongside the main road every day, and next to him stood his dancing bear. The bear was standing on his hind legs, holding a censer in his paw, and swinging the censer back and forth.

Just a few steps behind the bear stands Roubini's mother. But Roubini is not part of the picture; she is outside the dream.

The psalm ends, the Gypsy makes the sign of the cross over the dead body, Ashes to ashes, dust to dust he says, he's ready to go. Here, the last kiss. What can she write on the cross, Raraou wonders; but suddenly it hits her: nobody knows the cripple's name. He never told them, they never asked. And as she mulls it over, her mother steps forward. Wait just a moment, she says. Her mother is speaking. But it's only a dream and Raraou is not amazed that her Ma can speak; not in the slightest. Her ma moves forward, up to the edge of the pallet. Her ma pulls at the cripple's shoes. The lower part of his body snaps off and falls to the ground; his legs are made of wood.

'He wanted those legs so bad,' her mother says, turning to the bear. 'I rented 'em. Paid 2,000.'

And she hoists the wooden legs on to her shoulder.

The sun evaporates, vanishes. Raraou snaps awake to the shouts and curses of the cripple. Why is there that smell of incense, who was chanting? Then the heat floods over Raraou again and she starts calling out in a loud voice, hawking her wares, Step right up! Right this way, ladies and gentlemen, yours for only 2,000 (later they chopped off the three zeros and the thousand-spot turned into one drachma). The cripple is terrified, her ma tries to drag her away, but it's still too early, the shops haven't opened for the afternoon. And at the far end of the street there's a fire burning right in the middle of the road. How can we pass, Raraou thinks, it's impossible, we'll never get by, but they decide to leave because the three of them are thirsty and their water bottle is empty and her ma suddenly stiffens and her eyes roll back in their sockets and she collapses. Raraou fans her, slaps her on the face. The cripple wheels his cart over, pulls her by the skirt, and hands her a bottle, Drink, he says. Raraou stares, stares at him. What's that? she says.

'Elixir,' he answers. 'Take some, I stole it a couple of days ago from that pharmacy, took it from the bench, give her a slug.'

'What is it?' asks Raraou.

'How should I know. For sure it's medicine, it's bound to help her.'

Raraou shakes the bottle; liquid, she says to herself Let's give her some to drink instead of water. She takes out the stopper and tries to open her mother's mouth; nothing, her teeth are clenched tight. So she stuffs the neck of the bottle into the side of her ma's mouth, her ma starts choking, but she comes to, fortunately. Raraou takes a sip of the elixir.

'Give me some too,' says the cripple.

She hands him the bottle, he takes a mouthful, Bitter, he says. Let's get out of here, maybe we can find a café open, cool off a bit.

They start up the hill. Fortunately the fire has stopped. Raraou loops the rope over her shoulder, holds her mother's hand and they move forward effortlessly, why, if I only had a scene like that to play in the movies, she thinks, I'd show them what it takes to be a star. Now she says 'movies' instead of 'motion pictures'.

They move forward, the heat as intense as ever, her ma has recovered, but Raraou is holding her tightly by the hand as they start their way up the slope. Everything is closed tight, the corner café too and the cripple damns the heat, damns it's mother, come on, he says, we'll ask for water at some open window.

The houses are all one-storey affairs with two stairs, scraggly mulberry trees in front, shutters closed tight. One of the houses, the one there at the corner has its shutters open, someone's standing there. Let's knock, says the cripple. They advance cautiously lest the cart squeak, two caryatids look down on them from high atop the tile roof; the window is open, someone is watching them from inside, motionless.

Raraou is about to say 'kind sir' in a low voice, the window is in deep shade and the man inside is motionless, eyeing them. Perhaps he's been watching them all this time. Raraou leaves the cart, goes up to the window with the open bottle, says 'good day' and is about to ask for water. She raises her eyes to speak; the man looking at them is a statue, a statue of a man's bust standing on the windowsill. She goes back to the cart and they continue on. The cripple picks up a stone from his cart and flings it at the window as they go by.

'How come you're stoning the place, no-legs? We don't even know them,' says Raraou.

Now they're going downhill for a bit. And her ma is feeling better.

She lets go of the rope and moves behind to guide the cart by the handles.

'I told you never call me no-legs, skag,' he says. And he picks up another stone from the cart, throws it and hits her ma in the back. Raraou sees, comes to a stop, brakes the cart to a halt, then

172

lashes the cripple with the rope, without a word. He tries to protect himself but Raraou lashes him, weeping wordlessly, in a trance. The cripple starts shouting, Police, help, police! Then Raraou releases the chocks, the cart starts moving, picks up speed, rams into a wall and stops. Now the cripple says nothing. Raraou goes over to him.

'How'd you like that? Want some more?' she says.

But he says nothing, her mum is waiting further down the street, Raraou grabs the handles of the cart and they move off again, this time towards the fish market. Her mother is staring straight ahead. Whenever they have an argument her mother stares straight ahead, as if she were gazing out over a valley full of birds and flowers.

'The food market's just ahead,' says the cripple, 'there's got to be a café open somewhere.'

At the corner a gypsy gives them water. His dancing bear is exhausted from the heat, sitting under a mulberry tree without its chain. But the gypsy's not worried the bear will run away. Where would it run to?

A little under-age whore, bedraggled and miserable, is standing in front of the bear. Business stinks, she tells the deaf-mute, even the Allies can't stand the heat. Still, she's good-hearted and high-spirited. There she stands, right in front of the bear, trying to catch its eye, to make it get up and dance, finally she ends up dancing by herself, the whore does, legs spread apart like she was pissing and the bear just sits there clumsily. After, she reaches into her handbag and hands something to the cripple, here, poor guy, she says.

Thanks so much, says Raraou, and the cripple nudges her to move on; how low can you get, taking charity from whores!

The sun burns down from on high, hotter than ever; it's nearly four o'clock but instead of lessening, the sunlight is becoming more intense. Let's try the fish-market, says the cripple; come on, let's get this show on the road, you're worse

173

than useless, the both of you; for nothing I put the bread on your table. Since the day Raraou threatened him with the cement, the insults flew more thick and fast than ever, but they hardly noticed, let him get it off his chest, she told her ma, all men are the same, let him yell, and let off steam. And the insults poured out, thanks to me you've got food to eat, free-loaders!

Freeloaders he called them, but he feared them too; at night when they chained him before they went off to bed, he didn't utter a peep. Only one time he asked Raraou, Hey, you, why don't you take me to see that MP of yours, maybe he can fix me up with a disabled veteran's pension. But the cripple didn't have any papers, couldn't afford a fake army discharge certificate. Besides, who would believe a man of forty-five had fought in the Albanian campaign? He didn't even have an ID card, in fact, he gave the police a wide berth, because he was mixed up in dynamite smuggling.

Raraou had never even considered saying a word to Doc Manolaras about the cripple, firstly, because she would have admitted to being a beggar, and mainly because she wasn't concerned about the cripple's welfare. In fact, she hated him, mostly because of the way he talked to her mum, calling her dummy like he did. But she didn't show her hatred, just let him talk until we're out of this thing, she reasoned.

And she towed the cart at a steady pace in the direction of the fish market. The bear had fallen asleep, soon the young whore gave up and lay down beside it.

It was roughly the time they always hit the fish market, because most of the fishmongers didn't have refrigerators, they kept their fish on ice in fish-crates. Come midday when the ice melted, poor housewives would flock to the market looking for half-spoiled fish at half price. When they couldn't sell every-thing, the fishmongers gave the leftovers to impromptu outdoor food stands which would fry them on the spot. Sometimes the odd rotten fish would be left over; those times the cripple would have priority over the other beggars who had their two legs, and those nights they'd have fish to eat; fry it enough and you hardly noticed the stink.

As they approached the cook stands, Hey, you two, the cripple tells his two women, get a load of that bloke with the gal on his back.

The sight piqued Raraou's curiosity. But when they got closer, they saw he was only a porter, a young man, and the woman on his back was a full-size plaster statue, probably a caryatid from some demolition site somewhere.

'Get yourself a little cart like mine, mate,' the cripple joked. 'Set her up in the market like these here women of mine do for me, and you'll be raking in the dough.'

The porter was wearing a woollen vest; he smiled at them, amused at the joke, and walked on by. The caryatid was lashed carefully to the young porter's back; her back was damp from his sweat-soaked vest. Raraou watched the caryatid bobbing along, face towards the sky with empty eyes, indifferent, what did she care, thought Raraou as she knotted the rope around her waist, they had begun to climb again.

She never could accept it, the cripple calling them 'these women of mine'; it was a little as though they were engaged, gave the impression he was the one who decided when they would go out together, but Raraou knew their cooperation was only temporary, before they fell asleep she would tell her mother, Don't let it worry you, we're only working with a cripple for the time being, us, our future is ahead of us.

Raraou tried to avoid the fish-market; they didn't have much water at the blockhouse, and what they did have they had to haul from far away, even though it was easier of late, they could use the cart to haul the can and the jug, instead of carrying them by hand; first they would leave off the cripple, then run off for water. Still, those half-rotten fish the fishmongers threw their way needed one hell of a washing. Plus, Mum's hands would stink of rotten fish for days afterwards, and there was Raraou, dreaming of a life of perfume, just as soon as the pension came through, imagine all the bottles and flasks she would accumulate when she became an actress.

And so she towed the cart along with a gleam of triumph, but deep down, unwillingly. Fortunately there were no fish today, and the cripple was cursing, Double-dealing bastard fishmongers, sell everybody and his brother rotten fish and for me, nothing, can't you see my wife is sick, and he pointed to her mum and Raraou picked up the pace, no sir, she didn't want anybody thinking a fine lady like her mum had a cripple for a husband. Just then a little boy appeared, timidly dropped two little bags into the cart and rushed off.

Raraou stopped; behind her the cripple was laughing and wheezing. She turns, looks at him; he'd opened one of the bags.

'Confetti! Nothing but confetti! Instead of charity we get confetti!' says the cripple incredulously, throwing a fistful into the air.

'Don't waste it like that,' says Raraou.

'Don't you worry, carnival's a long way off.' But he's afraid of her, doesn't throw another shred. Several pieces of confetti are stuck to his forehead. Her mother goes over to him, wipes it off with a handkerchief.

'Nice tidy little wife I've got here,' he calls out to the public, but nobody's there, and when he turns to Raraou his laughter stops abruptly.

'What are you looking at?' he goes. 'Come on, put some shoulder into it, let's head for home, can't you see there's something wrong with your mum? I'll throw in the rest of the day's take,' he says, pointing to Raraou's mom. 'For her. Something's wrong with her; must be the heat.'

Raraou looks at her mother. Something had come over her again, but she wasn't fainting, she was coming around, walking.

'I'm putting my mum in the cart,' Raraou tells the cripple. Not asking, telling him. But he erupts.

'You nuts? There's no room, the cart can't take the weight, you want to wreck my cart, is that it? Besides, you couldn't possibly tow the both of us.'

'I could so, I could so,' says Raraou; but now her mum runs on ahead; she doesn't want a seat in the cart.

'We're taking a short cut,' the cripple decides, pointing in the direction. 'Only it'll be tougher, climbing the hill, and you're worn out; can you do it?'

'Don't you worry about me, I can do it,' says Raraou.

And they turn off on to the short cut back to the blockhouse. Raraou with the rope wrapped around her breast is trying to calm her mother. And as her mother walks on, she turns first yellow, then goes white as a sheet. Every so often she takes a swig of water from her bottle, they'd stopped at a café, bought a bottle of soda pop and filled up their bottle with water. Raraou bought the soda for her mum, but Mum won't touch it, and the cripple sips away at it as they make their way up the hill. Now there are no houses to be seen, only red earth and the newly paved street. Got a real future, this place does, says the cripple, won't be long before it's full of apartment buildings, tell that MP of yours to buy a lot or two.

In front of them lay the hill.

Now they struggle past a cement factory. All around are walled-in lots with red earth, right next to the cement factory is a garden full of stark white statues. All for rich peoples' villas, says the cripple. Statues and fountains, a whole garden in marble. Maybe the garden's too small, maybe there are too many pieces, but the place looks congested, Raraou thinks to herself as they pass. Now she's learned to use Athenian expressions, provincial turns of phrase would be the kiss of death for her theatrical career, suddenly the statues became whiter, Venuses, nymphs with dolphins, and Christs with lambs, even some elaborately sculpted crosses draped with ornamental vine-leaves, the Christs must be for a children's graveyard, mused Raraou. As they go by her Mum slows to look at the profusion of statues: got to remember to bring her by this way another time, Raraou says to herself. Now they're making their way uphill. The landscape is nothing but hills, and a lone tree, not one of the decorative kind; a homeless tree, unwatered.

Her mother is trudging up the slope bent forward, as if walking into the wind. The incline is steeper now, but they've almost reached the blockhouse, See what I mean, how much quicker it is this way? the cripple tells Raraou. Sure you get a bit tired but we'll get there quicker and your mum can lie down. Remind her to drink the rest of the medicine. Or did she take it all?

Raraou said nothing, she wanted to save her strength. All along the way she did her best to conceal it, but now they could hear her breath coming in gasps, her mum turns to look, Raraou can't stop, the gasping was coming on its own, You sound like a donkey in heat, says the cripple. He says it to perk her up, to encourage her, he wants to help. Raraou understands, wants to thank him. They're just like partners, the two of them. Instead of saying it in words, she pulls the cart along faster. Her breath sounds like braying, she can hear it herself, yes, sounds funny, she thinks. Imagine what my public would say if they could hear me braying like a donkey on heat, she thinks. Fortunately I'm not on stage right this minute. And her little partner the cripple is urging her on, just a little further, he says, it's almost half past six, we're almost there. Let them have it, Raraou. Raraou, you're tough as nails.

Raraou wants to respond, say something nice but she can't go on, something's wrong with her knees, her knees start to wobble. She stops, doesn't fall, calls her mother to set the chocks under the wheels to keep the cart from rolling back down the hill.

'Just a little minute,' she begs.

'Take your time, partner,' says the cripple, 'take a breather'. And he looks at her with pride.

'I don't need a rest,' she pleads. Not angrily, but as if she's afraid of losing the race, today a prize awaits her, a crown of glory, what exactly she doesn't know, but today she's a star. She jumps across the drainage ditch, slices off a mulberry branch with her pen-knife, comes back, hands it to the cripple, and wraps the rope around her again.

'Here, take this switch,' she says.

'What for?'

'Take it, help me,' she answers. And she leaps forward. But she can't go on; her knees are about to desert her.

'Come on, Raraou, you flea-bitten nag,' the cripple urges her. He wants to help. Go to it! One more turn and we'll be there.

But Raraou is about ready to black out. She turns to him and says:

'Give me a hand if I can't move. Help me. If you see me stopping, whip me. With the switch. If you see me falling, whip me.'

And she throws herself forward with a fresh surge of enthusiasm. And the cripple flicks the switch through the air, shouting Giddyup, giddyup! Raraou's knees desert her, the cripple brings the switch down on her back shouting with elation, Raraou struggles forward groaning, Whip me, whip me hard!

As the cripple whips her, Raraou forgets to look off to the side at her mother, now the cripple is whipping her and Raraou is pulling more smoothly, if only my public could see me now, she thinks triumphantly. The cripple is shouting, but he eases off with the whip, and starts to sprinkle her with confetti, Raraou wants to take a bow, to say, Thank you, thank you so much, the confetti is sticking in her hair, her mum tries to shake it loose but Raraou shoves her aside, now she is a star, now there is no stopping her, and behind her comes the cripple shouting at the top of his voice, singing her praises, whipping her across the back, pelting her with confetti …

179

NOW WE'RE THROUGH the Pearly Gates, said Raraou, when they were safe inside the blockhouse. She helped her mum lie down, used up all their water with nary a second thought, gave the cripple a couple of swallows even. Him, he didn't want to go inside, Leave me here for a while, he told Raraou, I want to get myself some air, have me a good look at the city. So Raraou left him there, just as he desired, didn't even prop him up, Watch out you don't fall was all she said and went off to fetch Mrs Fanny. At the same time she took the jug to fill with water on her way back.

The legless man put on his glasses, a pair of cast-off sunglasses he wore when he was in a festive mood, and rested, gazing off into the distance towards the capital faraway. He never even realized he was dreaming; he was certain he was awake, participating in his life.

He dreamed he was seated upright in his cart outside the door to their refuge but the sun was not sinking; no, it hung there in the sky motionless, mocking him. He had his jacket on and scorn welled up in his chest, scorn for those people there in the capital, the people and those handouts of theirs, I'm worth more than any of them, he mused, as he scratched his throat, he felt an itching, a soft tickling sliding down inside his collar. He closed his eyes to scratch with greater abandon and once again brought his hand to his neck. The feel of living matter. He opened his eyes and pulled his hand away and looked down: through the opening of his collar an eel came slithering. A shiny grey-green eel, stretching slippery as it slithered down his chest. Now it had reached his stomach. The cripple raises his hand to grab the eel which had almost completely emerged from his shirt, but it has begun to wriggle through the buttons of his fly. On the floor of the cart he sees two more eels slithering towards his belly. He wants to call for help, turns towards the blockhouse door, and through the door a huge, rusty ship is bearing down on him moving sinuously like an eel, but how could a whole ocean liner fit into their tiny blockhouse? and the ocean liner bears down on him like an invading army, the legless man's only line of retreat is to awaken. He snaps awake.

Scared the hell out of me, can you beat that, he thinks, and calls out to the dummy. How's everything, he calls loudly, feeling better? Come on outside and keep me company, he says. Asimina comes out, sits down beside him on a low bench, now he's chattering away contentedly, You'll see, he says, a couple of years from now and all this here empty land will be part of town. More and more people are coming to Athens, no, you can't stand in the way of civilization: just a couple of years – I told you first, don't you forget it – and main street will go right by our front door and there'll be shops and a market and customers, lots of them, and us, we can do our begging and we won't even have to move from beside our doorstep, we won't have to slog hours just for some of their lousy crumbs, no, they'll come right to our door, we'll be living the good life, give them seven, eight years at the outside; you listen to me, I know what I'm talking about.

He chattered on until Raraou came back with Mrs Fanny and the water jug: she also had a thermometer.

'Heat stroke,' says Mrs Fanny. 'Fortunately. She's not feverish, no fainting spells, just doesn't want to eat. Still, you ought to get her to a doctor.'

She helped them move the cripple inside, and asked Raraou privately, How old is your mum?

'Thirty-four,' says Raraou.

'So young! So it's impossible,' she mutters to herself. 'But take her to the doctor all the same. And if you need me at night, just drop by and call.'

Next day the cripple stayed home while Raraou and her mother took the bus to Doc Manolaras' office.

'Here's Mum to see you, doctor,' says Raraou. She always called him doctor even though he was a politician now; shut down his doctor's office years ago. But he gave her a quick onceover while voters lined up to pay their bribes in the waiting room.

'Nothing wrong with you, Asimina, you're looking fine', says Doc Manolaras. 'She may be presenting minor indications of hysteria.'

He wrote them out a note, then sent them off for a free examination by some doctor political cronies of his, one of whom happened to be a gynaecologist. Two days they spent running from one doctor's office to another, the legless man was grumbling, but who cared about him. Could her mother hear? the gynaecologist asked Raraou.

'Of course she can. She's only dumb.'

'In any event,' says the gynaecologist, 'there's nothing to worry about, my child. Your mother has stopped having her period, for good. An unusual occurrence in such a young woman, but certainly not dangerous.'

'That's just what I suspected all along,' said Mrs Fanny that evening, 'but I didn't want to say a word till a doctor got a look at her'.

And so on the third morning they went off to work again, the three of them; the cripple was in a rush, two days alone in the shelter and he was just about dead with boredom, he wanted noise and crowds, so he claimed.

'Don't you worry, Asimina,' shouted Mrs Fanny as they passed her blockhouse on their way down the hill. 'So I've still got my periods, even if I'm fifteen years older than you. Look all the good it's done me.'

'Don't you worry Mum, said Raraou as they made their way towards the fish-market. 'You should be happy; it's all one big bother, month in month out, nothing but trouble. What's a period good for anyway? I still can't figure it out, all the fuss!

Wish mine would just dry up, you and me we're real sticklers for cleanliness the both of us, all these necessities of nature, well, we just don't approve, do we?'

Fact is they went out and bought two eels to roast over the coals that night, to celebrate the occasion. It was a waste of money, the cripple complained, but Raraou told him I bought them out of our share, so eat your helping and shut up!

Lately he'd got quite bold what with Raraou's mother's dizzy spells (quite normal, they'll last two or three months, said the gynaecologist) plus her mind just wasn't on her work. One night he tried to touch her again. Raraou had just finished boiling an egg for her mum and she poured the scalding water over him. He screamed in pain, and later he asked her plaintively, Why do you keep trying to stop me? Can't knock her up any more, that's for sure.'

That night, after several months of freedom, Raraou began chaining him down at night again. But now instead of looping the other end of the chain around the leg of her bed she wound it around her wrist. And if the clanking of the chain happened to wake her at night Raraou would yank it until she could hear him groan. Then she would drop off to sleep peacefully once more.

One day – spring was here – because of the terrific take, the cripple decided to wind it up early. They'd even collected a handful of foreign coins, which Raraou would take over to Doc Manolaras' office the next day to see what they were worth, They stopped off at a shop on the main road and bought pork sausage and wine. Let's have a party, said the cripple. On the way back they encountered huge machines widening streets and demolishing ruined buildings. Look, said the cripple, the Allies, they're coughing up the war reparations.

Raraou felt fine, because her mum was fine too. She'd been relieved of her monthly indisposition once and for all, the dizzy spells were gone for good and the cripple, he'd learned to spend

183

the night in chains, it didn't bother him, and besides, the take was on the increase, he was putting on weight and chewing Raraou's ear off, why doesn't she get her MP to pave the street right up to their blockhouse door. But Raraou would never think of doing anything so impolite, they'd given him trouble enough with the matter of the pension for a good two years now, A happy conclusion is not far away, he would tell her every first of the month when she went calling at his office. The voter registration cards were ready. No one will ever know a thing about the extra years; it was the only way we could get cards issued for you and your brother, you see. But I'm giving you another birth certificate that makes you years younger.

He passed on the greetings from her brother Fanis, he was doing just fine there on the island, faithful, productive worker that he was.

Raraou and her mum broiled the sausages, fed the cripple, ate their meal and then plonked him down hard on his pallet; he'd begun trying to feel the mother up again. That was when Raraou wheeled him straight to his mattress without taking him to the toilet first, flopped him face down on his bed, chained him, took her mother and hurried over to Mrs Fanny's place, the cripple's little transistor radio wasn't working any more, all you got was static, it needed repairs. Plus, Mrs Fanny had electricity.

As her mum washed the dishes Raraou leafed through a magazine, Mrs Fanny, she bought magazines to learn new patterns. Just about all she could do was leaf through the magazine, what with all the roaring of the earth-movers and the bulldozers you couldn't hear a thing on the radio.

Then one of Mrs Fanny's neighbours came up, shouting Mrs Fanny, come quick, bulldozers. But she had a paper from city hall; she showed it to the crew foreman, it certified she was a legal resident of the blockhouse, a civil war displaced person.

'They're heading for your place,' he tells Raraou, 'you don't have a permit, hurry if you want to save your belongings.'

Raraou took her mother by the hand and they started out for their blockhouse. And when her mother tried to run ahead Raraou held her back. They strolled along at a normal pace and when they came to the turn in the road, they saw their blockhouse and two bulldozers crawling towards it. They stopped, and Raraou held tight to her mother's hand.

'We're not going any further,' she said.

And they watched as the bulldozers heading for the blockhouse. Because of the distance they heard no noise. And when the first bulldozer hit the blockhouse it seemed to hesitate for an instant, then back up before ploughing it under. Then came the second bulldozer, driving across it at right angles, and where the blockhouse had once been now only flat ground was left. Only then did Raraou and her mother start moving again towards the place which, until just a few moments ago, had been their blockhouse.

'I didn't want to save a thing, not a rag,' said Raraou to her mother. By the time they reached the spot, the bulldozers were about to head off in another direction.

'Anybody live here?' one of the operators asked Raraou.

'Not that I know of. Nope, nobody,' she said, and her mother nodded her head as if to say, 'Yes, that's right'.

'The municipal development department has it down as uninhabited,' he said. 'But me, I could have sworn I heard voices; you hear anything?' he asked the other bulldozer operator.

'Voices? With the roar these babies make?' said the other man. 'What voices? You're hearing things. Let's get on with it, we got work to do.'

'No; nobody,' said Raraou.

They left.

Raraou took her mother's hand and they walked back to Mrs Fanny's. Spent the night at her place. About a week later came the good news; the pension had finally come through.

Some dogs, strays most likely, came sniffing around the flat spot the bulldozers had left, sniffing persistently; but finally they went trotting off frustrated. And when the paving machines had done their work, the dogs disappeared.

FIRST TIME IN MY LIFE I ever lived in a house with wooden floors. Parquet, even. So when I walk in the door I say to myself, Roubini old girl, I say, you've arrived; I was so carried away I forgot to call myself Raraou.

Mum, she couldn't be bothered. Mum, I tell her, behold your house. In Athens, no less. Here's where we'll live and here's where we'll die, like high-society ladies; they'll have to carry us out of here feet first, when the time comes. So I want you to be happy, Mum. Happy, victorious, and every inch a lady.

Her name I changed to Mrs Mina. My mum, Mrs Mina, I told them down at the bakery, will be coming by for the roast. Made sure Mrs Fanny got it right too: my mum, Mrs Mina. And on the cross on her grave I had them carve 'Mrs Mina M.' No last name. Just M. Making amends.

With the money Doc Manolaras gave me from the sale of our house in Rampartville, first I bought the plot, then the apartment. Me, you won't catch me being a provincial ever again, even after I'm dead. The graveyard, it's just a little place around the corner, but my fellow actors I tell them, You know, got my mum buried in the First Cemetery. My enemies, let them eat their hearts out, plus it tidies up Mum's memory, socially speaking.

The gravestone I bought secondhand. While we were still living with Mrs Fanny, at her place. Small but tidy; but full of her provincial hand-me-downs and trinkets plus the furniture she brought along with her from Rampartville. Once a provincial, always a provincial, that's Mrs Fanny, even today. There, I said it; but she's a well-meaning sort all the same, and when we came up to Athens, she took us in without us even asking and we stayed at her place for about two years, till Mum's pension came through and we sold our house. We had to stay with her, to keep her company, she insisted; we were doing her a favour, even though there was an abandoned house not far away, just like hers. Furniture, carpets, all our valuables, everything, we sold it all back in Rampartville before we left.

Still, we were much obliged to her for her warmth and hospitality for two whole years.

The only thing I brought with me from Rampartville was the clothes on my back, and Mum's wedding photo. All the rest I gave away to the needy ladies in our neighbourhood.

Me, when Doc Manolaras announced the house had been sold all I could think about was my little pullet. Did they respect her memory? But later on I told myself, she doesn't need their respect. By now she'll be burrowed down deep to the centre of the earth, I imagined, just let them try and find her and drive her through town with their bulldozers and graders and humiliate her publicly.

As soon as everything was settled I went out and bought furniture. Bought one bed only, a double bed for the two of us, with a soft, bouncy mattress. Now for the bridegroom to break in real nice, said the mattress man who delivered it. The console I bought a bit later, Markezinis was in power then; meanwhile I'd paid the place off. Enjoy your dowry; now for a husband to mess it up, said the cleaning lady.

You heard what I said, the cleaning lady. Comes twice a month, she does. Thought Mum would like it, but instead she just got upset. What I mean is, I had the other tenants in mind too. Mum would be needing a cleaning lady when I was away on tour, I mentioned it to the lady (some 'lady', anyhow!) who runs the dairy downstairs.

Because now, now I was in the theatre. All because of Doc Manolaras, wonderful man God bless him. He'd done really nicely for himself too, what with being a member of parliament for Athens, we're climbing the ladder together, Mr President, I say to him one day. He wasn't president of anything, but show me a politician who doesn't like being treated like a big shot. Call him Mr President I wrote to our Fanis. Him I always give advice even if he is older than me. Well, he may be older, in my mind and in my soul he's still thirteen years old. That's the reason why Doc Manolaras and me, we arranged to have the apartment in my name. Eliminates transfer problems and estate taxes later on, he said. After, he gave me a note to this stage director he knew, saying, The bearer of this note is a party friend, please arrange for her to get work.

As it turned out, maybe the bloke talked like a patriot but he was a dirty old man. Past forty-five. So he invites me over to his place. I go, he asks me in, starts to caress me, gives me fifty drachmas and then he does something to me which I won't say what it was.

'Sweetie,' he says to me as we're going towards the door, 'you've got great prospects as a whore.'

'What do you mean, whore?' I say respectfully. 'I came here to become an actress, what's this about whores?'

'Whore, sweetie, is what you just did, right here.'

'But I don't want to be a whore,' I say.

'But,' he says, 'you already are one. Best of luck.' And he points to the fifty drachmas in my hand.

Fortunately Doc Manolaras knew lots of people in the theatrical world, so he sent me to see someone else. This one hired me on the spot. Just what I'm looking for, he said. He was an old man too. What am I talking about? Maybe he was forty-five, no more, but they all looked like old men to me back then. Talk about lustful! But when's the last time I met a man who wasn't? I've got it in my blood, so it seems. I ask him if I had talent for the stage. Come to my office tomorrow an hour before rehearsal, he says. Make sure you're squeaky clean and wearing your fresh underwear. After I'll tell you if you've got talent for the stage.

Next day I went off, light-hearted. Gave my mother a kiss and off I went. All squeaky clean and ready to go.

'For your basic successful actress,' my agent told me, 'the trick is to show up nicely washed on the inside, especially when the stage director invites you to his dressing room. She should always be clean and nice during work hours, and never have her period on work days. Those are the the the Ten Commandments of the successful actress. Obey them and she'll make progress.'

Progress I made. I was always obedient, everything my stage director said to do I did. But he was always telling me, Hey Raraou, you've got a hole in the head where your brain should be.

That got around to all the troupes as time went by. No matter though, always had plenty of work, I did, Doc Manolaras's little notes were a big help, fortunately most of the impresarios were good nationalists so I was never out of work. You name it, I played there. Why, I learned the whole geography of Greece upside down and inside out. Just ask me the name of the town, any town, and I'll tell you what prefecture it's in.

Of course I haven't really reached my peak as an artiste yet, haven't really got the recognition I deserved, not even now when I'm about to start drawing my actor's pension. Never really got to play any of the great roles; usually what I got was the non-speaking parts or the dead people. Never went to acting school you see; I'm self-taught, whatever I know I learned on my own. A few times I got to speak lines. I remember, once I had a line that went 'Look, 'tis the wife of the bishop'. Well, I said 'Look' twice, just to expand my role. Still, all the impresarios would pick me. Always squeaky clean, fresh underwear, and condoms in my bag – at my own expense – I'd give them a break on the wages, let them know what the other actors were saying behind their backs because me, ever since I was born I feel grateful to anyone who looks after me and I know how to show my gratitude. So that's how my mother Mrs Mina never wanted for nothing. Why, I got her a radio and a fridge and even a telephone, she couldn't do a thing with it but I figured so what; never said a word again, in fact. Bought her a TV too, just recently it was, the year before she died and did she ever enjoy it. Went out contented, I treated her like a queen, yes indeed I did. You think I'm going to sit there and take it just because the other actors dump on me, call me fink and stooge and such like? What do I care about them? And when they went too far and started slapping me in the face say, or kicking me, I'd head straight to my MP, Doc Manolaras. He's in fine shape, still alive and raring to go, even made it to deputy minister for a little while. Good old Doc Manolaras, always stood by me. One day I said to him. Doctor, you've always treated me as a mother.

At the start of my career he gave me recommendations for a lot of impresarios from our party. Back then, in fact, he made sure I got acting lessons, free. For two months the teacher taught me everything there was to know, a real lecher the guy was, your original red-hot lover. Tonight we're going to sleep together, he'd announce every morning first thing. Two months straight the guy gives me a bum deal, literally, I mean, being as how he had peculiar tastes in bed. But I don't mind; he taught me plenty. So what if people say I got nothing but a hole in the head where my brain should be. But all the impresarios went for me, seeing as I was always squeaky clean and willing and ready to go. And when you get right down to it, it was an honour, I was never so much known for my looks anyway, really. Raraou, I'd say to myself, you're not in the same league as Vivian Romance so whoever makes a pass at you he's doing you a favour. But all the same, I was a cutie, young; for them I was like candy, old men, all of them. Now wait just a second I can hear you say, how come you're calling them old when they're only forty-five-year-olds, and you're over sixty. Well, I'm over sixty and proud of it!

When you come right down to it, people always said I was a real sex-pot and passionate at that, word got around the troupe, how Raraou was real dynamite in bed. Nonsense; I fooled them, all of them. It was all an act, I was only playing a role in bed.

Never really liked it either but I pretended to out of courtesy and, besides, it paid. Me, my laurels I wanted to earn up on the stage. Plenty of times while some Tom, Dick or Harry was panting and puffing there on top of me, I'd be memorizing my lines, the lead role, I mean to say, and that way the time would pass gloriously.

When I turn thirty I say to myself, Roubini, I say, you ought to get your head examined. You're going to have to put up with it so you might as well enjoy it. Plus, you're paying the shot for the condom, right?

So, a little bit at a time I learn to enjoy it. Takers I had, that's for sure. So I was nothing special, but this agent or that was always inviting me to come up to his office. The guy was no Tyrone Power, of course, but still, he was a male. And when we were on tour I found out that people in the provinces were just wild about actresses, whether your name is Iberio Argentina or Raraou. Not too long ago, last year I think it was, I had a thing going with a gentleman who was only free after eleven at night. He was a fine fellow, don't get me wrong, but if I don't have a show the next day to keep me wound up I've got my night cream on and I'm ready for bed by half-past ten, all this while Mum was still alive. And the guy's got this thing about kissing me while he's doing whatever else he's doing, kissing me all over the face, like suction cups and sucking off all my face cream. One night as he's kissing me I say to myself, Holy Virgin, there goes three drachmas, every kiss was costing me three drachmas' worth of face cream.

When I realize what's going through my mind I freeze. Roubini, I say to myself, if all you can think about at the height of passion is your three drachmas, then maybe it's time to retire, sexually-wise, I mean. So I dumped him. Our hours don't match I told him.

No more sex, please. Better the night cream and the soft skin. So I get myself an unconditional discharge from sex. Thirty-eight years' service is plenty, I say to myself. And my panties I started calling my little pensioner. And that nasty little cop down at the police station (when was that exactly?) ...

Patient: Meskaris Roubini (Raraou), actress, retired. Member, National Federation of Stage Extras

CERTIFICATE OF PSYCHIATRIC EXAMINATION

Following examination, at Division V of the Athens Police Department, of the above-named patient, I herewith certify the following:

I have treated the above-named individual on several occasions. The insured is a member of the Federation of Stage Extras. Patient is quite harmless. Though placid, she engages in innocuous, non-directed misrepresentations arising from a powerful urge to communicate best described as a 'compulsive confession' syndrome. In the course of said confessions, motivated by a desire to conceal the identity of certain individuals referred to in her narratives, patient employs distorted first and last names of said individuals as well as of place names. Or, put more clearly, to protect such individuals from the 'dishonour' they might incur through being overtly connected with her. Patient consistently conceals the identity of the city of her adolescence, referring to it with a fictitious, non-Greek name. Furthermore, patient insists on utilizing her stage name, and presents symptoms of dementia praecox if addressed by her given name.

In my considered opinion patient has been apprehended and incarcerated due to ignorance and excessive zeal of the arresting officer. According to his report, patient was detained 'while impeding circulation of traffic on a central thoroughfare.' Though reclining on the paved surface at risk of serious bodily injury to herself, she was not engaged in indecent behaviour; patient was simply summoning a person named 'Roubini' to come to her assistance. As you will certainly appreciate, she was calling upon herself.

I recommend that the Police Department no longer concern itself in the event similar behavioural patterns on the part of the above-mentioned patient be repeated. Patient is entirely harm-less, well-intentioned and simple of mind.

I must further report that following gynaecological examina-tion as required by the Morality Division, and ordered by myself so as to allay certain suspicions, the above-mentioned Meskaris Roubini was certified to be a virgin.

Signature

SEAL

And generally speaking, there's only one thing concerns me now, what with Mum gone and all. I keep seeing sort of like TV shows in front of my eyes, they come and then they go away. Or I never see them again, maybe I'm only dreaming. I don't know. Take that funeral, the one with the old hags, for instance.

I dream I'm at the fish-market, at the crack of dawn. The same place where the fishmongers sell their spoiled fish half price to the cheap restaurants, and whatever the cheap restaurants don't take, they throw to the beggars. What I'm doing in such a place I don't have the faintest idea, but it's six o'clock in the morning and it's about to rain. Me, I never get up so early, what am I any-way, some kind of worker, or cleaning lady? Anyway, it's just after six, and you still can't see the Acropolis there above the fish-market; the Acropolis comes back to earth around half past seven. And over there, the spot where the Parthenon touches down, there's only a dark cloud. I'm thinking, shame on me, the Acropolis was always my dream as a little girl in the provinces, and now, here I am today, a sixty-year-old woman, and I never had the chance to climb up to the top. Make that over sixty. The fish-market, it's dead still, nothing moving, just like in a photo-graph, not a customer in sight, nothing but a fine layer of broad fish scales the colour of mallow even if the sun isn't shining, it's too early for the sun. And the breeze hasn't even begun to blow.

What's got into me, coming out at this hour of the morning, fortunately the panhandlers haven't showed up yet, imagine if one of my fellow actors, or one of my admirers were to think that it was me, Raraou in person, begging for spoiled fish.

Just at that moment a funeral procession comes through a neoclassical archway. The four of them, silent women, slipping and sliding on the precious scales which shine like Byzantine mosaics. The women are prostitutes, not low-class streetwalkers though. High-priced call girls. August women, women of stature. They look like a three-piece folding screen, each panel loaded down with necklaces, beads, glasses, hanging like votive offerings. Decorated like triangular church candlesticks; like holy icons in elaborate frames; like saints coming to sin.

The four are carrying a wide board high above their heads, an open casket, without a lid is what they're carrying. But the casket is encrusted with sequins and flower petals and gold threads and strings of beads reaching down to the ground, swinging to and fro. Not a voice, not a sound. The beads are touching the fish scales which are the colour of violets.

The dead woman is invisible, completely covered, she too is a prostitute. Her beads are like a suit of armour. But the woman is my mother, I know it from the dream, there beneath the beads my mother's face is hiding. Her body does not exist. Nobody's ever given me the assurance, but in the dream it's clear that they're transferring her, taking her away for reburial in a children's cemetery, something more in keeping with her life. Among the little children they'll lay her to rest. That means problems for me, seeing as how they don't put crosses on the graves and now I'll have to put a little chocolate candy on every grave and sprinkle a few drops of cologne on every grave, just in case I miss Mother's.

The four prostitutes carrying the casket are smoking cigarettes, dressed up like Byzantine icons painted in brilliant colours, colours straight out of a cheap musical comedy, bright and sassy colours, and they wear those colours with such serious expressions on their faces, no objections allowed, no comments. Their faces look more like masks. They're smoking cigarettes.

Something is missing from the picture. That's it: the funeral is ending, and there's not a clergyman to be seen. And instead of the mourning relatives there's a bear, without costume or makeup. And the bear showers the casket with confetti, and beside it stands another prostitute – a young apprentice, also without makeup. She is the bear's servant, and stares at it in admiration, but she walks along stiffly, like a hanged woman.

They march past me without a greeting, without a glance. Maybe they don't even see me. Then they vanish into the neo-classical fish-market. Meanwhile, I'm standing there holding a tambourine in my hand, but I'm not allowed to follow along behind; that's understood too. Even if wanted to, I couldn't. Because all of a sudden the funeral turns off and ventures out across the surface of the sea, the calm, motionless sea of dreams. And there the heads of eels stick out of the water and watch the bear as it passes, without sinking.

I lower my eyes with respect, as one must at funerals, and there, beneath the surface of the water swims the blue corpse of a woman, staring at me with boundless blue eyes. Just a minute, I say to myself, those aren't eyes, they're eye-sockets full of water, I was always crazy about blue eyes, me with my eyes black as a cast-iron frying-pan. The blue corpse is flat, as if it was made of cardboard. I lift my head, walk out over the surface of the water, and unlock the door to my apartment. What was I doing in the fish-market at the crack of dawn anyhow? Got out of there before the panhandlers showed up. Fortunately. But the doubt still gnaws away at me: the animal, was it a bear or a monkey? And the apprentice whore, how come she was its servant? That's all.

I don't know.

Me? My mind? Never had a care in the world; why, it's just about as down-to-earth and rock-steady as you could hope to

196

find. Let them talk, all those theatre people, let them think I got nothing but a hole in the head where my brain ought to be, why do you think I spend all my time at the hairdresser, hiding it with my coiffure. These days, of course, they've all forgotten the whole thing. They all greet me, Hi there Raraou, you old hole in the head, just as familiar as you please, just proves how young and vibrant I am.

Right here, in Athens for the most part. Don't get all that many calls for tours these days, that kind of stuff's for beginners, second-raters. Still, I could go for a tour or two, you get respect from the small town public. Not like my baker, I walk into his shop and the guy doesn't bat an eye-lid.

Not that I wasn't a bit of a sensation with the Athenian public. They made me what I am today, in fact. I remember how jealous fat little Mitzi used to be; good actress she was, all the talent in the world, but when it came to slender waists and sex appeal, she just couldn't keep up with me, but the public just wouldn't warm to her. Got so bad she up and married this shoemaker in Patras, right in the middle of a tour. Got a couple of kids and a boat. Send's me a box of Turkish delight every so often, but how am I supposed to eat it, I've got to mind my silhouette, plus my diabetes you know. So I pass it around wherever I've got an obligation, mostly to Doc Manolaras, still alive, he is.

One year we were playing in Athens and Mitzi comes backstage after the curtain, and says to me – she's laughing her head off – Raraou, there's this admirer of yours waiting outside, hurry up, you're in luck, and it's about time.

Me, I overlook the snide remark; what's his name? I ask.

'He'll be waiting for you outside,' she goes, oozing that sarcasm of hers. 'Looks harmless. An old country yokel'.

Took my own sweet time taking off my makeup, an old politician's trick, that, I always slow down when people are waiting for me, why I just about missed Mum's funeral, thought it was a performance. So, like I was saying, I take off my makeup and go out the stage door into the street. Not a soul in sight. Fat-face was putting me on. Just then an old man steps out from behind a newsstand. Not dressed all that bad, but still small town.

'Is that you, Roubini?' he asks.

I'm startled. Who's this guy that knows my past? I take another look at him. Then I recognize him, from the wedding photo: it was my father.

'Daddy, how are you?' I ask. Without emotion. Hadn't seen him for forty-seven years, since back then at the railway station the day he left for Albania, with the twenty-drachma coin.

My first thought was, O my Lord, now what do I do? He's alive. There goes my pension.

'I've been following you for a long time. I heard you were in show business, saw some photos of you years ago in Arta. Outside a coffee house.'

'How is your mother?' he says.

'Died year before last,' I retort with a little lie. Didn't know what his intentions were.

He asked me about the boys. He didn't know Sotiris left home during the Occupation. I told him; told him our Fanis has a good life, but I didn't say where.

'I heard about you in Arta, years ago, saw your photos,' he said, repeating himself. 'Always wanted to come and see you, kept putting it off, waiting for something to turn up. Finally I had some business in Athens, so I decided to come and get to know you.'

He didn't have much else to say, kept talking about my photos back in Arta. After, he invited me to dinner in this little taverna. I accepted just in case he wanted me to invite him to my place, but all I could think about was the pension, better kiss your pension goodbye I said to myself, it's a goner for certain.

Over the food we had a couple or three glasses of wine, the two of us, and we got more into things.

'So your mother's dead,' he says. Me, all this time, I'm touching wood and nibbling fried eggplant, even if it gives me indigestion.

'Never could stand her, poor woman,' he says. 'Well, may she rest in peace.'

Me, I didn't say a word about Mum's past; he told me about his. Lasted two and a half months on the Albanian front, he said. One night he says to himself, What am I doing here, what am I fighting for? What country? What did my country ever do for me? Guts to wash, that's all I got, my country never even set that up for me.

'So I decided to turn back,' he says. 'I play dead in an attack, they leave me lying there, I get up and start walking, nobody says a thing, they've got a whole war to fight, me they're going to worry about? I said to myself. So I end up in this little village not far from Arta to get me some rest, so this widow with some land gives me work and before too long she says, If you're unattached I'll marry you. I thought it over real hard, what's the point of going back, all that slogging just to wash tripe, to go back to Asimina, never could stand the poor woman; all that way, and for what? So I told the widow, Yes, had ourselves a pair of kids. Gave a fake name, Arnokouris Diomedes from Sarande, Greek from Albania. Had a good life. And I'm still alive.'

No sooner had he finished his story than I breathed a sigh of relief. Almost felt sorry I told him Mum was dead.

'Daddy', I say, 'everything came out just fine in the end, for all of us, the whole family. Fanis is taken care of, you're doing fine there in the village. And I'm living the good life here in Athens. I'm drawing a pension, on account of you're dead on the battlefield. So don't come here again. You're doing fine, so what do you want with me?'

'Nothing, Roubini my child,' he says. 'Just curious, that's all.'

I was terrified how he would take it. What's this stranger want from me? I kept saying to myself as he chewed his food and stared at me as I spoke. The father I knew was a twenty-five-year-old leaving for the Albanian war with a twenty-drachma piece who made me feel good back then when I saw him naked as he was changing clothes. But this man here, he was the same age as me. All the time we were eating I tried my best to love him as a father, to feel even a little warmth. I couldn't. I was more interested in the life of our cashier at the theatre.

I told him so. He gave his word to keep out of my life. You're right, he said. We're all getting on fine.

He paid for the meal, and we said goodnight at the entrance to the taverna, and he was gone; I never saw him again. But the fear was there, gnawing away at me.

Since then, whenever I sign anything, I always add 'fatherless orphan'. Like an alibi. And after my encounter with my father, when even I go to the bank to collect my pension I wear grey, with a black armband to make my claim even stronger, and hold my passbook in my hand. There are three queues, and I know which window is mine. But I stop right in the middle of the bank and call out:

'Which is the queue for orphans?'

And every first of the month when I go for my pension I put on the mourning, on my arm or my lapel, either one, and always ask where the orphans are supposed to queue. At any rate. I don't care whether that twerp of a teller who waits on me laughs or not, Henry is his name. He's always whispering something to the woman next to him, I picked it up, they're talking about me, even though that Henry's always making eyes at me. Well, good for him; he's got cute eyes. Still, better I should really make sure of my pension.

Doc Manolaras's office I dropped by too, pretending to ask after my brother Fanis, and he greeted me in person. Fortunately my Dad kept his word and didn't give a sign of life. I was terrified he might have gone and told Doc Manolaras.

But still, I couldn't put it out of my mind. What if he gets it into his head to show up, then what? For years I was on pins and needles. Till last year an envelope comes to our association, from some clergyman. I open it, and there's a clipping from a provincial newspaper, the 'Obituaries' page.

Diomedes Arnokouris, loving father and husband, passed away on etc., etc. ... his wife Ioanna, his children so and so and so and so. And after their names it said: Sotirios, Roubini, Theofanis.

Must've confessed to the priest.

I didn't know what to do next. Of course, it was one big load off my back, for sure. Imagine, losing my pension and being exposed as a parasite living off the public purse. You can be sure I never breathed a word to our Fanis. First I thought I'd send a condolence note (I have cards of my own printed up, with my name and profession in decorative characters), but then I say to myself, sit tight my little Roubini, you never know these days, what if some new brother or sister pops up and claims the apartment. So I never sent the note, he never did a thing for me anyway, apart from the meal he stood me in the taverna. Just let him rest right where he is, I thought.

But I had this funny feeling inside. I'm the adventurous type, you know, emotionally speaking, is what I mean to say. And I like observing the niceties. I just love to send out cards. Always send out cards on the occasion of the New Year to my impresario Kozylis Konstantinos and best wishes to his wife Eugenia, her name day is Christmas eve. I always send him a card because of when his mother left us the walnuts on our windowsill. May be of course I've got a bit of an ulterior motive, after all, maybe he'll take me on. What I mean to say is, he did hire me one time, a couple of years back, just after the incidents at the Polytechnic. A left-wing play unfortunately, but it was a job. I didn't have a lot of work back then, as I recall, so I say to myself, Why not give it a try, that pipsqueak Kostas, he'll recognize me and give me a half-decent part. I call him pipsqueak because back in Rampartville, when we used to play in the drainage ditches down near his place, he was short with a big head, and I was taller than him and I kept on smacking him on the head or beating him up and he went and splashed water all over my drawers.

So I showed up and they gave me a part. I played a dead Communist. She's dead at any rate, I said to myself. But he didn't hire me on as an old friend. He saw me, looked me over, said to a helper I can use that face there. Didn't even remember who I was. At which point I say to myself, don't bother to let on you know him. When I start up my own troupe, then we'll see. That was always my dream. Of course, I had well-founded suspicions that his leading lady, who happened to be his wife Eugenia, was jealous of me. She's got the most gorgeous eyes in the capital, I've got to admit it, still, she was jealous of me but I wasn't jealous of her, why should I be jealous? It's all fate. Not that I want to run down the girl, far from it, still, if I'd been born twenty-five years later and if fate had given me eyes like hers and talent too, well, we'd just see. Furthermore, there's one thing I had her beat at hands down: me, I've performed in 1,860 small towns. Her, she's only played in a couple of capitals.

But that little runt Kostis didn't recognize me. Better that way, I said. Didn't want him asking after Mum, after all. So I played the dead communist part and he wished me a pleasant good night after every show, just like he did the rest of the cast. Right up until the end of our run, he didn't recognize me. There, that's what being far-sighted will do to you, I said to myself. Because I haven't changed a bit in forty years, physically speaking. There were times ofcourse when I wanted to ask after his parents, to see if they still had that tangerine tree in their yard in Rampartville, the one I used to scale the wall to pick tangerines off and one time my drawers got caught on the rock and ripped. But I never did. Don't bother, I said.

Still, I kept on sending them cards every New Year's day, even after. Only forgot it this year, slipped my mind completely.

One time, in fact, I took Mrs Kanello to one of his shows. Her he remembered, the ingrate. I ran into her at a meeting, at the office of the new MP for Rampartville, right here in Athens. Journalists all over the place. Mrs Kanello got up and praised the politician, but she put her foot in it, as usual; she'll never be a diplomat, the poor woman, and not an ounce of femininity. The politician, a certain Mr George, he's from one of the best families, I can't mention his name so as not to compromise him. So, as I was saying, this Mr George is from Rampartville too, from a good family, and people in polite and not-so-polite society talked about him for two main reasons: because he had a talent for languages, because he went with men, even though he was a nationalist. Because he was plump and inexperienced, anybody who wanted to could do it to him, and out of politeness he wouldn't say no. The high-school student who taught him English taught him other things, disgusting things. The high-school student who gave him French lessons gave George lessons in doing dirty things. His mother used to say, There's nothing we can do, our little boy has an anomaly. Am I supposed to kill him, or what? Even took the kid to a fortune-teller, but nothing came of it. Then she sent little George off to a priest to say prayers for him in the hope he would cut out the men, but they say the priest did it to him, so we heard from this other priest George confessed to before communion. So his mother accepted it, it's God's will, she said, he'll only stop when he gets married.

As soon as I got back home from Kozylis's show where the ingrate remembered Mrs Kanello but didn't know me from a hole in the ground, there was a lovely little consolation waiting for me, a surprise: a letter saying my Actor's Fund pension had come through. Now, I said to myself, they can all eat my shorts, all of them, calling me extra and fink for all these years. Moneywise I don't really need their pension, but artistically, it's recognition of my contribution. I've still got my main pension, the one from Albania, that's why I never married, so I wouldn't lose it. You can count on your pension better than on any husband. It's warmer, too. So maybe I'm cheating the nation but I don't regret it for a minute. How come they sheared off my mum's hair, just tell me that? I accept this pension mainly as if it was the nation begging for pardon from Mother, for the disgrace they made her suffer back then.

Years ago I used to have this nightmare: that somehow they never paraded Mum through the streets and humiliated her, and that Daddy came back from Albania thirty years later, and I had to pay back the pension to the government. Now I'm used to the nightmare. And when it comes I just dismiss it, it's only a bad dream I say; they pilloried Mum and Daddy is dead and buried, no worry about the pension. I've got no regrets; when you get right down to it, all Greece is on a pension. I know what you'll say, you'll say What's wrong with her, I'm not Greece, I'm Raraou, artiste, and my country is my two pensions. How come I'm always feeling so sad? My future's all looked after, my health couldn't be better, I look just like I did forty years ago, so eat, drink and be merry, Raraou, Mum's gone to her reward and socially rehabilitated, what's there to worry about?

So a couple of days ago I made up my mind. Since the year before last I've been thinking about my father. Me, I'm the adventuresome type, emotional-wise, I mean to say. Poor Daddy, I say. So, I kind of sum up my life: so far my career really hasn't exactly taken off, and I'm over sixty. For a dowry all I've got is a couple of corpses. Buried in different places. My little pullet back in Rampartville. By big brother Sotiris buried God only knows where. Unless maybe he's still alive. Mum here in Athens, in Athenian earth. Recently I've been thinking about her a lot at one point in particular; standing there in the truck with her hair sheared off, pointing at me and saying, Why is that dog barking at me, get that dog away from me!

So one Sunday I get this flash. I'll make a pilgrimage to my Daddy's grave, I decide. Sure it's a bit risky for the pension but then, you only live once, right?

I took the bus and a real uncomfortable trip it was, the passengers weren't really my class of people. At Arta it was all I could do to find out where his village was, finally I locate it, go to the cemetery, me wearing dark glasses – I didn't want my admirers recognizing me – and I find the grave. Here lies Arnokouris Diomedes. Him too, with a stage name. I think to myself. Here he lies, artistic-wise. I left him a bit of earth from Mum's grave. You never did become of one flesh but at least you'll end up of one earth, so just try and work things out between yourselves from now on because me, I'm a big girl now.

I get home and I'm worn to a frazzle, home at last, home sweet home ... no more wild goose chases for me, that's it, finished.

So that's how I remarried my parents, and now, what've I got left to my name? I say to myself. A couple of graves. Each one all by its lonesome. But isn't that how it's supposed to be? Who am I to complain? Because I'm going to die? Alexander the Great died didn't he? Marilyn Monroe too; who am I to say I shouldn't die? Whatever I need, I've got it. Mum all fixed up in her own plot, the fridge full of eggs, remember back in the Occupation how you couldn't find an egg? Back then for an egg you'd have to put out, for the older girls I mean. And now all I have to do is open the fridge and count my eggs and my heart soars, believe you me. Got my cassettes, lots of left-wing songs, and that's just fine with me, they've got the pizazz. And at election time when we stay home, I put on my tapes with the left-wing song at full volume so my left-wing neighbours will think I'm on their side, being on the winning side is the best idea, the sidelines never did suit me.

Of course, maybe some of those snot-nosed little creeps from down the street make rude remarks when I go by, but I don't care, only thing wrong with kids today is they want to live. Then too, I go to church a lot. Not that I'm religious, but I do light the odd candle now and then, besides, if members of parliament from our party can go to church every day, why can't I? Of course, what they're lighting is the big tapers, not the little oil candles. But my pension's one thing, their's is another. When I light a little candle it's to say a big 'merci' to heaven, you never know what happens to us after death. But when it comes to prayers, I never say the 'Our Father'. Me, I've got no Father in heaven, I mean, you think I'm stupid or something? I just make out I do, that's call. There's no such thing as God, I know it, you think he's so stupid, to exist? All I know for sure is my mum exists. And my little pullet. They may be under the ground, but at least they exist.

Still, better to be on good terms with everybody, now that I'm a bit over sixty. Never said so much as a bad word about a soul, not once in my life, well, at least not to his face. Because, I said to myself, tomorrow I might need the rotten bastard. Can't bring myself to use rough language; my femininity forbids it, you see.

Movies I get into free, thanks to my special pass. Not to mention all the theatres, go on in Raraou you old wheezebag they say, and I walk in proud as you please. Raraou, the extras all tell me, you're just like Greece, you never die.

Frankly I couldn't care less if Greece lives or dies, one way or the other. What did Greece ever do for me? I'm supposed to care if she lives on dies? Greece, she's like the Holy Virgin: nobody ever saw her. Only nut cases and con men. Me, I can see my eggs in the fridge. My pension, I can see that. I'm a success. I'll slip into my mustard-coloured outfit, the one I had seized from this actress back when we had the colonels, the rotten slut wouldn't pay me on account of her son was getting it on with an army officer, so I'll slip into my mustard-coloured outfit like I say, and go out for a French pastry and let the men fight over me. Anything wrong with that?

What's all this fuss about evil, anyway?

I spend a lot of time thinking things over lately, unemployment you know. How come what they all 'evil' should be forbidden, and even worse, condemned? First of all, we like it. You know how it is when when you think of a lemon and your mouth starts watering, well, that's how my hands get, hungry for murder, as if they're starving to wrap themselves around a man's thighs. How come I can't just go and murder somebody? Wouldn't bother me a bit, just so they don't catch me.

Lots of times, coming back from my nighttime stroll, I go down a little street behind our place, right past a basement apartment with the lights on and the windows open. Looks like a working-class family living there, happy and contented; a drooling baby, a daddy with striped pyjamas and a young mum wearing an apron. They're so happy and smiling it makes me furious. I walk right by their place on purpose, so I can get good and mad. Maybe I'll think of some way to ruin that mindless pleasure of theirs. Maybe take a can of petrol one night, splash it all over them and light it with a match? Because mindless pleasure isn't allowed. I don't allow it. Plus there's a button missing from his pyjama bottoms. I'll douse them with petrol and light a match and walk away just as happy as you please. And nobody will ever know who did it.

Never did get around to it; the fire, I mean. I'll leave it for later, to have something to look forward to. The petrol and the matches I've got; just about broke my back hauling the jerry can home with me. And the more exhausted I got all because of that guy with the missing pyjama button, the more I was steaming and burning with rage.

Lately I've taken to studying at the sky a lot. I look up and I say to myself, all that sky! All that sky, for nothing. Fortunately I got my two pensions. Only just now I figured out what the sky is. The sky is the ceiling of an ocean. We live and walk around in the ocean, just as normal as can be and we look up at the ceiling over our heads and we call it sky. We look at it while we're eating our pastry and then we head back home to sing our mother to sleep.

My mum I treat like a queen. With two pensions even. Wherever I go, to the dairy or the bakery, everybody says Mademoiselle Raraou, those are really classy clothes Mrs Mina wears, right out of the fashion magazines. And in the living room there's this big gilded crown made of plywood hanging on the wall. Stole it from a stage set back when I was working in this patriotic review. Back then I wasn't really getting out much, seeing as how Mum was under the weather. But I never expected she'd just die on me. I was basting a roast when I hear my old name: Roubini! Roubini! Must be hearing things, I say to myself, nobody here knows me by Roubini. I open the oven door and I hear it again, Roubini, my child, I'm dying. It was the voice of an old woman. I close the oven, go into the bedroom, Mum, I say, you hear anything? As if she could answer me. Never crossed my mind the voice could have been Mum's. It was an old woman's voice, I remember Mum's voice when she was young, even back then on the truck when she was shouting, Get that dog away from me.

'Roubini, my child, I called you' and I see it's Mum speaking to me, with an old woman's voice.

'Mum! You spoke!'

I didn't want to admit that old voice had anything to do with my own mother. I was almost insulted that she suddenly found her voice.

'Come close to me, Roubini my child.'

Mother never did accept 'Raraou'.

'Mum, your voice, it came back?'

'Come close to me; I'm going to die. I never lost my voice. I just didn't want it no more. From back then. Don't cry.'

I wasn't saying a word. I was paying attention to her voice; it came out twisted, with effort.

208

'Yesterday when you were out, Roubini my child, something happened to me. It was serious. I knew it, but I didn't call for help. If it comes again, I might die ... or lose my mind. Come close, I want to give you my blessing; and to say thank you. For everything. For all these wonderful things and for then. For the water you gave me, back then ... there on the truck. You did the right thing, not to get married.'

She caressed me, then drifted off.

'Mum, I ask her, all these years you could talk and you didn't?'

She stared at me, then looked at the wall.

'What for? It wasn't worth it,' she says. And fell silent again.

'Do you want anything, Mother. Water? Shall I call the doctor?'

'I want, Roubini my child. My little Roubini, when I die I want something special: bury me here. Don't send me back. (She didn't say the word Rampartville.) I don't care how you do it, but get me a lifetime grave.'

'It's bought and paid for, Mother. A two-placer. And it's ours, for all eternity Mother. So don't worry.'

'I never made you do anything else. Don't you ever let them take me back, not even my bones.'

Then she fell silent.

A few days later she had her second stroke and she was gone.

After they buried her there was only quiet to keep me company. Only then did I figure it out: death isn't the big thing; the big thing is the dead.

God bless and keep her.

Every Holy Week I go and visit Mum, on Easter Sunday, in the afternoon. All around are mourners, a lower class of people for the most part, decorating graves with plastic flowers and washing and scrubbing the gravestones. Makes you feel good, mourning gives you a good feeling, like drinking a glass of wine to the health of the dear departed. I strike up a conversation

209

with the ladies even though they are from a lower class of people and I don't feel like quite such an orphan.

Everything's so nice and quiet. So lovely, I say to myself. Death comes and goes, only the dead remain.

When I do a little meditating or watching the sky I think how I'll be heading for paradise, and how nice I've arranged everything, just so, my conscience is clear, no doubts in my mind, nothing. Only one thing that bothers me: what's God's name? Mine is Raraou, the other guy's name is Harry, let's say, but what's God's name? That's what I wanted to get straight in my mind the other night when I didn't feel like going straight home.

Because the other night on my way back home, after a delightful little get-together with some other pensioners from the theatre it was, I didn't really feel like unlocking the door. Come on, Mademoiselle Raraou, put your key in the lock, I say to myself. But I stand there in front of the keyhole and I can't move. And then it hits me like a bolt out of the blue, there's nobody waiting for me in my apartment. And I didn't want anybody waiting for me, now that Mum was gone all these years. Still, I was frightened. A big fright. I pull the key out of the keyhole, almost creep across the street, and I stay right there in a kind of fenced-in vacant lot and I won't leave before the light comes on in my apartment. Right away I make up my mind: you're not going to put anything over on me, no way. I'm not setting foot in there unless you open the door. No, I've got conditions, I said: somebody's got to be there to greet me.

And so I went off for a little stroll; it was quarter past two, on the dot. A little stroll. Give them some extra time to open the door for me. The officer who escorted me back home at twenty-five after four treated me properly, said he wouldn't run me in for disturbing the peace, he recognized me, for sure.

'Merci,' I tell him. And ring my doorbell. Off he went. But they just ignored me, wouldn't open the door. So that's when I go and ring all the bells in the apartment building and it was only later in the ambulance when I finally realized the truth about the sky. The sky is alive. A living beast. Never could figure it out before, seeing as it's blue beast and it never moves during the day. Never moving. Lying in wait for us. But when night comes and we aren't watching the Sky beast starts crawling towards me. Like a lily. Far as I'm concerned, I say, well, it's an honour, still all these Lilies and Annunciations? Me, a grown woman, with two pensions at that? Now that I can't conceive any more?

I'm in the ambulance, does that mean I'll pull through like everybody else? Every night when it gets dark, Sky beast comes to life and starts moving, just imagine what it's doing to us and us, we don't even realize we're defenceless.

That's why I avoid going out after dark. Who needs the lily, anyway? So I sit and watch television, bought a colour TV with easy payments; paid it off last spring.

Nowadays I go out mornings mostly. Call on actor friends of mine, look at the posters, visit Aphrodite's mum, Mrs Fanny. Still doesn't have a phone. One day I ran into Mary, Thanassakis's sister from Vounaxos village, the son of Anagnos the schoolmaster. Recognized me right away, Roubini, you still look as spry as ever, she said. She's looking well, not like me of course, but then, what can you do? She told me about her brother who's getting ahead in Boston, he's got a university of his own over there, why he's even been honoured by our government, kind of a half-national benefactor is what they'll declare him, seeing as he brought civilization to our country.

'See Mary,' I say to her, 'when you come right down to it, we all succeeded, all made it in Athens, all us kids from Rampartville. Kostis the pipsqueak as a stage director, our own little Thanassakis in book-learning, me on the stage, all us poor kids from Rampartville, we all got our heart's desire. Me, for instance, I've got my apartment, my stereo and my record col-

211

lection, free medical care, pensions, recognition. Why should we complain? We've all arrived.'

She had to admit it.

Just what Mrs Kanello and I were talking about a couple of days ago. All her kids are doing fine, and now Mrs Kanello is a happy granny. As provincial as ever and proud of it, but then, who doesn't have their little shortcomings. She keeps me up to date. Rampartville isn't what it used to be, of course. Before the war there were four elementary schools and a municipal brass band and now only two of the schools are open. Not enough kids for the other two. Even the graveyard where we kids used to play hide and seek, it's gone to seed. Most of the graves have been forgotten and the statues have lost their paint. Only Mrs Chrysafis, the dead partisan gendarme's mother, she's still a regular. Didn't they call him Valiant? His ma still visits his grave but not so much as she used to. Only on Saturdays, nibbles a bit of earth and lights a candle, she's got to be very old now, but she keeps on begging, God Let me live so I can come to my little one, because if I die I'll forget him.

Well, that's progress for you. Most of the inhabitants of Rampartville moved up to Athens. And they're all doing just fine. Lottery sellers, doormen, Aphrodite's mother in her blockhouse, you should see how she's fixed up the place, a dream. All she does is crochet. Must be close to eighty, and she's still bringing in the money, what good is it to her, at her age, God forgive me!

Strictly between you and me, I looked into buying a little piece of land myself, but it didn't work out. I said to myself, what're you going to do with the land, Raraou? It's nothing but earth. I can't for the life of me figure out what I wanted to do with it.

Another time, when some officer escorted me back to my place I refused to tell him where I live. So he opened my handbag looking for my ID card and my address, but he never spotted my age, the brute. And all the while I was waiting at the police station for the officer to escort me back home, the cop on duty keeps asking me my name and where I'm from. And it all came to me.

'The place where I come from was a little girl name of Roubini,' I say. 'Who had a little garden under her bed and her best friend was a little chicken with bright coloured feathers.'

And then I understood right away why everybody loves and respects the earth, why they want land: the land is full of graves.

Nothing sad about that; why should it be sad? That's the way life is: full of death. Nothing to be sad about, it's a natural thing. Natural, like how my mother stopped speaking.

Doesn't bother me one bit I have trouble remembering Mother's eyes. Forgot which one of Fanis's hands is the busted one. Can't even remember the colour of his hair. Forgot how to be sorry. Makes me sad, a little. All the colour is running out of my sadness.

But what can you do?

Me, I remember my little pullet. I've got the trick now if I have a fit when people are asleep. Stick a hankie in my mouth and that way the neighbours can't hear a thing, all right, so I learned it from the moving pictures, you're going to say, but anyway.

That's right, doctor. But I don't have my fits anywhere near so often any more.

I got my little pullet to remember, doctor. With those bright-coloured feathers of hers, died of hunger in my mother's house. She was the only friend I ever had. Turned and looked me in the eye before she fell over and died.

Me? Who will I look at?

No matter.

By now my little darling will be part of the earth.

And so will I. One of these days.

Maybe two or three centuries later, I say to myself, when my pullet and me will be nothing but dust without a care in the world (that's what I hope), maybe one day the same soft breath of wind will raise us up and unite us in the air for an instant. Just for an instant, together.

End